SO
NOW
GO
TELL

SO
NOW
GO
TELL

SUSAN SACHON

Matador
Unit E2 Airfield Business Park,
Harrison Road, Market Harborough,
Leicestershire. LE16 7UL
Tel: 0116 2792299
Email: books@troubador.co.uk
Web: www.troubador.co.uk/matador
Twitter: @matadorbooks

ISBN 978 1803137 605

British Library Cataloguing in Publication Data.
A catalogue record for this book is available from the British Library.

Typeset in 11pt Adobe Caslon Pro by Troubador Publishing Ltd, Leicester, UK

Matador is an imprint of Troubador Publishing Ltd

To my parents, who taught me to love books,
and believed in dreams.

ONE

'Smooth runs the water where the brook is deep...'
(Henry VI, Part II)

I was drowning.

Silty water invaded my ears and nose; water lilies slapped against my cheeks as my legs heaved then dragged, too paralysed by the March cold to keep me afloat for long. Above the surface, my flailing arms cleaved a brief pathway through the vegetation: a precious gap into which I pushed my face to suck in air.

And then I saw him, standing by the bank, watching me: the man in the hooded sweatshirt who had slipped in and out of my life over the past few days like a silent, olive-green ghost. I'd never managed to catch a glimpse of his features except for a tuft of rust-brown beard and sandpaper cheeks. Even when we'd bumped into each other in the job agency, he'd kept his head well down, the hood falling around his face like a monk's cowl, and at first I'd never dreamed he could be following me. But now here he was: a black shadow curling over the water, the hood rippling as the wind blew. As my body stilled and the cold closed around me, I wondered fleetingly if it was he who had pushed me – and why. One moment I'd been firmly on the bank, admiring the pale sun's rays on the weed; the next, I was hitting the water, my coat bloating around me like a mushroom until it gave itself up to gravity and dragged me under.

I'd fought hard and shed the coat, but had no chance of winning against the cold. There was no air in my lungs to scream, and no one to hear me – except him, and it seemed that shock had frozen my fear.

As I drifted momentarily, distant sounds of a siren were swallowed up by the water sucking in my ears, and an eerie calm wrapped itself around me. The thought slipped through my mind that the hooded shape of my unknown stalker was the last thing I would ever see. I was a forty-year-old woman, divorced and newly redundant, who would only be missed by her best friend, and who had achieved precisely nothing in her bleak little life, except...

My mind lit momentarily as I returned to the few weeks of my life when I'd felt 'worth something'. To a random comment on the night my school had performed a Shakespeare play that I'd actually directed, and a woman in the audience told me I had 'a rare gift'. Even if that was an exaggeration (and my mother had assured me it was), I'd treasured those words. They'd come back to me in the job agency that morning, even after twenty-four years.

I'd read about people who'd had near-death experiences, and they often said the last few moments seemed like a lifetime. That must be what I was feeling, now. Perhaps I was no longer breathing; the horrific ache in my lungs had gone. As the water squeezed around my ears like a tired heart valve, my mind committed its final act of spilling out the secrets I would never tell. My mother's face glimmered before me in the water, the flesh shrunk against her bones as her white fingers reached for my hair to wind themselves within its splayed curls. *"You can never tell anyone, Jenny. Not ever. You understand that, don't you?"* her voice whispered in my head. I'd kept my promise, because all I'd ever wanted was to escape the past that pulled me down, like the strips of weeds now clinging like manacles to my feet. I'd craved the sort of life other girls had: ordinary, loving and safe. And when I realised I would never have it, I'd learned to improvise. Pretending was something I could do. From an early age, I was adept at making up stories, and my make-believe worlds were my sanctuary. For the rest of the time, I learned to curl up small and go largely unnoticed.

Except for him. He had noticed me. It seemed he had even been following me... and now I would never know why.

A flurry of light and bubbles exploded suddenly somewhere above me and streamed past, its wash rocking my body. As I followed it with my eyes, a crab-like figure grasped me from behind, winding its thighs around mine and pulling me upwards. I couldn't think or feel, only stare at the fat-bellied hood that trailed behind us like a gaping mouth as we surged towards the light. And then the water weighed down my eyes.

"It's okay. I've got you."

His voice stirred the remnants of my consciousness. There was something about its tone… something I recognised but had spent half my life striving to forget.

How strange, I thought, as I slipped into the liquid darkness. My mother always said that the past had a way of coming back to claim you.

TWO

'So, ere you find where light in darkness lies,
Your light grows dark by losing of your eyes.'
(Love's Labour's Lost)

"Jenny?"

Mags. She was a long way off, but I could hear her, calling over and over. My head felt heavy, my mind confused. Was I still underwater? I opened my lips a tiny amount and sucked, and a blessed draught of air reached my lungs. *Thank God.* I tried calling Mags's name, but only a husk of a sound came out.

"Jenny!"

I opened my eyes, and awoke into darkness. I could hear someone breathing, feel fingers grasping mine, but I was in some kind of blackout room where I couldn't even make out a human shape. There were no windows, no shadows.

Blood started pumping in my ears as I tried to move. Everything hurt. "Oh, God, where am I?" I heard myself choke. "I can't... I can't see anything..."

5

"It's okay," said Mags's voice. "It's fine. You're in the hospital. You, um, had a bit of an accident." Terror got the better of me, and I let out a wail of panic. "Stay here and don't move," she said, quickly. "I'll get a nurse. Oh, *shit.*" Something tipped over with a crash, and I heard her calling, but all I could do was heave breath after breath into lungs that never seemed to fill. I was sliding into the distance again: fading away from life.

"No!" I struggled up, my left arm dragging as something sharp and painful pulled on my hand. Footsteps sounded, and more breathing in the darkness.

"Steady there, Jenny. You're quite safe and you're going to be fine." Another voice, male this time, spoke in my ear as a pair of larger hands pushed me gently backwards. My fingers flew to feel for the edges of whatever I was lying on: a bed or trolley of some kind. Slivers of light flashed at the corners of my eyes, and I blinked, furiously. *What was going on?* "You need to lie down, Jenny," said the man's voice. "You're all wired up, here. Just relax; you're safe, now. You're in hospital."

Another tide of fear engulfed me, leaving my body rigid in its wake. "I'm not fine!" I screamed, panting and grasping the arm that was propelling me. "Why can't I see? I can't see!"

I could hear my friend Mags crying in the background, and my terror climbed.

"It's okay, it's only temporary. Just temporary," the male voice said, and the repeated word finally arrested me. "My name is Doctor Asan. You had a fall, but there's nothing seriously wrong." He paused while I took in his words, my breathing still ragged. "We've run a number of tests overnight, and the results have just come back. Everything is clear, including your brain scan and your vision. We believe you have a condition known as functional neurological system disorder: a form of temporary blindness brought on by stress." On my other side, Mags burst into tears again, and I heard her rummaging in a bag, then blowing her nose as my mind rocked with all this news.

Stress? Well that made sense. My thoughts flew back over the last few weeks: the terrible interview in HR; the heartless way I'd been marched from the building without saying goodbye to anyone. I hadn't made any close friends, but they were people I saw every day, and a reassuring part of my tiny world. Mags's sniffing brought me back into the room. Someone was pouring water into a glass or cup, and the sound spiked my heart rate again. A pair of hands was wrapping what felt like a blood-pressure cuff around my arm.

"Who pulled me out of the river?" I asked, raking the room with my eyes as though that would force my sight back into operation. *Was it him?* my mind whispered. *Was he here, in the hospital?* My legs and arms began to shake. "Only… I think I might need to talk to the police." There was another silence, so long that my stomach rolled in dread. *Why didn't they answer?*

"Jenny, I think you must have had a nightmare," the doctor said, gently. "You've been unconscious for a while, but as I said, all your X-Rays and scans are normal. You fainted in Stevenage town square and banged your head as you went down. The whole episode appears to have been brought on by a panic attack – which is what you're having, now. I'm just going to give you a little something to calm you, so keep still for a moment. There you go." Something briefly stung my arm, and within moments I felt my body relax and my chest expand.

"Jenny." Mags's fingers found my right hand again, and squeezed it. "You phoned me. Don't you remember?" Her voice was blocked with tears. "You'd been to three job agencies, then felt exhausted and were on your way to Starbucks by the fountain, for a coffee and a rest. That's when you rang me. You said you were losing your sight, and were terrified you were having a heart attack or something. I called an ambulance from my car, but you were already unconscious when we all got there. There was a guy with you, looking after you."

"The man in the hoodie?" I whispered. *And if he wanted to drown me, why had he saved my life?*

Another pause. "Jen, the man who rescued you was the security guy from your office building," said Mags, softly. "He was just coming back from his lunch and saw you collapse." She went on, clearly speaking to Dr Asan this time. "She said something like this in the ambulance, when she came to for a moment. Something about a man in a green sweatshirt. We thought it must have been someone she saw, just before she passed out. She kept saying he was following her."

"Don't worry," said the doctor, from my other side. "Jenny, I think what you're remembering is a dream. This sort of thing isn't uncommon under the circumstances. You may be confused for a while. What you need is lots of sleep and no worries. Do you have any family we can call?"

I swallowed, my throat like cardboard. "No; I don't have any family in this country, only an aunt and uncle in New

Zealand." *Who I haven't spoken to in years.* "Um, Mags here is the closest thing I have to… to a family."

Mags sniffed again. "She'll be staying with me," she said, and I heard a tissue rustling. I couldn't say anything, I just hung onto her hand as though I'd tumble off the edge of the world if I let go.

"I've got such a headache." I tried to lift my free hand to my head and felt the sharp pull of a needle lodged in the back of it.

"Don't worry," Dr Asan said. "We'll give you something for that, and you'll sleep. When you wake up, you should feel much better. Then we'll talk again."

His footsteps receded, and were replaced shortly afterwards by another, lighter set. Their owner told me she was a nurse, come to help me take some painkillers. It was strange, feeling the little plastic cup of water at my mouth, but seeing nothing. The nurse settled me down against my pillows before she left, and I turned my head, trying to locate Mags, desperate for her not to leave.

"It's okay, I'm here," she said, and took my right hand in hers again. She sat with me while the medication eased through my limbs, weighing them down as my sodden clothes had in the river. Then I remembered the doctor saying all that stuff about drowning was only a dream… and yet, why did it feel more real than being here, shut inside this awful darkness? An image of a dark hood, flaring wide in a watery scream filled my head, and as I fought to stay awake, I thought I felt the chill of those crab-like thighs encasing me. Dragging me downwards.

"You're shivering. Yet it's so warm in here." Mags pulled my covers up over my shoulders, and I resisted the urge to lock onto her arm with both hands and not let her go. "I'm here," she said, as though she knew. "I won't leave you."

"I was drowning, Mags," I whispered, as I slipped into sleep. "And he was there, just watching me."

THREE

'Fortune brings in some boats that are not steered.'
(Cymbeline)

The sharp rattle of crockery bouncing on a trolley broke my dreams, and I awoke to find myself in a small room bathed in pale, early light from a steel-framed window. A snore brought my head round to Mags's diminutive form lolling in a blue plastic chair beside me, her short peppery hair sticking up in tufts, traces of mascara icing her thin cheeks, and her brown tweed coat wrapped around her. On the scratched white wall at the end of my bed, my reflection looked back at me from a misty mirror. As the last scraps of sleep left my mind, I lifted a bemused hand slowly to my face, tracing its pale reflection. It was warm and pliable. I fingered my chestnut curls, and stared back into the grey eyes that were wide with anxiety. There was a yellowing bruise down one side of my left cheek, and I appeared to be wearing a blue hospital gown with a round neck. *So many colours.*

"I can see!" I whispered, my heart thumping. Mags's chair scraped loudly as she leapt awake, then groaned as she put a hand to her aching neck.

"Jenny!" she croaked, discarding her coat. "Oh, that's wonderful! Wait, I'll call the nurse."

Before I could get used to my new state and surroundings, I became the centre of a whirl of activity that lasted the best part of half an hour. Nurses came and went, followed by a dark-eyed doctor: all making checks and asking questions while my eyes roamed continually around, noting every crack and blemish of the little white room as though it was the most precious thing I would ever see.

"I'm confident we'll be able to discharge you, later today," Dr Asan said at last, as he glanced down at my chart. "But we will need to keep a check on you for a while. From what you've said, the condition was probably brought on by your sudden redundancy; but often there's a much deeper-rooted cause that needs addressing. I'd like to suggest some talking therapy, if I may. A one-to-one appointment will take months to arrange, unfortunately, but there's a form of group therapy that has an excellent track record for helping to ease stress through building self-confidence. I'll send the details on to your GP."

He must have seen the spasm cross my face at the despised word 'therapy', because his brows rose. But the past was one place I would never revisit voluntarily; I'd made a promise long ago, and breaking it wasn't an option. My mother's voice whispered through my mind, as it had so many times when I was a child. *"You can't tell anyone, Jenny. Not ever. You understand that, don't you?"*

"What you need to remember is that this condition

can recur in moments of extreme stress," said Dr Asan, gathering up his clipboard. "And I'm afraid you won't be able to drive until we're sure you're fully recovered."

It was a blow, but I wasn't going to let it sour my elation at the thought of being discharged. I was alive, I told myself, and I could see again. It was enough. After the doctor left, I managed to devour every scrap of my breakfast, much to Mags's joy, and we finally had time to talk.

"So – you remember what happened, now?" she asked, a cautious look in her eye.

I nodded. "Yes. I think I was just exhausted, after that last agency interview." My brow wrinkled. "I mean, I must have been; I remember burbling on about Shakespeare, which really confused the woman there – because she thought I was looking for an office job. I also remember feeling pretty groggy while she was interviewing me. Maybe I was dehydrated or something."

Her eyes rounded. "Shakespeare! Whatever was that about?"

My cheeks heated. "Oh, I directed a play at school, when I was sixteen, and it went really well – had me dreaming about working in theatre, for a while." Though my mother had soon squashed that idea. "So, one of the questions on the agency form asked if there was anything I was particularly good at, and – can you believe it? I put 'Shakespeare'! I was clearly out of it, even then. Maybe I'd taken a few too many headache pills."

For a moment I was back in the tropically heated interview room with its logo of blue waves and its slogan emblazoned across the window: *New-U Career-Moves Employment Agency. We don't just find you a job. We help you find yourself.* The young woman there, Denise, had been particularly sweet about my sudden bewildering plunge into theatrical waters.

"I'm not suggesting I should look for a job involving Shakespeare," I'd said, trying to shrug off my skin-curling embarrassment with a laugh. "It's purely an interest. A hobby. Something… I should have pursued a long time ago."

The thought stirred another memory as I lay there in my hospital bed: of a man in an olive-green hoodie crouched over a desk in that same agency, filling in his own application form. It was odd, but I'd noticed him several times over the past few days, emerging from shop doorways or hovering on street corners, waiting to cross. It seemed too much of a coincidence that he'd been in the agency, too; but then he was entitled to look for a job, like the thousands of others who were unemployed. Including me.

My thoughts drifted back to Denise's unexpected reaction to my burst of confidence. "You know," she'd said, blushing faintly, "I did Shakespeare myself at school. Some of it sounds so beautiful, doesn't it? My favourite's that sonnet; you know – *'Rough winds do shake the darling buds of May'.*"

It was as though her words gave the room a shot of oxygen.

"It's one of mine, too," I'd said, eagerly. And before I knew it, I was filling her in on my school production of *Julius Caesar*, the open-learning courses I'd done since, and my early dream of being a director. Only when the room fell quiet had I faltered, my mother's blighting words ousting every other positive thought. *"For pity's sake, Jenny.*

One teacher lets you help her out of the kindness of her heart, and suddenly you're a professional. Have some sense!"

She was right, of course. Loving Shakespeare wouldn't pay the rent, and without a job I would soon be homeless.

That sobering thought brought me back into my hospital room with a jerk. *Dreams are for fools,* I told myself. But as though the universe had heard me, my phone burst into life inside my bag.

"Bloody hell!" swore Mags, as the opening bars of Beethoven's Fifth blasted out, and we both jumped. I stared. She never cursed, and this was the second time in twenty-four hours.

"How do I turn this thing off?" she demanded, thrusting the phone at me.

"Sorry. New ringtone." I glanced down at the screen, and saw that it was an unknown number. "Maybe I need to get this," I said.

Mags's head shot up. "No! The doctor said—"

I ignored her. "Jenny Watson."

The voice at the other end sounded vaguely familiar. "Jenny! It's Denise, from *New-U Career-Moves.* You know, you came in to see us yesterday morning?"

"Oh! Right; yes." *Agency,* I mouthed to Mags, with a fizz of nerves, and she dragged her chair in closer.

"Well, look – I think I may have something that's right up your street. A guy rang this morning, looking for someone to manage a pub in a little Northamptonshire village. It's live-in, all bills paid except food, plus £300 a week."

"A pub?" My mouth fell open. "Oh, no, I'm afraid I don't know anything about running—"

"No, wait; here's the thing." She could hardly contain her excitement. "Apparently there's a retired bar manager who can train you up, and your boss will take care of all the licences and insurances involved. What they *need* is someone with a knowledge of Shakespeare, to revive the two annual festivals they used to hold there. With – and I quote – 'some directing experience'. Which you have. How amazing is that?"

I gazed at Mags. This definitely had to be a dream. Or maybe I'd died yesterday after all and was now in a parallel life. Mags's eyes were almost popping – and I could well understand why. Although we shared an interest in theatre (in fact, we'd met at a local drama group), we'd only ever worked backstage on costumes or props. My determination to keep a low profile had precluded any forays into acting or directing.

"Hello?" came Denise's voice. I hastily pulled my attention back to the call.

"I'm sorry. Are you serious?" I asked.

Denise bubbled with laughter. "I know – I couldn't believe it, either! But the pub's just changed hands, and this Mr Norwich only took over a few days ago. The thing is, he works abroad, and can't run it himself, so he wants someone interested in promoting the place: really putting it back on the map. It's over four hundred years old, and has quite a history."

I hesitated. History was another passion of mine, especially of that period, but… no, I couldn't be other than honest. This was way above my remit.

"I don't think I'm the right person, Denise, to be honest," I said. "I mean, I know I spent a few years with an am-dram group, but that's not really—"

"Jenny, listen." Denise lowered her voice. "Apparently, it's really unusual for this guy to call in person. He hates talking to people on the phone; does everything by email – which I know is a bit odd. But when I told him about you, he jumped at the idea. Said your mix of enthusiasm, admin and directing experience sounds perfect. He wants *you*, Jenny."

I swallowed hard. What on earth had she said to the guy? For all I knew, job agencies were like estate agents, and she'd made me sound like an ex-director for the Royal Shakespeare Company. But a nagging little voice was telling me I'd be insane to let this go. What if I passed it up, and never got another chance like it? It was the *actual* dream come true. And, deep down, I was pretty sure I could direct a play with an adult cast. I'd helped enough amateur performances come together, so… shouldn't I at least find out more? An interview wouldn't hurt, and if I met the man face to face, I could be totally honest about my lack of experience. Then if he still wanted me – well, that was a different matter.

"I tell you what," Denise said. "It's Friday tomorrow. Why don't you go and take a look around the place over the weekend? He says there's a key-holder who could let you in, if you're interested. I can always email and check."

I raised my brows hopefully at Mags, who came out of her trance. "Have you got any plans this weekend?" I hissed.

"No. But, Jen…"

A strange exhilaration was now coursing through my veins. Maybe after all that had happened, this job was meant to be. And anyway, it couldn't hurt to look.

"I may need to bring a friend with me," I said to Denise. "I don't have a car at the moment."

Mags choked.

"Again, I shouldn't think that's a problem; the guy sounded very amenable, and really keen to get someone in right away. But again, I'll check for you. There are a few other things I should mention. The job offer is strictly on the basis of a four-week trial, so you'd need to show some good progress by then, for the post to be confirmed."

A month. God; it was hardly any time at all.

"Mr Norwich is abroad for the next few weeks, but your wages will be paid by bank transfer," Denise went on. "He'll arrange to visit when he gets back into the UK. There's no one else living in, so you'd have the place to yourself. It's a bit of an unusual arrangement, I know – but do you think it might be acceptable?"

"It's fine by me," I said, recklessly. "But what do we do about an interview? Could we use FaceTime or something?"

"I'm afraid not; he's apparently not comfortable with any form of virtual conferencing. To be honest, he said he was happy to trust my judgement." Denise's voice held a tremor of pride. "I sent over your details, and he said 'yes', straightaway. He must think you're a perfect fit!"

"No interview?" said Mags, her ear almost glued to mine.

"Well, I think the trial period sort of replaces it." Denise sounded confused at the change of voice. I manoeuvred the phone out of Mags's reach, thinking hard. This was all moving at incredible speed. But for once in my life, my inner voice was pushing me to ignore all doubts.

"Okay. So, what's the next step?"

"Well, if you can come in ASAP, I'll run over the contract." Denise's smile lifted her voice. "I can't tell you how pleased I am, Jenny. It's just so perfect, isn't it?"

It was. Almost too perfect. But after what had happened yesterday, now wasn't the time for doubts. I ended the call and turned to confront Mags.

"Look, I know what you're going to say. But I mean, a Shakespeare job! What are the chances?"

She stared back at me, unblinkingly. "I can't get over the fact that you directed a play, and I never even knew about it. We've been friends for, what, eight years? In a drama group, too; and you've not so much as mentioned it."

"It was a long time ago," I said, with forced lightness. "Not a big deal. But if the guy's willing to take me on with that level of experience – well, why not? I've got nothing else."

Her eyes stayed on my face. "Jen, I think you should tread carefully. If there's a month's trial, will you need to keep your flat in case the new job doesn't work out? And how is this guy going to judge your performance, if he's not even in the country? You're only just about to be discharged from hospital, and you're supposed to be keeping away from stress, not diving headlong into it."

I avoided her gaze. "Listen, I can't afford to renew my lease on the flat, so I'll just have to take the risk that I don't end up homeless. But whatever; I can't let that stop me, because this is more than a job, Mags." I swallowed, and raised my eyes tentatively to her face. "For once, I've the chance to do something that excites me; something that doesn't make me feel like a waste of space. I know it seems random, but I've never wanted anything so much in my life."

In the silence that stretched between us, I kept my eyes riveted on her. I could do this without her, but I so wanted her blessing. At last, she drew herself up and gave me a tight little nod.

"Okay. Okay, I get it. I'll even drive you over and help you move in, if you're that sure."

"Oh, Mags!" I could hardly suppress my tears.

"No worries," she said, trying to smile. "Now I need some coffee. You rest, and I'll get us some from downstairs." I nodded and settled back in bed, grateful for some time alone to think. I was doing the right thing – wasn't I? Yesterday, outside Starbucks, the shock of thinking I might die had shaken me out of the feet-deep rut I'd been wading through since the day I started work. But now I had a new job: a second chance at life, and I couldn't let anything stop me from seizing it, however difficult it might prove.

For the second time in twenty-four hours, I threaded my fingers together and offered up another prayer heavenwards, in case someone or something just might be listening.

"*Please, whoever you are,*" I whispered. "*I'm seriously begging you. Don't let this go wrong for me.*"

FOUR

'Enter a clown…'
(Titus Andronicus)

"Wethershall-End!" Mags muttered, as her car lurched along a mud track like a giant tortoise with a hip replacement. "World-End, more like. We should have started out earlier. What's the name of this pub again?"

I fished my phone out of my bag and studied Denise's email.

"The Old Bell. And it's only supposed to be a few yards along the road."

"It had better be," growled Mags. "Even the fogs aren't making much difference in this lot."

The light mist that had descended as we'd entered Northamptonshire had thickened into witches' cauldron fog level, and in the chill afternoon, darkness was already gathering.

Mags flashed me a glance. "How's your vision, now?"

"Much better," I said, averting my eyes. I wished she

wouldn't keep asking, as though I might succumb to a relapse at any moment. "Did you bring the wine?"

"Yes, and some brandy – that should help us relax! And I put two hot water bottles in with the bedding, in case we stay the night. That's assuming there's somewhere to sleep, of course."

"Denise reckons the place is fully furnished," I said.

"You have reached your destination," announced the satnav firmly, as it guided us to the entrance of a fog-bound field.

"Blast!" Mags let down her window to peer out, and her back went ramrod-stiff. "Oh, my God. Jen, don't panic. But I think there are a couple of cows looking at us."

I opened my own window. "They're just trees, Mags," I said impatiently. *Now* who was the jumpy one? Then my senses sharpened. I could distinctly hear the flow of water nearby.

"For goodness' sake, go carefully!" I hissed, as Mags reversed and her bumper biffed a tree. She glowered at me in the dimness.

"It's your bloody agency, giving us the wrong postcode!" Her car graunched in protest as she changed gear. "God, I hate finding new places. I should've brought more wine; we may end up drinking the stock. You'd better ring the agency and check the directions."

"Hello, there." A voice at my shoulder sent my breath hissing into the windscreen. Mags slammed on the brake and fumbled for the interior light.

"It's all right; don't panic, my dears." A man's face, stubbly and topped with sleek silver hair, looked in at my window. His blue eyes twinkled in calm friendliness. "I was asked to come and meet you. Which one's Jenny?" His voice was rich and crumbly, like butter shortbread.

"That's me. Are you Mr Southcote?"

"Aye, but George will do. Good to meet you." He lifted his hand to my window, and I skewed around to grasp it. His fingers were knobbly and rough, like fresh root ginger. "The agency said half three, but you were a bit late, so I wandered down in case you'd got lost in the fog."

"That's very kind," I said. "This is my friend, Mags."

George gave her a friendly nod, then rested his eyes on my face.

"I've been wondering who'd take over the place, now old Jake's gone. I worked for him nigh on thirty-five years, you know, as barman. He were a good man."

"Jake?" I said, all at sea.

"Jacob Reeve. Used to own the pub. He passed on a few weeks ago. His solicitors did say he were leaving it to a friend – but not anyone we know from round here."

"Oh, it's a Mr Leo Norwich," I said. "But he's working abroad at the moment, so he's taken me on as his manager."

"Aye, so I understand. Well, you're very welcome." George scratched his chin, and surveyed Mags's attempts at reversing. "You know, I think I'd best guide you in," he said. "We don't want you ending up in the river. The pub's only a few hundred yards from here."

With a sigh of relief, Mags followed his directions, and within minutes the car eased through a gap in the trees into the huddled presence of a building, lit fitfully by an old security light that drooped from its gable.

"One thing bugs me," murmured Mags, in my ear.

"Why should this Jake Reeve keep the new owner a secret from the locals?"

I blinked back at her, as George fumbled with a set of keys.

"Perhaps he's a stranger to these parts. Anyway, what does it matter?"

"Just asking," said Mags.

"How long has this been shut up?"

I wrinkled my nose as George turned left out of a tiny porch into a big lounge bar crammed with dark, round tables and squat barrel stools. The aroma of sour beer hung in the air; it seemed to be coming from a row of stained beer towels, draped like last-post flags over the chrome taps that lined the bar.

"These'll need a scrub," muttered Mags, running her finger across a sticky-ringed table top.

My spirits sank. I wasn't quite sure what I'd expected, but not this run-down shabbiness. Even with the light on, the room felt weighty with gloom – probably due to the dust-encrusted casement windows.

"It just needs a good clean," I said, trying to sound upbeat. "Are the beams original?" I rested my palm on one of the great blackened pillars that supported the walls.

"They are, that," smiled George. "Oh, aye; there's over four hundred and fifty years of history in this building."

Mags tugged her coat around her.

"Mmm. It's probably that long since it was heated. You could hang half a pig from those rafters, and it would still be fresh next Christmas."

"Okay, it's cold," I said. "But we can soon fix that."

"Oh, come on, Jen. The guy can't seriously expect you to live in this? You'll end up with pneumonia."

"It soon gets warm, when the fires are lit," said George, and I brightened at his kindly tone. "I'm afraid the heating's not working too well at the moment. You'll need to get an engineer in to take a look at it. But meanwhile, the fire's your best bet. I've been coming by and lighting it from time to time since Jake died, just to keep the damp away. And no need to worry about soot falls; I've had the chimneys swept."

Soot falls? I peered up into the enormous brick chimney that dominated the wall adjacent to the bar, half expecting a ton of the stuff to come stuttering down. But it remained at peace, the ashes of its last fire puffed and grey in the grate.

"There's another hearth in the Croft Bar, next door," said George, picking up a fallen log and adding it to the pyramid stacked on one side of the fire. "It gets quite cosy when both are lit. And there's a big supply of logs in the cellar."

"We're going to need them." Mags shivered. "*If* we stay. For goodness' sake, think twice about this, Jenny. It's a total dump," she whispered as I passed her on my way to one of the windows. I'd spied a cosy jumble of faded hardbacks, crammed along its wooden sill. The sight of books always cheered me.

"Shakespeare," said George, as I peered at their titles. "Every last one of them. Jake were very fond of the Bard."

My face split into a smile.

"Bit of a fan, yourself?" he asked, his eyes twinkling.

"You could say that. I'm… here to revive the festival, actually."

"Are you, now? Well, that's the best piece of news I've heard in a long time."

"Did you see any of the performances?" I asked hopefully. I'd been wondering how to find out more about the festival organisation.

"I ran the bar for over thirty of them."

Okay. George was definitely someone to befriend.

"Jenny!" Mags's voice called from somewhere beyond the bar.

"She'll be in the kitchen," said George. "There's a corridor leading to it from behind the bar, but watch your head. It's low." We threaded our way into a small room with a pine dresser, a bare, scrubbed table and some crude shelving. The walls, once white, were yellowed from oil and smoke, and a faintly mouldy smell emanated from the fridge.

"Talk about taking 'distressed' to a whole new level," muttered Mags.

I smothered a laugh. "At least it's got a modern kettle."

"If it works," she said. We followed George out into a small private lounge. A feeble light penetrated its casement windows, either side of which sat two comfy-looking armchairs in red leather and a low round table. In the centre of the room, a dark wooden staircase led up to the second floor, and underneath stood a rough slatted oak door with a latch.

"That's the cellar," said George. "There's all manner of stuff down there, I can tell you. There's another way into it through the trapdoor under the bar, but we only use that for changing barrels. Still, you won't need to worry about that for a while," he added, as I gaped. "I'll soon show you."

"If she ever gets any customers," sniffed Mags. "By the looks of the dust behind that bar, most of the stock's been untouched for a decade. It's probably rank."

Oh, give it up, Mags, I thought.

"Aye. Well, it's been shut for the last two years, you see, while Jake were ill," said George. "Though the new owner's taken an interest, of late. A firm of builders and an electrician were sent round last month, to assess the place and do some quotes on what needs doing. And the electrician came back only a couple of days ago – did a few repairs, and said he's to quote for a rewire. Seems the old place might get a new lease of life, after all."

"Oh?" Mags raised her brows at me. "Well, that's something, anyway."

"What's the upstairs like, George?" I crossed my fingers, praying I wouldn't have to share a room with a family of cockroaches, or sleep on a mouldy mattress.

He beamed. "Ah, well that's in much better shape. There's a couple of decent bedrooms, and Jake had a lovely new bathroom put in not long before he died."

Mags sighed in relief.

"Thank God. I was expecting a shed with a hole in the ground, and a stack of newspapers."

I giggled, and it lightened my mood. George grinned.

"There's a door by the kitchen, leading out the back to the river," he said, nodding towards it. "And another in the Croft Bar. The grounds are pretty extensive. The festivals were open air, though we did put on plays inside in the winter. But I wouldn't go out there in the dark; that river's quite deep in places. Now, I'd better check that the bulb's working in the cellar before I go. You won't want to go down there in the dark, either. That is, if you're planning to stay? The woman at the job agency said you probably would."

"Ah. Denise," I nodded.

"Aye; the new owner apparently gave them my number. They must have got it from Jake's solicitors. He named me as key-holder in his will, you see, until the new owner was ready to take over."

That seemed to make sense. And somehow I found it comforting, that Jake's solicitors knew Mr Norwich. "Yes. We'll be staying," I said.

Mags rolled her eyes. "Right," she sighed. "Well in that case, I'm going to bring our overnight bags in, Jenny. You go with George – but be careful if the light's not too good." I flushed at her reminder of my 'problem'.

George toddled stiffly to the cellar door, lifted the latch and felt for a light switch inside. "There you go," he said, moving aside for me. "It's a bit chilly down there, but there's no damp. The heating only went a month or so ago."

A bare bulb cast swathes of yellow light over a set of worn stone steps that wound into a vast underground room. A thin, rusted banister ran from top to bottom, and I grasped it for support as I peered down. I needed to, for spread out below was a feast of theatrical treasures.

"My God!" I whispered, and George chuckled.

"Be my guest." And I felt my way down, step by step. It was like entering Aladdin's Cave.

A battered copy of *Henry V* peeped from a crate. Boxes and chests spilled over with material of all colours. I fingered some mustard velvet poking out of what looked like a black metal World War One soldier's trunk. The material felt cold to the touch, but quite dry. Painted stage flats leaned against the walls, with pots of paint, brushes and rolls of lining paper heaped in front of them. On the far wall, an imposing plaster bust of Julius Caesar lay on its side. But none of these sights prepared me for what I encountered at the bottom, where the steps curled round on themselves.

A tall, white Roman pedestal stood alone in the yellow light, its base covered in cobwebs. And perched on top, a sallow, bony casing framed a pair of black hollows that stared into emptiness. The bone was pitted here and there with pin spots of black. Below a central triangle of darkness, a monstrous set of protruding teeth curved in a gruesome smile.

"That's a skull," I said, my voice like dry parchment. I looked instinctively up at the cellar door.

"Oh, aye, that's our Henry," said George calmly. "Well, it's either Henry or John; no one quite knows which. He's been in this cellar for as long as anyone remembers. The story is he grew up, here – this place has a long history. He does have his own cardboard box somewhere, but he needs airing now and then." He passed a fatherly hand over the skull's pockmarked pate.

"Er, right," I said, taking a step backwards.

"Local legend has it he were once a clown, desperate to play in one of Shakespeare's tragedies, but it were a dream he never got to fulfil." George gave a soft laugh. "P'raps that's why he's still here. Waiting."

In the silence, the cold closed around us. I began to wonder how long it would take me to get upstairs, if necessary.

"Anyway, that old story were enough for Jake to keep him around. As I said, he did love his Bard. He were a good man, old Jake. Ran the festival here for years, until he got too old, and no one's wanted to take it on since. He had no children, you see."

I stretched out a tentative finger and touched the skull's bony brow, expecting it to feel damp, but it was oddly light and dry. A sour smell wheedled its way up my nostrils, and I hastily stuffed my hand in my pocket, wiping my finger on a tissue.

"Ah, we had some fun in those days." George sighed. "Productions outside, and in the barn; rehearsals upstairs. And we once ran a pageant, down by the river. Oh, the costumes were something, I can tell you."

I pulled my eyes away from 'Henry', wondering what I'd let myself in for. I mean, what sort of man was Jake Reeve, to keep a human skull in his cellar? And did Mr Norwich know?

George gave me an appraising look.

"Well, I must get back, or my old woman'll have the police out looking for me. Doubtless you'd like to explore a bit more down here, once you're settled. I'll bring a new bulb up, though, they tend to go sudden-like, and it's no fun being down here when that happens."

I could imagine. Shivering, I followed him upwards, looking back every now and then at the pale, fleshless face below.

"I'll be seeing you again," said George, wheezing as we arrived upstairs. "I'm only ten minutes away, across the bridge. Oh, and I run a taxi service, by the way. With better rates than most in the area." He dug a card out of his back pocket and handed it to me. "Though I don't expect you'll be needing one, with that car of yours – but you never know.

Now, I promised Jake I'd help out wherever I can, so you let me know if there's anything you need."

Here was my chance.

"Actually, I was wondering if you had any advice on finding actors for the festival play," I said in a rush.

His face eased into a kindly smile. "Ah. Well, your local drama groups are the best place to start. If you pop into the library in the village, they'll give you a list of contacts."

"I'll do that," I said, gratefully.

"And come to think of it, somewhere or other I've the old checklist we used for organising the festival." George scratched his head. "If I can find it, I'll bring it by."

I offered up a silent prayer of thanks. "Oh, that would be amazing."

He held out his hand once more, and it felt warm and corky in my grasp, the way some trees do when you press your palm against them in the heat of summer. "Welcome to Wethershall-End, my dear," he said. "And The Old Bell."

And off he went, leaving me wondering what Mags was going to say when I told her what – or who – was in residence at the bottom of the cellar steps.

FIVE

'Such stuff as dreams are made on...'
(The Tempest)

"Have you seen this other bar, Jenny?" called Mags, as I carried a pile of bedding inside. I dumped it in the lounge bar and went back into the porch, turning the opposite way this time, and found Mags perched on a red velvet-lined settle on one side of a cosy fireplace.

"You'd half expect to find Anne Boleyn and Henry VIII in here, cuddled up on one of these," she said. "In their happier days. Mind you, it smells as if it hasn't been cleaned since then, either. Oh, good Lord!" She recoiled as I opened the nearby door to the gents' urinals.

"Genuine Tudor water closets," I grinned, peering behind the adjacent door. "The ladies isn't so bad, though. This must be the Croft Bar George talked about." I glanced around the snug space, crammed with dark wooden tables and benches, while Mags peered up the winding metal stairs in the far corner.

"It's going to be fun, getting everything up there."

"We can use the stairs at the back," I said, heading into the lounge bar. "They're wider. But first, I think I'll try and get a fire going, till we can sort the heating out." I seized a metal bucket from behind the bar.

"Jen, you can't seriously be thinking of taking this on, now you've seen the place?" Mags asked, as she followed me. "It'd take weeks of work to make it suitable for customers. And you've got a month. No wonder the guy seemed so keen to have you. He obviously can't find…" she bit her lip, her cheeks reddening.

"Anyone else stupid enough? Thanks," I said, grabbing the fireside shovel to scrape up the ash.

"I didn't mean it like that! It's just that with your lack of experience… you know." She took the shovel from me. "Here, leave that to me. I grew up with an open fire. Jen, I'm sorry. But surely you must see that the job's impossible?"

"No, I don't, actually." I straightened up. "I'll go and have a look at the bedrooms. But you don't have to stay overnight if you don't want to."

"Don't be ridiculous. If you're staying, so am I. How are you going to get home?"

Damn. I kept forgetting that I didn't have my car.

I gathered up our bedding and trailed it behind the bar and up the oak staircase, irked by her negativity; and yet, deep down, a little voice whispered that she had a point. Perhaps that *was* why I'd got this job; no one else had agreed to take it on. Well, it gave me an opportunity to prove myself.

The stairs led to a narrow landing, where a dormer window with a broad ledge gave onto the foggy drive. I turned right and encountered two low oak doors that hid a bedroom apiece.

"Wow, that's what I call a bed." I peered into a rangy old room with bare floorboards, on which a sturdy four-poster stood square, a carved oak chest flanking its foot. "Talk about Wolf Hall," I murmured. The room had been stripped bare of personal belongings, but it was full of presence. This must have been Jake Reeve's room. I couldn't invade it. But Mags wouldn't have any such scruples, so I dropped her bedding inside. As I poked my head into the smaller blue and white room next door, which thankfully held no evidence of cockroaches, my phone pinged with an incoming email. Dr Logan, my GP. She'd recently gone techno-mad, sending all her communications direct by text or email.

I sat down on the white wooden bed tucked under the eaves to read her message.

Dear Ms Watson,

I've received an email from Dr Brasier about your hospital admission, and you will receive an appointment for the talking therapy he recommended in due course. I understand that waiting times are currently around six to seven months. Meanwhile, below are details of the self-help group he mentioned. They can be contacted directly.

Kind regards, P. Logan

Underneath was the website address for the confidence-building group, Speak Out. I gazed at it, my insides simmering. My first instinct was to conveniently forget about it and get on with my life.

But I'd promised Mags. Her outburst at the hospital was still fresh in my mind; I couldn't forget the anxiety in her eyes. Didn't I owe it to her to at least go to one meeting, and see what it was all about? I didn't have to commit myself to anything. I seized my phone before I changed my mind, and in seconds was scrolling through details of the various Speak Out groups around the country. There was actually one in Northampton (there *would* be, I thought), run by a woman called Louise Wainwright, who said you could go along and try a session before booking in properly. I felt a stirring of dread as I read the 'description of activities'. It sounded like some awful version of Alcoholics Anonymous and would most likely prove a waste of time – but I gritted my teeth and clicked on the times and dates of meetings. *Monday evening.* This Monday. That was far too close for comfort! But then, maybe it was better not to have too much time to think. There were directions by road to the church hall where the meetings took place, and numbers of buses that stopped nearby. The trouble was, I had no idea where to catch one from. Remembering George's taxi service, I decided that maybe I should book him for my first visit. It would be stressful enough without adding public transport into the mix.

Okay. Sucking in a breath, I keyed in a message to the group leader, giving my name and email, and saying I'd like to attend. My fingers had hardly left the keypad when a reply dropped into my inbox.

Hi, Jenny. We'd love to see you! Please see further details about us below.

My eye ran over the rest of her friendly email as I heard Mags moving about downstairs. I wouldn't tell her until I'd been to my first meeting – just in case I couldn't make it, for some reason. *In case you bottle out*, my inner voice whispered. But somewhere in my heart I knew I couldn't do that, this time.

Wandering back along the landing, I found a dazzling white shower room and toilet – Mags would love it! – then the landing opened into another roomy, open-plan space, all oak beams, off-white walls and wooden floorboards that creaked their age beneath my toes. The top of the metal corkscrew staircase protruded like a crown in the far corner. So this was the room above the Croft Bar. George's words drifted through my mind: *"We had some fun in those days. Productions outside, and in the barn; rehearsals upstairs."* This must be the room they'd used, but it looked more like a storeroom now. I wondered what the faintly musty smell was, and then noticed that its walls were lined with metal clothes racks on wheels, shrouded in thick white polythene. As I plucked at the nearest, dust motes puffed into the light like a swarm of gnats. A rainbow of colour met my eye, and I gave an exclamation so loud it brought Mags pounding upstairs. She panted to a halt beside me, and both our mouths fell wide.

Tunics of rich red brocade were jammed among cloaks of black satin and thick, grey fur; long, heavy-sleeved velvet dresses in canary yellow, scarlet, emerald and olive trailed to the floor; beautiful Tudor doublets in black, brown or mulberry sat stuffed and substantial on their wooden hangers, silken shirts visible beneath their slashed sleeves.

On the floor, covered in sheeting, were boxes of hats from every era; jewels and sashes; boots, shoes and slippers. Behind the door stood a cluster of stage foils in a rusting umbrella stand.

We trod around the room like newly arrived customers at an exotic market for theatre lovers. My brain ran riot, imagining my own cast of actors, decked out in all this finery.

"Oh, Jen," murmured Mags, holding a mulberry doublet reverently to her cheek. "What a find! How often did we long for costumes like this, in our old group? They must be worth a fortune!" She sneezed as she pulled the polythene off a second rack.

"They could do with an airing," I said. "But at least they're not damp. They just need some TLC."

She sighed. "Only give me the chance. God, I'd love to have my own costume business."

I shook my head, thinking how little I knew of her dreams.

"Really? Don't you get enough of sewing all day long?" Mags ran a small but successful garment repair business called 'The Stitchery' from her home.

"This is different. These all tell stories. They must have taken thousands of hours of somebody's time." I looked at the glow in her eyes and wished with everything I had that the costumes were mine. I'd give them to her.

She squeezed the doublet back into its rack.

"I've been thinking," she said, head down. "And I do get it, why you want to do this. I know I get over-protective – you're a bit like a sister to me. Better, actually. I can't imagine having a conversation like this with Victoria, or Caroline;

maybe it's because they were quite young when Mum died, and I had to take over from her. I think they resented me a bit." She swallowed, then shrugged. "I don't think I did a very good job, because they left home, first chance they got. I felt as if I'd lost my whole family in the end, because Dad was never the same."

I blinked at her, my throat pricking at this sudden rush of confidence. I hadn't any experience of sisters, though if I could choose one, it would be Mags. But, as ever, the words I wanted to say and the questions I should have asked knotted in a painful lump somewhere between my gut and my gullet, and the moment passed.

"Anyway, I was thinking," she added, her cheeks blotching. *Shit.* Now we both felt awkward. "If you're set on this, I'd really like to help you. How about I come and stay over Friday to Monday, if you can manage in-between? I've someone to cover The Stitchery at weekends, and to be honest, I'd love a change of scene. Especially now I've seen these." She ran her hand over a silk-lined cloak. "What do you think?"

"Mags, I'd love it!" I said, and cast myself on her for a huge hug, trying to transmit with my body the things I couldn't say. We emerged laughing, a bit ruffled and slightly wet-eyed.

"You know, some of these are going to need dry cleaning," she said, running her eye over the costumes. "Do you think your Mr Norwich will be happy to foot the bill? I mean, we're going to need them for the festival, aren't we?"

"I'll have to enquire." For the first time, it occurred to me how odd it would be, having a working relationship with someone purely through email. Still, people had all kinds of long-distance relationships these days, didn't they? Perhaps it wasn't so unusual.

"Come on, let's rustle up some food," Mags said. "And then I'd love to see all the stuff down in that cellar."

I wondered if she'd still be so keen when she encountered Henry at the bottom of the steps.

"Let's open a bottle of wine while we cook," I said. I had a feeling she was going to need a glass or two.

"I still can't believe someone would keep a human head in their cellar!" exclaimed Mags that evening, as we finished up our pasta by the crackling fire. The pub felt drier and friendlier already. "Or that you're even okay with it! I think that knock on the head must have addled your brain, Jenny. I mean, have you not thought that the old owner could have murdered his wife and chopped her up – and that skull is her head? Don't you think we should inform the police?"

"What? Of course not!" I grabbed my laptop, and started scrolling through an email from Denise. "George said the skull's really old; probably an heirloom. And he may come in useful, if we put on *Hamlet*. A real skull would be great publicity."

Her brows arched. "*He?*"

My ready flush rose up. "George said it's a 'he'. He's called Henry." Mags cast her eyes upwards. "Anyway, look. Denise has sent over the contract, and the job sounds completely manageable. The festival performances aren't till May, so I've plenty of time, and Mr Norwich will take care of all the licences, correspondence and stuff."

"How's he going to do that, if he's hundreds of miles away?"

I peered at the screen. "He's thought of all that. I'm to take photos of all correspondence and email it to him. He says the first priority is the festival. That means getting a play cast and into rehearsal as quickly as possible; then we'll talk about opening the pub."

Mags frowned. "Well, that's weird in itself. So he's prepared to pay your wages without getting any customers through the door. Surely it should be the other way around? Did he send any guidelines on running the festival? I mean, you've never done any events organising, have you?"

I sighed. As fond as I was of her, discussions with Mags sometimes felt like a run-in with the Spanish Inquisition.

"No," I said, "but George has. And he's going to advise me."

She turned this over in her mind. "So does the contract say when you get paid?"

"I have to work a month in hand."

"Oh, goodness – I hadn't thought of that. Are you going to be able to manage?"

"I have my redundancy money, remember; that will keep me going. Besides, I'll get two months' money when I leave." Though I hoped it would be a good while before that happened. I looked around the bar, so much more cheerful now, in the dancing light of the fire. A good clean would soon make the place homelier. "Look, if I want the job, Denise says I should sign and return this contract by tomorrow evening. And that's it. I can stay on."

I waited, hoping she wouldn't make this difficult.

"O-kay," she said. "I suppose that means you'll need to fetch your stuff."

Shit. This car thing was going to be a real issue out here. "Listen, why don't I stay over for the weekend, then I can drive you to the flat Sunday morning and help you pack? We can bring the urgent stuff over on the same day, stick the rest in my garage, and I'll ferry it across, bit by bit. I mean, it isn't as if there's a lot."

I sprang up and gave her another bear hug. "Oh, Mags. I owe you big time for this. But I'm paying for the petrol and food and everything. Okay?"

A sudden tapping at the window made us both jump.

"What the hell was that?" whispered Mags.

I opened my mouth to say it was probably some ivy blowing against the glass, when her fingers dug hard into my arm. In the orange glow of the pub lights, an unmistakable shape was sliding slowly across the casement windows. The head and shoulders of a man.

"Who is it?" I said, my chest tightening. Mags put a finger to her lips and drew me out of the light.

"Did you lock the front door?" she breathed.

"I... don't know. I think so."

Her face quivered. "I'll check. Get your phone. We may need to call the police."

Heart pattering, I made for the kitchen, while Mags trod softly towards the front door. I spied my phone on the table and swept it up. *Oh, God.* No battery! I'd meant to charge it earlier and forgot – and I had no idea where I'd put my charger. Mags's bag sat, lean and neat, on one of the benches, and I felt inside it with shaking fingers. No phone there, either. A familiar ache radiated upwards from my neck, and in the corners of my vision, two mottled patches appeared.

*Christ; no. It couldn't be happening again. I was better –
wasn't I?*

I took a few steady breaths, forcing myself to count. The
patches didn't advance. Okay.

I slipped back to Mags, who'd just reached the porch.
"My phone's dead, and yours isn't in your bag!"

Her pupils expanded. "Upstairs!" she hissed. And then
a metallic click froze us where we stood. Slowly, smoothly,
the front door latch was lifting.

My eyes flew to the bolts at the top and bottom of the
door, and I could have wept with relief. They were both in
place. Mags gripped my arm.

"Use the landline," she murmured in my ear. Thank
God she'd noticed we had one. "It's on the bar."

I edged back into the lounge, keeping to the walls,
trying to ignore the murky blotches in the corners of my
eyes. *I'm fine. I will be fine, as long as I stay calm.* A little black
phone sat in a cradle next to the till. I snatched it up with
clammy fingers, pressed the 'call' button and glued it to my
ear, as Mags threaded her way towards me. But there was
no comforting burr; only a dry click. She met my eyes, her
own deepening in fear.

"Upstairs; run!"

Panic rising, we shot towards the little lounge – and as
our hands grasped the banister, a brisk hammering burst
from the back door. We both leapt with nerves, Mags's
hand coming out to grip my arm. My eyes followed her as
she lifted the other, and silently pointed to the two bolts.
They were both undone.

But I'd locked them. I *knew* I had!

Mags breathed hard in my ear. "Hang on," she

murmured. "Are we being a couple of idiots, here? A burglar wouldn't knock on the door."

A faintly familiar, cheery voice called out.

"Hallo, in there! Sorry to disturb you so late. But I've got something for you."

"George!" I grasped the banister as my legs gave way.

"Oh, for f... pity's sake!" Mags never used hard expletives, so that little slip spoke volumes.

"I'll let him in." I took a step forward, but my legs sagged as though they were stuffed with straw. "Hang on, George!" I quavered.

"Let him in? We ought to damn well send him packing!" Mags snapped. "What does he mean by going about lifting door latches without knocking first? Are you all right, Jenny?"

"Mags, don't," I said, tottering across the little lounge. "He's really sweet, and he worked here, remember? He's probably been used to walking in whenever he likes."

She pursed her mouth as I heaved the door open and George appeared, beaming at us as though we were long-lost relatives.

"Ah, there you both are. All settled in?" He glanced from me to Mags, and his smile faltered. "Oh, I am sorry. I shouldn't have knocked so late," he went on, "but I was on my way over to see a friend and thought you might like this." He held out a yellowing, typewritten sheaf of papers headed WETHERSHALL-END SHAKESPEARE FESTIVAL.

"You found it!" I exclaimed. "Thank you, George. You're a lifesaver!"

He grinned. "Aye, well – it's a bit behind the times, but chances are it'll get you on the right track."

My eyes scanned through line after line of 'action points'. There was enough work here for months. Licences, Fire and Safety Regulations – I hadn't even considered those.

"It looks worse than it is," George said, kindly. "Well, look – I'll get off. But you let me know if you want any help updating it."

"Thank you, I will. And there's one other thing I wanted to ask you. How do I find out more about Hen – the skull, George? I thought I might use it to drum up some interest in the festival play."

George nodded. "Thinking of doing *Hamlet,* are you? Makes sense. Old Jake put it on a few times, but none of the actors could ever bring themselves to handle a real skull." He scratched his head. "There's not a lot known about old Henry, I'm afraid. Only a few folktales. One thing they do say is, he were hanged, poor beggar, just for stealing a coin. I've always thought it were a poor end for a chap who made his living making people laugh."

I remembered those empty eyes, staring into their own darkness. Here was a fool who'd dreamed of playing a tragedy and ended up living one.

"There's a little museum in the village that can tell you a bit more about the pub's history," suggested George. "Next to the library. Quickest way is out the back, over the bridge and turn right along by the river. Takes about twenty minutes."

"George, you're a marvel." I followed him to the back door, then locked and bolted it once he'd toddled off into the night.

"You know, I'm really sure I bolted this earlier," I said, half to myself.

"You couldn't have done." Mags frowned at me. "Jen, are you sure you're happy being here on your own? I mean, the place is really remote, and there's no proper security."

"Of course. I'll be fine." Though I'd certainly research cheap burglar alarms.

She grimaced. "I need a brandy."

My laptop pinged with an incoming email as I followed her into the lounge bar. "Oh, great. It's from Mr Norwich, my new boss. He says he welcomes me to the pub and looks forward to our working relationship."

Mags sniffed. "And that's it?"

"Well, it's good of him to get in contact so soon," I said. "I expect he'll write more once I've settled in."

My fingers hovered over the keyboard, ready to reply – then stilled, as an unwelcome thought slid into my mind. Mags was rooting about behind the bar.

"Mags?"

"Mmm?"

I hesitated, not wanting her to think I'd become neurotic.

"Um, we're assuming George tried the front door, then went round to the back, is that right?"

"Yes. What's up?" She surfaced, clasping two brandy glasses.

"Well... it's just that George has got really stiff legs, and he doesn't walk very fast, does he? This building is quite big – and he got round to the back at the same time we did. In the dark, too. I mean..."

I stopped, as her eyes turned slowly back towards the window.

"I know what you mean, Jenny," she said, grimly.

SIX

'There is nothing either good or bad, but thinking
makes it so.'

(Hamlet)

"What I still don't understand is why you have to ask
his permission to call the police."

Saturday morning, and Mags and I were huddled in the
kitchen in our coats, finishing our pancakes and the last of
the coffee from Mags's cafetière. Pancakes were her favourite
breakfast, which she said she needed after she'd 'hardly slept
a bloody wink'. My laptop sat on the table beside me, with
Mr Norwich's late-night email open on display.

"Because it's in the contract," I said.

"*What?*" She lowered her mug, staring. "You haven't
signed it, yet – have you?"

"Not yet. But I went through it with Denise when we
visited the agency, and there's a clause that says I must
inform the proprietor of any 'complaints, disturbances or
altercations' before reporting them to the authorities."

"You have *got* to be joking."

"I expect he just wants to be kept up to speed," I said. "Look, Mags: it is a pub, after all. There must have been 'disturbances' in the past, and he's responsible for the place. It would be pretty awkward to get a call from the police, and not have a clue what they were talking about."

"That's nonsense – you're the manager! Surely the police would approach you, rather than him, anyway?"

I shrugged. "Possibly. But as the owner, the buck stops with him. And at least he cares!"

The cafetière clinked ominously as she slapped it down on the table.

"*You're* the one living here. And all that rubbish about it being a customer who thought the pub might be open. All the locals must know how long it's been shut."

"I've told you – he explained all that!" I said, turning my laptop screen so that she could read Leo Norwich's response to my panicky message.

Dear Jenny,

I'm certain your 'visitor' was an old customer who saw the lights on inside and assumed the pub was open. I'm told people used to travel for miles to visit it. The fact that the guy left quietly, as soon as he found the door locked, speaks for itself, so I don't think there's any cause for alarm. Please try not to worry, and do let me know if you have any further concerns. Good luck with settling in, and I'll look forward to receiving your first weekly progress report.

Kind regards,

Leo Norwich

His calm, measured tone had instantly reassured me. Not so, Mags. It had taken all my persuasive powers to restrain her from calling 999.

"He got back to me really quickly," I said, "which shows he was concerned."

She snorted. "If he's that bothered about your welfare, he should get the heating fixed. I bet you didn't put that in your email, did you?"

"Not yet. I'll mention it next time."

I rubbed a hand over my neck, and Mags looked sharply at me.

"Headache?" she asked.

"*No.* I'm fine."

She ignored my frosty tone. "Why don't you get some fresh air while I'm having a shower, and take a walk into the village? The fog's cleared, and we could do with a few groceries, now we're staying on. There's a list by the kettle."

I had to smile. Of course there was. If we went on a sailing trip and ended up wrecked on a desert island, Mags would produce a 'to do' list she'd prepared earlier.

"Good idea," I said. "I'll take the shortcut George spoke about, over the river. I'd like to check out this library."

If I only had a month to get a play cast and in rehearsal, I'd no time to lose finding some actors.

Heaving open the old back door, I found a tiny patio, set with a round metal café table and two chairs, facing the mid-March sun. Just right for morning coffee in summer – if I managed to pass my month's trial. *And I would.* Of course I would. I'd already settled on a play, and maybe by this evening, I'd have a mailing list of potential actors.

Pulling my coat around me, I tentatively circled the building. Its rambling spread enchanted me. To someone brought up in an urban world, its grounds were bewilderingly extensive. Behind the Croft Bar, I discovered a spacious gravel patio, on which a number of wooden trestle tables stood, grey with wet and spotted with moss. An expanse of rough, green lawn stretched beyond them to the river, where a neat wooden bridge curved across to the other side. On the opposite bank ran a footpath, bordered by a grassy verge that gave on to woodland. I squelched my way through the grass, down to the water, and stood there for a moment, sniffing the mossy air and wondering what the river's green, sluggish depths would be like in summer. For a blissful moment, I imagined living here always; seeing this view every day for the rest of my life. Mr Norwich was a lucky man. Well, I'd have a shot at making a life here for a while anyway, and the change of pace would be better than any therapy.

My spirits skipped at the sight of a great willow, trailing its rough, brown hair in the river, and I wondered for a moment if our own willow tree – the one I'd helped my father to plant as a child – was anywhere near as big by now. A smile hovered; I could still catch the faint timbre of my father's voice in my head, as we'd lowered the young sapling into the hole I'd helped to dig – though I could no longer picture his face. *"Willows are full of life, Jenny. Even if you strip everything off a willow twig, if you stick it in a pot or in the ground, it'll grow."*

I lingered briefly beneath the pub's magnificent tree, watching beads of moisture tremble on its branches: tiny globes in which miniatures of the old building behind me danced in the morning light. The grey and brown stone pub looked as though it had emerged from a long sleep, with its dappled roof of red tiles gleaming; its dormer windows protruding like faces eager to find the sun.

Two other trees stood between it and the river: an immense oak and a cherry. I'd read somewhere that you could calculate the age of a tree by the number of times your arms reached around it: each circumference reflecting a century. In a moment of abandonment, I thrust my arms wide and circled the oak like a schoolgirl, its rough bark against my cheek. If the story were true, then this tree must be over four hundred years old. Was Henry alive, when it threw out its first shoots?

Adjacent to the pub stood a black vault of a barn, with a mossy, brown-tiled roof. I made my way inside. It felt like entering a church: deep and sweet and silent, and George's words flashed through my mind: "*Productions outside and in the barn; rehearsals upstairs. And we once ran a pageant, down by the river.*" I looked around, trying to imagine the eager audience, and anticipation swelled inside me: everything I'd secretly dreamed of, but had never dared to hope for. Once again, the idea that some happy trick of fate had sent me here flickered in my mind. And all I could think of was, *I mustn't mess this up.*

My phone pinged with a text from Mags:

I'm locking all the doors, so text me when you're back. M x

The memory of our evening 'visitor' disturbed my pleasurable thoughts, and I hunched my collar around me as I made for the bridge. No, it had to be a customer. We had no reason to think otherwise.

The village of Wethershall-End was quaint and colourful, with a parade of shops set higher than the pavement, accessed by uneven stone steps, trimmed here and there with black, twisted iron railings. The library operated from an old Victorian schoolhouse of gentle grey stone, tucked away by the village pond, with the small museum next door. I lost no time in obtaining a library card from the young receptionist, then bore down on a glossy copy of *The Witches of Wethershall-End: Myths and Histories* that was sitting proudly in the window display.

"Could I take this out, please?" I asked the angular-faced librarian who was arranging books nearby. She looked up, her eyes blinking behind her spectacles.

"Oh, yes, dear, that's a wonderful book. Half a sec, and I'll have it all done for you." I followed her as she whisked my choice over to the loans desk. Her eyes flicked over my card. "New to the area, are you?"

"I've just come to live at the pub: The Old Bell."

In the fiction aisles, several well-coiffured heads popped up over the tops of plastic-clad novels.

The librarian broke into a delighted laugh. "Well, now, isn't that a coincidence? Jake Reeve's old place? We had someone in here just this morning, asking why it wasn't open. Are you a relative of Jake's?"

I felt a prickle of apprehension. "No, I'm the new manager, actually. So... did you know the person asking about the pub?" I got the question in just as she opened her mouth to fire off one of her own.

"Oh, yes, that's old Ted Hernshaw, bless him. He used to live in the village, but moved out, years ago, to be near his son. He was on his way home from visiting some friends, and thought he'd pop in for a drink; catch up with Jake. He looked so upset when I told him the news."

Well, at least we now had an explanation for last night's debacle. If George had come along the riverbank and over the bridge, he would naturally have knocked at the back door, while this other visitor came to the front. Strange we hadn't heard a car, though, or seen its lights. Perhaps he'd parked up the lane and walked to the pub, or someone had dropped him in the village. Oh, there were a dozen explanations. Mags and I were clearly getting paranoid because the place was so lonely, and neither of us were used to it.

"Well." The librarian handed me my book. "You'll find a bit on the old pub in here. And it's got loads about the witches' hangings, of course." I smiled, weakly, not sure I wanted that much detail. "There's probably a lot more myth than history," she went on cheerfully, "but it's a good read. And if you're interested in finding out more about the village, the museum has a nice little collection. It's closed this morning, though. Open again on Monday."

"Thank you," I said. "I'll pay it a visit. And… could you give me some contact details for local drama groups, please?"

There was a rustle among the books behind me.

"Yes. Of course. We have a list online. Let me write the link down for you." She scribbled on a card and handed it to me. "We had a local group until a couple of years ago, but sadly it closed down. Your nearest now would be in Mile-End. Some of our old members go there. In fact" – she waved a hand towards the door – "a few of them often meet on a Saturday lunchtime at the café across the road.

If you ask Glenys, behind the counter, she'll point them out to you. We'll look forward to seeing the old pub open again, then!"

I thanked her, jittering a little at my new challenge, and bore my book off towards the café. As I crossed the road, I glanced up; a thick-set man in jeans, a black puffer jacket and a grey woollen beanie hat and scarf was lounging against the wall at the end of an alleyway, between a newsagent's and a butcher's shop. He dropped his head into the scarf, and disappeared quickly into the alleyway, but I had the strange feeling he'd been watching me. Then I shook myself inwardly; the guy was probably just taking a break from work. I stepped aside to let a blonde woman pass me on her way to the café, and edged towards the alley. It was empty, but at the top I spied what looked like a print shop. Maybe he worked there. Yes, that had to be it.

SEVEN

'Make not your thoughts your prisons.'
(Antony and Cleopatra)

Gathering up my flat white and plate of lemon drizzle from the counter, I followed the direction of Glenys's finger.

"Over there, dear," she beamed. "By the window. Gordon and his wife. They're into all that am-dram stuff."

Normally, I'd run a mile rather than go up and accost a pair of total strangers. *But this is for the job,* I told myself. So I ignored my gurgling insides and approached the couple: an older man sporting slick, silver-grey hair and a soft, tan leather jacket, and a plump, wavy-blonde woman in a summer-blue sweater that matched her eyes.

"Hi," I said, with a nervous smile, as I sidled towards the seat opposite theirs. "Is anyone sitting here?" The man glanced around at the virtually empty café, and I cringed at my ineptness. But the woman's face broke into an eager smile.

"Oh, hello. You're the lady from the library! Yes, do join us. I'm Diana." She held out her hand. "This is Gordon, my husband. You're new to the village, aren't you?"

"Diana, give the poor girl a chance to sit down, before you start interrogating her." Gordon rose with a smile for me and an impatient glance at his wife.

"Jenny Watson," I said.

I slid into the spare seat, slopping my coffee into its saucer. *Not* the smooth impression I wanted to give.

"So, you're managing The Old Bell?" Diana steamed on as though Gordon was invisible, and his grey eyes silvered with annoyance. "I overheard you talking to Liz in the library. We thought that old place had had it, you know – rumours went round about it being permanently shut up. I'm so glad it won't be! You said you were looking for a local drama group?"

I nodded, slightly dazed by her enthusiasm.

"Diana and I were members of the Wethershall-End Amateur Players," explained Gordon.

"'Were' being the operative word." Diana sighed. "It got too expensive for us to perform at the school, you see – and that's the only place with a stage. Then the membership dwindled away completely. So now we're with the Mile-End Players, down the road. We're doing *Othello* at the moment."

Well, that was hopeful; it could mean a ready supply of Shakespearean actors.

"If you're interested in joining, I can give you Helen's number?" suggested Gordon. "She's our current director, and a good friend of my wife's. We're always on the lookout for new members." He ran his eyes over my face. "I'm sure she'd love some help backstage."

I choked a bit over my coffee. He didn't seem to think much of my chances as an actress. And what was wrong with working backstage, anyway?

"Oh, for goodness' sake, Gordon!" snapped Diana. She leaned forward with a wink. "You can see why he's playing Desdemona's father. You know: bad-tempered and despotic. Type-casting, of course." I couldn't help feeling a ripple of liking for her.

"Don't start, Diana," muttered Gordon. He drew a clean serviette towards him and scribbled a number down on it, and an email address, then pushed it towards me.

"Here you are. I'm sure Helen would be delighted to hear from you."

"Actually, I'm glad you mentioned Shakespeare," I said. If I was going to get them onside, it was now or never. "That's why I'm here, you see. The pub's new owner wants to re-establish the festival, and I'm organising and directing it. So I'm looking for some actors."

I felt a sliver of satisfaction at their stunned faces – particularly Gordon's.

"Wow!" Diana's eyes ran over my face, as though reappraising me. "We were aware that Jake had left it to a friend, but he was a very private man, so none of us had a clue they might be a theatre buff! You'll have to tell us all about him – or her. And I can't believe you're taking on the festival!"

"You'll certainly have your work cut out," said Gordon, grimly, and my smile wavered. They made it sound like organising a NATO conference. "What's the opening play going to be?"

"*Hamlet*," I said, with satisfaction. He couldn't find fault with that.

"Mmm." Gordon tipped his head to one side. "Bit of an obvious choice, but I suppose it'll do."

My mouth fell open. Who on earth did the man think he was?

"Oh, Gordon!" sighed Diana. "I'm sure Jenny knows what she's doing." Her blue eyes smiled into mine and my ready flush rose up. "I expect you've loads of experience at this sort of thing, haven't you? You'd hardly be here, otherwise. Where have you worked before?"

Shit. Now what did I say?

Should I lie about this – or at least embroider the truth? *No*. My tell-tale blushing gave me away every time – sometimes even when I told the truth. There was only one thing to do. Withholding information couldn't be classified as lying.

"Actually, it's my first time running a festival," I said. Diana's eyes popped a little.

"But I'm sure you've directed plenty of productions," smiled Gordon.

I carefully avoided his eyes. "One or two." My cheeks had now reached scorching point. Gordon and Diana exchanged glances. "Actually, I wondered if you could give me some advice," I said. Diversion was always good. "I need to hold my auditions quite soon, so I'm looking for some help to spread the word."

Gordon sat back, tenting his fingers, watching me. It felt like my bloody HR interview all over again.

"I see. How quickly?"

"Um… I need to get the play cast in the next two weeks."

"Really? That's hardly any time at all. When's the performance?"

"End of May," I said. He frowned, and I began to regret having approached him.

"Are the actors getting paid, at all?"

I took a sip of coffee, trying to look casual and in control, but my hand shook, and some of the hot liquid spilled onto my sweater. "No. I mean – it's not a professional production."

I reached for a serviette and glanced down at my chest, watching the stain sink slowly in, my hand itching to scrub it away. But I didn't touch it. If you rubbed a spill in, it would never come out – I'd learned that the hard way. An image of stained sheets flashed into my mind; of my small hand scrubbing and scrubbing, my stomach full of knots. I closed my eyes, pushing nausea away, trying to focus on Gordon. But my mind kept pulling me back to the warm patch on my sweater. *I couldn't let it stain.*

"Right. And how many performances?"

"Er… six."

All I could think of was getting to the ladies and trying to blot my sweater before the stain set. I couldn't leave it much longer.

Gordon's eyes rested on my face. "You might be pushing it a bit, trying to find a cast in a fortnight," he said.

I kept my hands locked together in my lap, but the stain on my sweater grew and pulsated in my mind. I had to get to the toilets and deal with it.

"Oh, honestly, Gordon! Stop giving her the third degree!" Diana broke in.

"Would you excuse me a moment?" I said, scrambling up. "I need the loo."

"Of course! Up the steps," called Diana, helpfully, as I

hurried off, trying to hold my sweater away from my skin without being too obvious.

I thought I'd got over all this. It hadn't happened for months. Thankfully, the toilets were empty. I soaked my serviette in cold water and began to sponge and sponge and sponge, then dab, dab, dab with shaking fingers, as my mother's words hissed through my head, like steam from an over-hot iron. *"You've been clumsy again. Haven't you, Jenny?"* I bent over the sink, trying to fight the dread that blossomed in my belly: the leaden realisation that what I'd done could not be undone. *There were only consequences.*

"Jenny? Are you all right? You've been ages."

Diana's voice made my whole body judder. I pitched the serviette hastily into the bin and covered the stain with my hand.

"Yes. Fine, thanks. Sorry." I glanced in the mirror, knowing I probably felt worse than I looked. I'd had years of practice, covering up moments like this, and most people never had an inkling of the turbulence I carried within me.

"No problem." She looked at me, full of concern. "We were only a bit... look, would you like another coffee? We're having one."

"Oh... no. Thanks." I turned, with a resolute smile. "I've got to get home. Lots to do."

She smiled at me in the mirror, as she fluffed up her blonde hair. "You know, I think you're very brave, taking on the festival," she said. "And I'd love to help – if you need any, that is."

My knee-jerk reaction was to deny any such need and get out of there as fast as possible. But the kindness in her eyes and my desperation not to fail at my new job stopped me. I couldn't keep running away.

"Actually, I'd love some," I said, with shaky resolution. "I'm far from brave, and to be honest – I'm not quite sure how I'm going to manage it all."

I hadn't made such an admission to a stranger since childhood. But there was something about Diana. Something I yearned to have – a carefree joy in everything she did and said. Where had it come from? Could it be learned? If there were classes to teach that, rather than picking over a past that was best left buried, I'd attend them like a shot.

Diana opened her bag and extracted a card. "Look, this is me. Email me your audition details, and I'll see they get around to the right people. And don't let Gordon put you off. He can be quite negative when he wants to be. He spent years at the helm of a huge company; misses having the control." She grinned. "Doesn't really work, when you're married to someone like me. What days and times were you thinking of holding the auditions?"

"I hadn't decided," I said.

She nodded. "Well, the sooner the better, then. Maybe one evening this week, as you've not much time. Social media's so instant; it's better not to give people too much time to think."

My breathing calmed, and, in an unguarded moment, I lifted my hand to push some hair off my face. Diana's eyes went straight to the stain on my sweater, and my cheeks flamed anew.

"Ah. I noticed you'd had a bit of a spill. Here." She fished in her bag and brought out a navy scarf.

"The colour's not amazing with that sweater, but no one will notice," she said. "I always carry a spare, because I'm constantly spilling stuff. Gordon says I need a bib."

I glanced at her; she seemed so well groomed, I couldn't imagine a stain coming anywhere near her.

"Borrow it," she said, pushing the scarf into my hands. "I'm sure we'll run into each other soon. In fact, if you're opening the pub, we could pop round for a drink or a coffee one morning. Meanwhile, shall we settle on this Thursday evening for a first audition? At the pub, I presume?"

She took my breath away, but I nodded. Her enthusiasm was refreshing yet unnerving at the same time. But I already had my list of contacts; surely I could attract some interest if I emailed everyone? So I thanked her as I arranged the scarf around my neck.

"See? No one would ever know." She winked at me. "Our little secret."

I followed her back into the café. If only all secrets were that easy to hide.

Gordon smiled up at us as we arrived back at our table. His eyes travelled to the scarf around my neck, but he made no comment.

"So, Jenny, you were going to tell us who's taken over The Old Bell?"

"Ooh, yes, do give us all the gossip!" said Diana at once, slipping back in beside him.

I hesitated. "Well... I really don't know anything about him, other than he's called Leo Norwich, and he works abroad. Germany, I suspect, because his email address ends in .de."

Diana's face sharpened with curiosity. "God, this is a real mystery! We'll have to get to the bottom of it, Jenny."

"All in good time." Gordon leaned towards me. "There *is* something you could possibly help us with, though. Jake had a big store of costumes – he used to let us borrow them from time to time. I wondered, if they're still there, could you ask this Mr Norwich of yours if we could hire some, for *Othello*? We'd be happy to pay going rates, of course."

Wow. That was the last thing I'd expected.

"Yes, of course I'll do that," I said. "If you give me the dates and let me know exactly what you need."

"Excellent!" He rubbed his hands together. "Tell you what, jot down your email address and I'll get you a list." He pushed another serviette and his biro towards me. "And in return, send over your audition stuff, and I'll ring a few people. Do what I can to drum up some interest."

In a flutter of relief, I scribbled down my details, then gathered up my coat. I had to find a shop that sold some good stain remover.

"And do me a favour: email me your CV as well," he added, and those silver eyes glinted into mine for a second. "People need to know who you are."

My spirits sank. Well, that wasn't going to happen... unless I made it a work of fiction.

EIGHT

'What's past is prologue...'
(The Tempest)

Monday morning came so quickly that Mags and I were in a daze as we crawled back and forth from the pub, packing her car. Clearing out my flat, plus a major spring-clean of the pub kitchen and the gents' loo had left us both stiff and aching. I probably now had housemaid's knee, not to mention hands. But I daren't complain; Mags was a brick to help – despite her obvious lack of enthusiasm for my exciting new job.

"We'll have a go at that lounge bar next weekend," she said, bundling her quilt onto the back seat.

"Remember we're invited over to the *Othello* rehearsal at Mile-End on Saturday night. You know, the prospective costume hire I told you about."

"Oh, yes." Her eyes gleamed. "I'm glad that so-called boss of yours agreed. He should be pleased you're making him some money."

"He is. Thanks for offering to do the measuring up, though, Mags."

"No worries." She gave me a quick hug. "You know I'm happy doing it. I've had a great weekend, despite the work. And don't forget to air as many costumes as you can when you've got the fire lit."

I smiled. "Will do."

"Now listen, are you sure you don't want to change your mind, and come back with me?"

"Mags, we've been through all this," I said, with an exasperated laugh. "I'll be fine. I've got bags of work to finish; I probably won't have time to sleep. Joke," I added, as her eyes narrowed.

"I wish you'd set the auditions for Friday, so I could be here."

"Diana said Thursday's a better night."

"And you can manage by yourself?" I rolled my eyes like a teenager. "I'll call you," she shouted, as her little car rocked away over the gravel. "And I'll bring some fan heaters down with me on Friday. Keep the fire going!"

I waved until she drew out of sight, then turned back into the pub. After a weekend of companionship, I'd rarely felt so alone.

Opening my laptop, I pulled up the tenth version of my fictitious CV. Mags had told me not to be so precious about it. "Gordon's not your employer," she'd said. "He's hardly going to check all the details."

But although I occasionally stretched the truth in conversation, writing bare-faced lies was another matter. Perhaps if I shipped the audition details over to Gordon without my CV, he wouldn't notice. I prepared my email and sent it off, then made quick work of the library list e-shot advertising for *Hamlet* cast members. A reasonable first attempt, I thought: short and punchy, and headed up with an image of a skull I'd found on the internet, to hook people's interest.

"Now what?" I said to the empty pub.

It remained as dumb and silent as a museum; an apt description with Henry lurking beneath my feet in the cellar. I remembered the actual museum in the village. Perhaps I should visit it to see what I could find out about my new home, and have lunch at that cosy café across the road.

I grabbed my coat and went to lock up.

Inside, the museum building opened up like a stone Tardis, stretching up and back, with light walls and dark, polished wood doors and floor. An oak staircase, encased in twisted white metal spindles and topped with a sweeping mahogany banister, wound to the upper galleries.

The room was dominated by a broad oak desk, at which a young woman in a black skirt, matching jacket and cream blouse stood, bent over a computer screen. Her dark bob swung back and forth over a tiny face made studious by a pair of Clark Kent glasses. Probably late twenties/early thirties. Despite the 'Reception' sign at her elbow, she seemed disinclined to register my presence; but when I enquired tentatively about the history of The Old Bell, she looked up, surveying me as though I was an unpalatable nibble she'd been offered at a business seminar. Then she inclined her head towards the stairs, and went back to her work.

"First floor, second room." Her gold and black name badge glinted in the light. *Sarah Lander.*

"Is there anything on local theatre?" I ventured. She sighed her reply, without looking up.

"Same room. Entertainment is all in one place." Her face looked so bored and resigned that I found myself imagining her thoughts in caption form, like the T-shirts you find in tourist shops. *I applied for the Natural History Museum and ended up here.*

I left her to it. Perhaps it was just a bad day.

Wandering around the creaking floors and glass cases, I found a bewildering array of jumbled artefacts – far too many to take in on a short visit. Then a case of old correspondence caught my eye; in particular, a scrap of parchment, faded and worn at the edges. Its writing was difficult to make out through the glass, but a label below declared it to be '*a fragment of a letter found among Edward Bennington's household accounts'.* The next two lines had my breath steaming up the glass. '*It mentions a local performance of a play in 1593. Though the play isn't named, scholars believe it may have been Shakespeare's* Titus Andronicus.'

A local performance! Could that be possible? I'd read that only licensed acting groups were allowed to perform publicly in Shakespeare's time. But 1593; surely that was one of those years when the London playhouses were closed due to plague? If so, the various troupes of players would have been forced to split up and tour the countryside. Maybe – just maybe – this fragment referred to such a tour.

My attention was arrested by a couple of words I could just make out, scrawled near the margin. I might be imagining things, but they looked like 'our clowne'. And then, in the next line along I found 'the players', and a spidery scrawl that could easily have been 'Lundun'. Rubbing the glass clear, I ran my eyes down the document; and there, on another line, I found the words 'Roman' and 'tragedie' – and surely that word before 'tragedie' was 'bloodie'? I fixed my gaze on the last word, my fingers curling. Only one Shakespeare play I could think of fitted such a date and description: *Titus*. It all made sense... except the mention of 'our clowne'. Did that mean a local actor had taken part? *Titus* did have a clown; a tiny part, normally doubled with another in performance.

Then I remembered what George had said about Henry. *"Local legend has it he were once a clown, desperate to play in one of Shakespeare's tragedies."* No, it had to be a coincidence, that old story? Though even the suggestion of truth would make a great PR article. Excitement prickled through me. A play that had actually been performed here, in Shakespeare's time! Oh, surely I would earn some Brownie points from my new boss for this! Unfortunately, *Titus* ranked as the only Shakespeare play I'd read that I couldn't bear; I'd had to study it briefly for one of my courses, and found it disturbingly violent.

The clack of heels behind me made me jump: the bob-haired curator had come upstairs to check on me, her hands wrapped around a clipboard. She was followed by a man in a tweed hacking jacket and brown chinos. He had a mop of floppy brown hair that kept falling into his eyes, so he had to keep pushing it back. She consulted her clipboard, led him to one of the shelves of old books that lined the room, and indicated a substantial volume.

"Here you are, Mr Whitaker."

I almost gasped as her face split into a smile.

"Thank you. And as I've said before, the name's Ben, okay?" he said, the skin around his eyes crinkling attractively.

A faint flush spread over her cheeks; another person with my own affliction.

"If you need anything else, you only have to call."

What a U-turn in attitude; perhaps he was a museum official or something.

"Excuse me, could you tell me any more about this item?" I called after her, as she tapped back towards the stairs. She halted, turned and approached, trying her best to look accommodating, no doubt because Mr Whitaker was still in earshot.

"I can try, of course, but we know very little. It was donated by a local family, the Benningtons, sadly all gone now. The last surviving family member left us a collection of their old household expenses, going back to the 1500s, and one or two other papers were found tucked inside it, including this. It caused quite some excitement when it was found. The ink in this fragment is so faded that it's only possible to make out a few words, but I'll give you a transcript of what we have." She sifted through some folders in a cabinet nearby, and handed me a sheet. It confirmed the words 'tragedie', 'Lundun', 'Roman' and 'bloodie', but not 'clowne'. When I told her what I suspected, she showed a spark of interest, as did the man in the tweed jacket, now seated at a table with his book.

"You could be right," she said, peering into the cabinet. "But it's really so faded, I don't think it was picked up. You have a very sharp eye," she added, not entirely approvingly. "I'll make a note of it; perhaps we can get it checked out."

She scribbled on her clipboard while I went back to the transcript.

'There is evidence to suggest that a troupe of actors from one of the London playhouses was touring the area between 1592–3, when the playhouses were closed due to plague.' Yes!

"Would it be at all possible to see the rest of the accounts?" I asked, excitedly. I'd read somewhere during my studies that Tudor household records could contain all kinds of detail – almost like a diary. Who knew what else was buried in there if the papers hadn't been carefully combed? "It could be really important."

She raised a pencil-thin eyebrow as dark and shapely as her suit.

"I'm afraid you'd need permission to access original documents. A letter from your college or university would suffice." *Which I don't suppose for one moment you have, at your age*, said her eyes, as they travelled over me. For a second, I ached for the courage to say something smart and withering. But, as usual, nothing came. She delivered her coup de grâce. "And of course, it would help if you're familiar with secretary hand – which is what the accounts are written in, being business documents."

I couldn't help my slow smile. "That wouldn't be a problem. I've done a course." Another of my mad ventures: an online course I'd filled some of my empty evenings with, and found fascinating. Her face quivered; and in the silence there was a scraping of chair legs behind us.

"Er, perhaps I could help?" The floppy-haired man strolled towards us with an easy grace, and a smile that brought the flush back to Sarah Lander's cheeks. I had to admit, he had gorgeous eyes. They were soft hazel and held a glint of humorous kindness. "Sorry, I couldn't help overhearing." He turned to me, eyes bright with interest.

"I'm a history teacher, you see – I work at one of the local Further Ed colleges – and I'm now burning with curiosity about this observation of yours. Ben Whitaker," he added, extending his hand. I took it, and it closed around mine in a firm, cool grasp.

"Jenny Watson," I murmured, my blush stirring.

"If Sarah has no objection, I'd be happy to lend you my pass. In fact, if you wouldn't mind me tagging along, I'm free this afternoon, as it happens."

I gazed at him in surprise. Sarah looked as though she'd rather swallow her own name badge, together with its pin, than give her consent, but she wasn't proof against that smile.

"Well… um, it could be arranged, of course – but we're about to close for lunch."

Ben twinkled at me.

"Right; then how about I treat us to a coffee and sandwich, over the road, while you tell me about your interest in that fragment? And then we can come back after lunch – giving Sarah a chance to assemble the papers?"

I hesitated. This all seemed far too quick, and a hint presumptuous. But the opportunity to have a look at the Bennington accounts was alluring, and his smile so reassuringly calm and friendly that I murmured my thanks. Sarah looked as though her badge had got stuck halfway down her oesophagus.

"Of course. Shall we say two-thirty, Mr W— Ben?"

"That's great," he said, and the pink tinge reappeared in her cheeks as she hurried away.

"I bring a lot of school parties here," he explained, with a soft, apologetic smile. "So I get preferential treatment.

Come on, let's have that coffee. I'm dying to hear why you're so interested in those Bennington accounts."

NINE

'I will believe thou hast a mind that suits
With this thy fair and outward character.'
(Twelfth Night)

"So, now I know why you're at The Old Bell, let's get down to how I can help you," said Ben as we finished off our lunch with hearty slabs of Victoria sponge. I surreptitiously loosened the button on my jeans; I'd be looking like a pumpkin by Hallowe'en, if I didn't watch it. "I've read about the alleged performance of *Titus*, of course. But I never realised the play had a clown. I thought it was all pretty serious and rather violent. Are you thinking of doing it for the festival?"

I shook my head quickly. "I'm doing *Hamlet*. *Titus* is – not one of my favourite plays, I'm afraid. And you're right, it is violent. But it also has this disturbing seam of dark humour, and the clown is part of that. It's a small role, but so important. That's one of the things I love about Shakespeare: the way he gives a real voice to minor characters. There are some who have a few paltry lines, or none at all, yet their personal tragedies can be as immense as, say, Lavinia's in *Titus*."

Ben's eyes deepened with interest, and it was so refreshing. My ex, Ross, had hightailed it out of the room at the first mention of Shakespeare. And though Steve had claimed to be a theatre enthusiast when we first dated, that had turned out to be one of the 'slight exaggerations' on his profile.

Ben leaned forward. "Tell me a bit more about this clown."

I quivered with the impulse to move back, but quelled it, telling myself not to be ridiculous. The man was just interested in Shakespeare.

"Well, he's there in the city to try to settle a dispute between his uncle and one of the emperor's men," I said. "But he ends up as an innocent messenger between Titus and the emperor, and gets caught up in the crossfire of their argument. The poor man's hanged on a whim, simply for being in the wrong place at the wrong time, without a trial or even an inkling of what he's supposed to have done."

He nodded, sipping his coffee. "And you think the scene's there to make that point?"

"Yes, I do. It's a total abuse of the justice system, you see. And such a common occurrence that the clown even makes a joke about it; a sort of knee-jerk reaction to hearing his sentence. It's a real Del-Boy moment. The audience is still laughing when he's dragged off, but you should hear it stop when they realise he's not coming back. If it's played well, the moments after his exit can be stunning."

"And there's no trial because he's from the lower classes?" suggested Ben.

"That's right. He's poor, and therefore insignificant. No one wants to waste the time. And of course, because he's a clown, it's all the more poignant."

Ben blew out softly through his lips. "Now that is a terrific piece of drama."

I pulled my eyes away from his mouth.

"Yes, that's what I think. And if I – we – can find out more about this local performance, it'll make the basis of a great PR story. That and the skull in the pub cellar."

"The what?" Ben's hazel eyes opened wide. They seemed to change colour according to the light or his fluctuations in mood. At the moment, they were tinged with amber.

"Henry," I said, and relayed what George had told me.

Ben shook his head. "Amazing. I've lived here for four years and never heard about this. I'll have to make George's acquaintance."

"He said Henry was hanged for stealing a coin. I mean, can that be true?"

Ben shrugged. "Depends on the sum. Stealing a shilling or more was a hanging offence at that time."

"Really? I knew it was a lot of money, then – but to hang someone for it?"

He rubbed his chin with a forefinger. "Yes. It seems so arbitrary, doesn't it? A bit like the clown's fate in *Titus*. You know, there's often more truth in these old folktales than you'd credit. I've a friend, Aaron, who works in forensics. If you could let me have a small bone sample from that skull, I might be able to get it carbon dated. That'll tell us how old 'Henry' is."

"Would you?" I breathed.

He grinned. "On one condition. That you let me help with the research."

Ah. I dropped my gaze, wondering what sort of 'research' he had in mind. "Purely on a professional basis, of course," he said, eyes crinkling again. "Seriously, I'd really like to follow this story through with you. Apart from my interest as a historian, the college I teach at has a really strong performing arts course – and I know some of the kids would love to attend a Shakespeare festival. We've nothing like that, locally. In fact, if you don't mind, I'll take some details about your auditions, so I can pass them on to our English Lit and drama tutors. That is, if you need any youngsters in your cast?"

"Oh! Yes, that would be great," I said.

His eyes folded into a smile again, and I pulled my sweater away from my neck a little, wondering why the place was so overheated. Then he lifted his coffee mug to his lips; and before I could stop them, my eyes went straight to his left hand.

"So, let me tell you a little more about myself, if we're going to be research colleagues." His grin confirmed that he'd seen my look; I was sure my face now matched the plastic poppies slumped in the squat little glass vase between us. "I'm divorced – about four years ago – with one daughter, Janie, currently at university in Leicester. She lives with her mother most of the time in the holidays, except when she descends on me and my life becomes utter chaos. I love my job, and am a total history bore, often to be found with my nose in a book. What about you?"

Me? I fluttered into nervous speech. "Um, not much to

tell, really. Divorced, recently redundant and really lucky to find this job, doing something I love."

He raised an eyebrow, waiting for more, but I took refuge in my coffee.

"Okay. Let's go attack the Bennington accounts, then," he smiled, and got up. "By the way, you were really sharp, noticing the word 'clown', like that. I'm eager to see what else we turn up."

I gathered my things, wondering where this was all going. He was undoubtedly one of the most interesting men I'd encountered, but for some reason, his assured, good-humoured manner stirred faint memories of my ex, Ross, whom I'd fallen for like a stone. But I wasn't sixteen anymore, and this was purely a professional arrangement, as he'd said. There was no way I was letting another man more than an inch into my fragile heart, however much I needed – and wanted – his help.

TEN

'Yet do thy cheeks look red as Titan's face,
Blushing to be encountered by a cloud.'
(Titus Andronicus)

"If you'd like to come this way."

Sarah Lander led us into a small back room to a pair of desks, on one of which was a laptop, and on the other some stout metal boxes. She ushered me to the laptop. The light levels were subdued, presumably to preserve the documents.

"You'll need to watch our online video on the care of old documents before you start," she said, her polished fingertips deftly bringing the file up on the screen in front of me. I slid my own less well-groomed nails under the desk. "The documents are considered valuable. These papers are purely household accounts and such, I'm afraid, but the Benningtons certainly had a strong interest in theatre: that we do know. Please handle them in line with the guidance on the video."

I sat down dutifully at the laptop and donned some headphones. Ben pulled on a pair of white cotton gloves that were sitting on top of the first box, lifted the lid and gently drew out a sheaf of long, thick, yellowing papers.

"What about you?" I demanded. "Aren't you going to watch?"

Sarah gave me a sliver of a smile. "Mr Whitaker is well versed in the care of our documents." I glared at her back as she marched off, and Ben's lips twitched, but he said nothing.

The minute the credits appeared, I shot across and joined him in scouring through a sheaf of household expenses dated 1575–95. It was painstaking work. Each page was divided into two columns, both sides covered in thin, spikey scrawl. Some years took up several pages; others were missing altogether, and the ink ranged from legible flourishes to parched indentations. No wonder no one had gone through it all.

"It's amazing this has survived," I said.

Ben nodded. "Well, the ink is iron gall: a combination of iron sulphate and secretions from gall wasps, found in oak tree galls. The type of paper helps, too. This was likely made from old rags: normally linen that was pulped and pressed. The plays were probably printed on good quality stuff like this, too."

I ran my gloved finger lightly above a line of ink, a smile hovering. "I wonder if Shakespeare used the same materials for writing," I said. "Imagine *Macbeth* or *Othello* written on linen undergarments that were once close to someone's skin – with ink made from the fluid of a stinging wasp. It feels so... apt, somehow."

"Particularly the ink, for some of the love stories," he said, dryly. "Anyway, we'd better get on or we'll run out of time."

An hour ticked by, and all we'd discovered were – as Sarah Lander had warned – endless lists of household purchases. It was among these, however, at the end of a second long hour, that I made a gem of a discovery. Part way down a heavily compressed page detailing events that Sir Edward Bennington had paid to attend or host was an entry dated 10th July 1582. It was difficult to make out, as the ink had all but disappeared in places, but what looked like the words 'acting troupe' had me up and running to the help desk, to beg a magnifying glass. I didn't want to tell Ben until I was sure I was right.

"You've found something?" Sarah said, her brows shooting up under her fringe.

"I'm not sure." I grasped the glass she held out and raced back, stumbling into my chair.

"What is it?" asked Ben. I pointed, and he leaned over my shoulder as we both peered at the faded entry.

For the carrying of a letter to Lundun, for the inn keeper, William Coates, on the problem of his Sonne, taken from his home against his will by the owner of a children's acting troupe.

There was then a line of lettering so rubbed away by time that nothing could be made of it, and the sum of money proved indecipherable. But the writing underneath was much clearer.

The man being unable to write for himself, I undertook to perform this servyce for him.

"A boy actor!" exclaimed Ben.

"And an innkeeper's son, too." I hardly dared to say what was in my mind, but Ben's face was full of enquiry. "George said that Henry had been in the old pub for as long as anyone could remember. The story is, he grew up there. And the pub is sixteenth century. So what if —?"

"The skull belonged to this boy?" Ben rubbed his chin with his forefinger.

"It has to be a coincidence," I said.

"No, it's possible. We need to find out how old that skull is." He bent over the page again. "But who would have imagined we'd turn up that little piece of history in household accounts? It's like a diary entry."

"Probably a note to remind him what the payment was for," I said.

"Yes, you're right. Do you want to have another look, see if there's anything else we can find, or have you had enough?"

"Absolutely not!" I scoffed, bending my head once more. Surely, surely there must be something else that would tell us what happened to young master Coates? But at the end of another half hour, we'd found nothing, and Sarah, though intrigued by our discovery, could enlighten us no further.

"And I'm afraid we're about to close, Mr Whitaker," she said.

"Ah." Ben glanced at his watch. "Of course. Sorry. I'll just make a note on my phone of where we're up to, and we'll be out of your way."

We emerged into the pale March sunshine and perched on the wall to talk.

"So, what we know – in terms of facts – is that there was a local performance of a play: most likely Shakespeare's *Titus*," Ben mused. "The fragment upstairs talks about 'our clowne', and you say there's a clown in *Titus*. The old folktale suggests that Henry was a comic actor who longed to play in a tragedy, and that he grew up in The Old Bell."

"Yes, and now we find that a local boy, the innkeeper's son, was press-ganged by an acting troupe and taken to London," I said. "It looks as though Edward Bennington was trying to help Mr Coates get his son back. It wouldn't have been the first time such a case was fought. It really does feel as though all these stories are tying into one common thread, doesn't it?"

"Yes." Ben pushed his hair back, as though combing through ideas in his mind. "It's a pity we can't hurry up this carbon-dating process. Aaron says it can take a while, and even then it might not be completely accurate. Still, just an idea of the century we're dealing with would be a start."

"But where do we go from here?" I sighed. "Ploughing through all those records could take months."

"Yes. But if we assume this boy actor *could* have been Henry – making him Henry Coates – then parish records are our best bet. You know, births, marriages and deaths. We're lucky; ours are stored here at the museum. Though even with the carbon-dating results, it'll be difficult to know where to start. And we can't even be sure it *is* him."

"Wait a minute!" I laid my hand on his arm. He glanced down at it, and I pulled away, flushing. "We do have a date for the performance, though."

"Yes." Thankfully, he seemed oblivious to my embarrassment. "But that could have occurred at any point in his life. Maybe we just have to keep going through those Bennington records, looking for more clues." We both sagged at the thought.

Then he sprang up, deftly clicking his fingers. "Of course. Simon!" I looked questioningly at him. "My mate who works at Kew. Yes, I do have more than one friend, believe it or not," he added with a grin. "Simon and I were at uni together. He owes me a few favours. Maybe he'd know where to find info on the troupes of boy players, to see if there were any kids of that name registered around the date of the entry we found."

"Kew?" I asked.

"National Archives. They're housed there. I'll drop him a message."

I switched my phone on and it came alive with messages. Two missed calls from Mags, several texts from her, and three other missed calls: 'number withheld', plus a text message.

Long time, no see. Perhaps we should meet for a catch-up.

It must be meant for someone else; clearly a friend. But then why on earth was the sender's number private?

"Problem?" enquired Ben.

"I've got a few calls from a withheld number, which is a bit weird."

"Probably automated sales calls. Ignore them. Well, look, as much as I'd love to stay and chat, I'd better get off. The next time I'm free for research is Saturday morning."

"Isn't the museum closed on Saturdays?" I asked, remembering my visit to the library.

"No, last week was an exception. Is eleven okay then?"

"Yes, of course." In fact, I was feeling far keener than I was comfortable with.

"We can firm up on Thursday, at your auditions," he said. "Do you mind if I come along?"

I looked up in surprise. "I'd love... you'd be most welcome."

A smile lit his eyes, as I felt myself redden again. "Good. Let me take your number."

As I recited it, I couldn't help feeling that our friendship was taking off rather too quickly.

"See you Thursday, then," he said. "Unless... I don't suppose you'd like to have dinner one evening?"

I took a step backwards. He was undeniably attractive and great company. But I couldn't help wondering exactly what 'dinner' would involve.

"I can't, I'm afraid. I've got a pile of work to do."

To my relief, he took my refusal in good part. "No worries. I'll pick up the bone samples on Thursday."

"Yes. Great." I gave him what I hoped was a business-like smile, but my voice betrayed me. I might have been calling about a job with one of those sex phone companies. It was bizarre; I hadn't even felt like this when Ross first kissed me – and I'd met Ben only a few hours ago, for pity's sake. I turned away, my face starting to glow. *Shit.* I hated this constant flushing that branded my skin with my thoughts, however hard I fought it.

"Do you need a lift home?" Ben asked.

I lifted my bag onto my shoulder, not looking at him. "No, I'm fine, thanks. All sorted."

And I walked away before he could ask any more

questions. He seemed a bit too sure of himself; I found myself wondering how long he'd been divorced, and how many casual liaisons he'd had since then. I had my own reasons for not wanting to start a relationship, and besides, my job was the most important thing in my life. I was actually living my dream, and nothing was going to distract me from it.

ELEVEN

'There's rosemary, that's for remembrance.'
(Hamlet)

I texted Mags, saying I'd call her before bed. If I rang now, she'd probably freak out that I was walking back alone, just before dusk. I'd meant to ask at the café if there was another way home, because the river path really was deserted, but at least it was quick. My phone pinged up the reminder I'd scheduled about the Speak Out therapy group as I walked. *Damn.* I hadn't booked a taxi. I quickly pulled out George's card from my bag, and keyed in his number.

"Jenny Watson! Well, now, there's a nice surprise. How's it going?"

George's delighted tone made me smile. "Good, thanks. I was wondering if I could book your taxi service for seven this evening."

"Of course! Where to, my dear?"

I gave him the address, then jumped as a bush crackled and a bird fluttered upwards.

"Shit! Oh… sorry, George." I shivered, pulling my coat firmly around me against the wind. Rain clouds were piling in overhead, and blocking what was left of the light. I quickened my pace, wishing I'd left sooner.

"You sound a bit out of breath, my dear," said George. "Is everything all right?"

"Yes. I'm just walking home from the village." My toes caught in a twisted root, and I shot forwards. It was getting hard to talk and hurry, and as the trees slipped into shadow I found myself glancing behind me at every snap of sound. "I'm sorry, George, but I'd better go. I'll see you later."

"Wait a minute. You did take the long way round, I hope?" The edge of concern in his voice brought my nerves swooping up under my skin.

"I only know this one. Why? Is that a problem?"

My breath hung around my mouth as I waited for his answer.

"How far along the river path are you?"

"Er… I'm not really sure. Hello? George?"

The line went dead. *No signal.* Should I go back? I was already over halfway; to return would be as far as going onwards.

By the time I reached the bridge opposite the pub, the last dull trace of daylight had been sucked into dark, and I'd travelled the longest twenty minutes of my life, listening painfully to every whisper of sound and stumbling over bumps and dips under my feet.

As my fingers closed in relief around the bridge's support rail, a scurry of wind seized the security light that hung from the pub roof, swinging it sideways, and I gave a choke of a scream. Crouching at the corner of the barn was the shadow of a man. The image was gone in a breath, but it sent me scrambling backwards into the trees, fingers of prickly gorse pulling at my jacket.

I stood silent, blood thrumming against my temples. Had he seen me? Inching my head out again, I peered fearfully at the barn, but the lamp had moved back into place and the barn sat humped in gloom. I had no idea if the intruder was still there; he could even have crossed the bridge by now and be behind me. I whirled around at the idea, my skin crawling under my coat as my eyes raked the dense darkness. Maybe running back towards the village wasn't such a bad idea.

Silently, I crept out onto the path. So far, so good. Then as I turned, a flurry of snapping twigs and snorting breath burst through a gap in the trees: something hit me hard on the shoulder and spun me towards the bridge. I caught a glimpse of pale cheeks under a dark hood flashing past me, and pitched towards the bridge, too shocked to scream as the figure thudded away up the mud path.

Straining my eyes to follow it, I caught a round, yellow cone bobbing against the trees, faintly lighting the shape of a man in dark grey joggers and hoodie. At least, it moved like a man. Its hood turned briefly back towards me, a trail of vapour wreathing around the bone-white face cased within. Then it was gone and I was alone, panting with relief. *Christ.* A jogger! What were the chances? I glanced down at my black coat, my pulse gradually subsiding. Better to wear something light in future; he obviously hadn't seen me. But then, who would expect to literally run into someone here, in the dark? The bastard wasn't going to stop to see if I was all right, though, was he? I leaned over the bridge handrail, my chest heaving painfully, and then almost fell into the river as a familiar voice rang out.

"Jenny!"

George came hurrying stiffly towards me along the bank, his torch lighting up his face.

"Are you all right, my dear?" he panted. "You know, it's not a good idea to take this route in the dark."

I wrestled with an overwhelming surge of tears, prompted by a fusion of relief and embarrassment.

"I think I've realised that. George, you haven't come all this way because you were worried about me?"

"That's nothing; I'm not more than a few minutes down the road. And I should have told you to come the other route, through the estate, anyway. It brings you out at the front of the pub. That river path's far too deserted for this time of day. Come on, I'll see you indoors."

"No, honestly, George, I'm…"

I glanced, quivering, across the river. The moon was edging through a hollow in the clouds, lighting the barn. Mags had hung the all-in-one boiler suits we'd worn for our cleaning duties on an old washing line she'd found, rigged up between the cherry tree and the barn door. She'd told me to be sure to bring them in – and of course, I'd forgotten. As I watched, the wind stirred the cherry's boughs, and the suits swung gently. One of them had slipped low down, and was flapping against the corner of the barn, its sleeves and legs bent as though embracing the wood. Please don't tell me that *this* was my 'intruder'. My insides curled like burned bacon as I imagined the local police turning up, all prepared to tackle a dangerous criminal and finding a clothes line.

"You're what, my dear?" queried George.

"Nothing," I said, and followed him meekly across the bridge.

The pub was so cold that George insisted on relighting the fire in the bar lounge for me, but wouldn't stay for a cup of tea.

"My missus will have the dinner on," he explained. "You'll be okay? Anything else I can do while I'm here?"

"Honestly, I'm fine," I said. Actually, I was feeling foolish, and doubly determined not to overreact to every little fear in future.

"I'll get off then. Oh, but wait a bit." George pulled a couple of new bulbs from his coat pocket, still in their packaging. "I said I'd bring you a couple of spares for the cellar. We don't want you falling down those steps in the dark."

I smiled and thanked him, the memory of the cellar bringing Henry to mind.

"Actually, there's something I wanted to ask you, George. I met a historian in the museum, Ben Whitaker, who says he can get Hen – the skull carbon dated for us, if we give him a small bone sample."

George's eyes brightened. "Now, that's a fine idea."

"The thing is, I'm not sure how to do it."

Would I have to saw pieces off? The idea made me feel queasy; and the last thing I wanted was to venture into that cellar alone.

George grinned. "Don't you trouble yourself. There were a few little pieces broken off anyhow, lying on the pedestal. So all I need is something to put them in. You stay here and I'll sort it."

I armed him with a plastic zip-lock bag from the kitchen, courtesy of Mags's supplies, and in a few moments he returned with two grubby bone fragments sealed inside it.

"That should be enough," he said. "Right, well, I'll go out the front way, as I've just time to pick my paper up from the newsagents. And I'll see you at seven. You make sure you lock up behind me, now. All right? You don't want folk thinking the place is open, when it's not. Give me a ring if you need me."

I nodded sheepishly. "I will. And thank you again, so much."

He toddled away into the night, and I was about to push the front door closed when I noticed something lying on the gravel just beyond it. A small bunch of tiny blue flowers on dried stalks, gathered in a scrap of black ribbon. I bent to pick it up, wondering how it had got there, and held it under the security light. I knew what these were. Not flowers, but herbs: dried rosemary. The question was, what was it doing here? And why hadn't I noticed it before?

As the light shone through the stalks, I noticed a minuscule hole in the centre of the sleek ribbon, as though the flowers had been pinned up somewhere. My eyes scanned the front door and, sure enough, two-thirds of the way down in the centre was a tiny pin-prick in the wood. I ran my finger over it. I was sure there had been no flowers on the door when Mags and I arrived at the pub. Bending to examine the gravel again outside the porch, I spotted something gleaming: a bright new drawing pin. Like the flowers, it was clean and untarnished.

I looked hastily around, half expecting someone to come looming out of the darkness, then panic took hold and I shot inside, slammed the door hard and rammed the bolts home. Had someone been here? Or was I really becoming paranoid? And if they had, why pin a bunch of rosemary to my door?

A line from *Hamlet* slipped into my mind. *'There's rosemary, that's for remembrance. Pray you love, remember.'* The words Ophelia says to her brother after their father's murder.

There was a copy of the play on the windowsill. I pulled it out and located the speech. At the bottom was an editor's note: *'Rosemary was traditionally used for funerals. Hamlet's mother, Gertrude, later throws some rosemary into Ophelia's grave.'*

Funerals. I fingered the black ribbon, then looked up and caught my reflection in the bar mirror. I'd never looked paler. The next thing would be another headache, then a visual disturbance. I snapped the play shut. What on earth was I doing, fretting like this over a little bunch of flowers that had probably been there all along – and Mags and I simply hadn't noticed them?

There was a light sigh as the fire guttered in the grate, and I dropped the flowers onto a table while I rushed to revive it. If I didn't get a grip on my nerves and my job, I wouldn't pass my first month's trial. This was my one chance to show what I could do, and I was sure my idea for publicity couldn't fail to impress my new boss. And though there were no replies yet from my emails to the drama groups, I was confident that with Gordon and Diana's help, there would be.

I plugged my phone in to charge, wincing as I saw how late it was. George would be back in no time. And as far as tonight's self-help group went, I'd go, but they'd have to put up with whatever I chose to tell them. Because no way was I sitting in a room with God knew how many others, baring my soul. It had done perfectly well so far with all its clothes on, a thick coat and a set of oilskins on top.

Moving on.

TWELVE

'Best safety lies in fear.'
(Hamlet)

"Sorry I'm a bit late," I murmured, as I ventured inside
the foyer of the little green and cream Methodist hall, where
the Speak Out meeting was being held. A skeletally thin,
elderly woman pushed a reporter's notebook and pencil
towards me.

"Can you put your tea or coffee order down on here,
please?" she whispered. Hastily, I obliged and made my way
into the meeting room. About a dozen women of various
ages, shapes and sizes were seated in a circle. One of them,
forty-something, with a rounded face framed by thick,
flaxen hair, looked up and raised her hand for me to wait.
The room was hushed, save for a single, halting voice that
was barely audible. Some poor woman, head bowed, was
wading her way through a harrowing moment from her
past. God, this was everything I'd feared. But the flaxen-
haired woman had seen me now – so I couldn't bolt.

The wooden chairs looked like they'd been bought as a job-lot from a Victorian school. I lowered my eyes, not wanting to intrude on the stricken woman's grief. No way could I do this; it was brave, beyond anything I could imagine. The women sat like stones in some ancient ritual, making me wonder what was going on in their heads. And this was supposed to be therapeutic?

Then, to my surprise, one of them rose, went quietly to the distressed woman and took her hand. Another joined her, and another, as though that first movement had sparked a synchronised act. They gathered into a nucleus, swelling in strength and I took a hasty step back towards the door. *No, this definitely wasn't for me.* I cast a quick look around for the group leader, who was now obscured by bodies, so she wouldn't notice if I slipped away. Then I saw that a solitary woman was still frozen in her original place. Her eyes were huge and empty, as though they'd glimpsed something so emotionally vast that they were incapable of returning to normality.

"Her name's Bridie," murmured a diminutive Scotswoman, as she passed me on her way back to her chair. "She lost her husband and two children in a car accident, and she's not said a word since. I'm Isla, by the way," she added.

I nodded and smiled. All I wanted now was to get outside into the air, but the elderly woman was standing guard by the front entrance. Inside the hall, the nucleus split and its members flowed back to their places. Their leader looked up and beckoned me over.

"Jenny Watson?" She held out her hand. "Good to see you. I'm Louise Wainwright. Take a seat." I lowered myself tentatively onto a chair made for a size six bottom, while Louise settled back in hers and swept the circle with her eyes. I kept mine firmly lowered; she was probably scanning for another victim.

"Ladies: I'd like to extend a warm welcome to our newest member, Jenny Watson," she said, and I jumped, dropping my bag. "Jenny, would you like to share something about yourself? It can be general – your name, occupation, hobbies. Anything will do, to get started."

Shit. It really was like Alcoholics Anonymous. I swallowed and looked up, past her shoulder, at the clock. It was an old trick we were taught as chorus members in amateur musicals: avoid direct eye contact with the audience, in case you see someone you know.

"Hi, I'm Jenny. I'm an office worker, and I was recently made redundant."

I paused, and Louise smiled encouragingly. "And I'm, um, divorced." That was fairly safe ground; lots of people got divorced. And still, she smiled and waited. *For God's sake.* "And I've recently taken a job directing a Shakespeare festival at a pub." The last bit came out in a rush.

Louise nodded. "Thank you, Jenny. I must say, your job sounds fascinating. Perhaps you can tell us some more about it next time. Now, anyone with something more to share?"

No one moved or spoke. It reminded me of 'awkward' lessons at school – when we were talked at about periods or sex.

"Okay, then," Louise went on, brightly. "Well, we've got quite a few new members, and it will take time for us all to get to know each other. Last week, we talked about

95

first days at a new job. How about going a bit further back, to first days at school? Who remembers their first day at infant or primary? What sort of experience was it?"

A rumble of conversation broke out, punctuated by spurts of laughter.

"Christ, you cannae expect us to remember that far back," joked Isla.

"Mine was horrendous," said a woman next to her, with a severe auburn crop and heavy blue eyeshadow. I sat quiet, lips closed.

"Jenny?" said Louise. And I felt my shoulders tense.

"I, um, can't really remember anything about my infant school," I said, truthfully. That was when my father was still alive; before the world changed.

"Your junior school, then?" she prompted.

I felt my eyes widening. Well, that was one place we were never revisiting.

"Okay. Well, it wasn't bad. My... my mother used to go there." *Oh, she had, indeed.* I could still see the school motto emblazoned in aggressive black paint on the headmistress's wall: *St Michael's: strong on discipline and faith.* I'd gone there the week after my father's funeral; it was one of the few independent schools still using physical punishment at the time. "But my first day's a bit of a blur, to be honest." I tucked my head down, quickly, as my blush betrayed me. I remembered, all right.

"Seven years old, Jenny Watson, and you're already a liar and a bully."

Miss Yates had a voice like a fork on metal. She was brought up in a convent, and to my mother, that made her word law. I was no bully. I'd pushed a girl in retaliation, but

I didn't mean her to fall, and she wasn't hurt – she even managed to smile when I was being punished, though she made sure Miss Yates didn't see. The memory invaded my mind as the meeting room faded around me, the mingled smell of disinfectant and chalk as pungent as it had been twenty-three years ago.

"She took my story!" I'd protested tearfully as I stood, eyes lowered, before Miss Yates's desk. *"She was going to tear it up."* I flashed a furious look at the smirking Samantha. It was a special story I'd written for my father. We'd always had our 'sharing' time before bed, and sometimes he read to me; sometimes we talked about what we'd done during the day. But that last evening, he'd asked me to read out one of my own stories. *"I want to hear your voice,"* he'd said. *"So I can always remember."*

"And this is your 'story' – is it?"

Miss Yates held my pages up between her thumb and forefinger as though she'd just pulled them out of the school cat's litter tray, and paraded them up and down the rows of desks. *"Tell me, children, what do you see on these grubby little sheets? Can you see any words? Any sentences, perhaps? The odd full stop?"*

I stood, stiff and straight as a rounder's post, while the other children stifled their giggles.

"It's just scribble, Miss," a boy at the front said. More spurts of laughter.

"It IS a story!" I choked, fighting back tears.

"Then I think you should read it aloud to the class, Jenny Watson, so we can all enjoy it." Miss Yates returned to my side. *"And as you read, you will follow each word with your finger, so I can see."*

My mouth fell open. But I couldn't do that. How could she not understand?

"That's not how I read it," I whispered. I could read books like that, very slowly. But not my stories. I'd written them this way since I was very small. Daddy said it was because my thoughts came out so quickly, and that it would *'all sort itself out, in time'*.

"Show me." She hissed the words in my ear, but I daren't shrink away.

I managed to stumble out a few words, while she stood at my shoulder, her eyes burning into the pages as they shook in my grasp. I couldn't see my story anymore, only a jumble of messy pencil marks on the pages – and of course, that's all they'd ever been; I realised that now. They weren't real stories at all, only thoughts in my head; my father must have known. He was just being kind.

"So we can't write or read properly, either?" Miss Yates snapped, whisking my story out of my hands. *"I think you should learn to walk before you can run, young lady. It's also high time you learned that telling lies and pushing other children will not be tolerated here, whatever you might have got away with at your last school."*

An expectant hush fell as she dragged open her big desk drawer and drew out a thin leather strap. My stomach rolled.

"Hold out your right hand, palm up." I hesitated, trembling. *"Do. As. You. Are. Told!"* she snapped, and I winced, wanting to run and hide under the desk, as I'd often done at home.

I quickly pushed out my hand and screwed up my eyes… and waited, and waited. Then it came: the stinging split of air and leather that tore across my palm like fire. I only yelped once, then managed by grinding my teeth together; curling my toes inside my shoes, counting each stroke. She did it twice more, and when it was over I buried my throbbing palm beneath my left armpit, but she wrenched it out and forced my 'story' into my aching fingers, spinning me by the shoulders to face my class. I was crying so much, they were a blur, and I didn't want to look at their faces anyway, because I was unbearably ashamed. Miss Yates made me walk back down the rows of desks and stammer my apologies to Samantha. Then I had to go with Miss Taylor, the class assistant, and kneel in the quiet room and think about what I'd done and ask God for forgiveness. But what about Samantha? I wondered, resentfully, as I prayed. Didn't she need forgiveness, too? She'd hurt me just as much, though you couldn't see it.

When I was released into the playground at lunchtime, I found the loneliest corner I could, by the dustbins, and, even though it smelt, I curled up there, fighting the shame that pulsed through me. I could see, now, that this school was like home. That was why my mother had chosen it when Daddy didn't come back from the hospital. *"We'll be doing things differently around here, from now on,"* she'd said. And life had never been the same. So, from now on, I'd keep myself as small and quiet as possible. The less I was noticed, the safer I'd be.

When the bell went for home, I ran as fast as I could, back to our garden, and heaved the lid off our big dustbin with both hands. Then I tore and tore my story into pieces so tiny that no one would ever see those meaningless pencil marks again.

I never told my mother my teacher had hurt me. I knew all too well what would happen if she thought I'd misbehaved.

"Jenny?"

With a start, I realised I was still in the Methodist hall. *Oh, God.* Had I said something I shouldn't, out loud?

The woman I'd met in the foyer was trying to pass me some pale tea in a blue fluted cup and saucer. I took it gratefully, and gradually the hum of conversation brought me back to the present.

"Well, you know, eating behaviours are often a manifestation of other issues," Louise was saying. "So perhaps we need to have a further think about that, Sam."

A sturdy young woman with long, blonde hair pulled back in a ponytail was nodding and trying not to look self-conscious.

"I know it's difficult to open up, in situations like this," Louise went on, with a glance at me. "My advice is, as I've said to all of you, start by writing things down, like a diary. Keep a note of your thoughts, your dreams and memories, and then read them through in quiet moments – or, better still, bring your notebook to our sessions, if you can, and read it to us. This is all about learning to be completely honest with yourself; looking beyond the surface, to what's going on underneath." She turned her eyes to me again, and I slopped some tea into my saucer. "All clear, Jenny? Is there anything else you'd like to ask?"

I shook my head, quickly checking my sweater. Thank God; no spillages. I'd have to start bringing a scarf with me just in case.

"Next time, perhaps." She smiled, and her eyes twinkled. "We meet again on Wednesday evening, ladies. Thank you all, and have a good start to the week."

It was over; I made good my escape. But just as I reached the door, Louise caught up with me.

"Ah, Jenny! Just a second. I've something to ask you." I eyed her warily. "It was so interesting, hearing about your directing job! And it's given me an idea. How would you feel about saying a few words next time, about your work? What you enjoy and hope to achieve, that kind of thing. Just a few minutes' worth, or whatever you feel comfortable with."

My mouth shrivelled inside, like a dried flannel.

"I, um, I don't know—"

"Have a think about it. You did so well today, I'm sure you'll be fine. You can always write something down and read it aloud, if that's easier; but I know everyone would love to hear from you. If you'd rather wait, then that's no problem, of course. See you next time!" And she bustled off to talk to Isla.

Write it down. I could give it a try. But surely all this effort was only adding to my stress levels, when it was supposed to be curing them, and what I actually needed was to be left alone.

On the way home, my mind wandered over the strange day I'd had. Such a good start with Ben at the museum, but then that weird walk home along the river path. I shuddered as I recalled the runner by the bridge.

"All right?" said George, glancing at me in the rear-view mirror.

"Yes, good," I nodded. "George, I meant to ask you something. Do joggers regularly use the river path?"

"Joggers? Well, they may do, but I've never seen any. Probably a few too many tree roots to make running comfortable. Why do you ask?"

I told him about my earlier encounter, taking care not to make it sound too dramatic.

"That's a new one." He shook his head. "Running in the dark. Some people haven't the sense they were born with."

He carried on chatting, but I wasn't really listening. As I replayed the episode in my mind, a chill crept over my skin. I'd assumed the runner had come from the same direction I had, so surely he must have been behind me for a while. And in that case, why hadn't I seen or heard him?

Into my mind came the small, yellow circle of light I'd seen bobbing ahead of him, up the river path. *He'd had a torch.*

In that case, why on earth hadn't he seen *me*?

Unless he'd been there all the time, a little voice whispered in my head. But no, he'd looked as stunned as I felt. And anyway, why would anyone lie in wait for me and then run past? That didn't add up at all.

THIRTEEN

'The play's the thing.'
(Hamlet)

Tuesday morning, and Beethoven's Fifth Symphony was thundering somewhere under my pillow. I tore myself from my dream and felt feverishly around for my phone.

"Hi, Jen!" sang out Mags's voice. "I've got a free half hour, so I thought we might have coffee together! Well, separately, of course, but you know what I mean."

"Mags," I croaked, sitting up and groping for my coat. I was already wrapped in my white fluffy dressing gown. "What time is it?" A small mist puffed up around the phone, and I shivered. *God, we need to get this heating fixed.*

"Half ten," Mags said, in surprise. I groaned.

"Jen, you're not still in bed, are you?"

"Not now." I pushed my feet into some furry slippers and headed towards the stairs. "I had a bit of a late night; worked till half twelve preparing the auditions." I didn't mention that I'd hardly slept, even when I had gone to bed. Every noise had had me up like an alarmed blackbird, convinced I could hear the stealthy creeping of an unseen intruder. But now in the daylight, my fears appeared foolish. For one thing: why would anyone be following *me*? As for the rosemary, I'd convinced myself that it had been there all along. So I only told Mags about my visit to the museum, even playing down my meeting with Ben – though I did mention his offer to get Henry carbon dated.

"That's fantastic!" she said. "You could probably get a piece in the local papers about that, or even a radio interview. So, what's he like, this museum guy?"

"Ben? Oh, you know," I said, airily. "Your typical historian." Now she probably pictured him as eighty-four, bent over and bespectacled, but I knew what she'd be like if she had an inkling how attractive he was.

"How did your boss like the idea of doing *Hamlet?*" she asked.

"He hasn't come back to me yet." I flicked the kettle on. "But I'm sure he'll love it! I've already started a press release."

"You have been busy."

There was a ping from my inbox.

"Wait a minute – he's replied," I said. "Hang on, Mags." I clicked on the message.

Dear Jenny

Thank you for the helpful suggestion re Hamlet. However, I have already decided on Titus Andronicus as our opening play, and I'm afraid that decision is final. I understand it was probably performed in the

village in the sixteenth century, so that should help
with publicity.

Good luck with the auditions. I look forward to
hearing the outcome.

Best wishes, Leo Norwich

"*Shit!*" I sat down with a thud on the kitchen bench.

"What? What is it?" she said, sharply. "Are you ill again?"

"No! Of course not."

"Isn't he happy with your suggestion?"

"No." I rubbed my forehead with an icy hand. "He actually knows a bit about the local history, and he's insisting we do *Titus*. Mags, I can't. It's the one play I really can't tackle."

"Jen…" she sounded bewildered. "Hang on a minute. Aren't you overreacting a bit here? I mean, I know I said *Hamlet*, but if *Titus* really was performed there, I can understand his reasoning. I wonder if he's a local man?" she mused.

"Yes, but…" I stopped, unable to tell her the real reason for my unease. "Gordon thinks we're doing *Hamlet*," I said, feebly.

"The guy from the Mile-End Players? Well tell him you've changed your mind! He's not running this show, you are."

There was no point arguing. The only thing for it was to persuade Mr Norwich that *Titus* was a bad idea.

"Listen, Mags, I have to go. I'll call you later."

Before we'd said our goodbyes, I was firing up my laptop and plugging in the dongle I'd brought; I would be faster using a keyboard. I started typing the second the 'compose email' prompt came up.

Dear Mr Norwich

Thank you for your swift response, and I understand the value of local publicity to support a production of Titus. However, I would strongly suggest we reconsider Hamlet for a first play. Titus is extremely violent, and not very popular, and I'm sure we'd get poor audiences, whereas Hamlet would definitely bring in crowds. We can still use the museum research to boost publicity, though.

I look forward to your reply. Very best wishes
Jenny Watson

Well, that was uncharacteristically assertive. As I pressed 'send' my phone burst into life again, but it was Gordon this time.

"Jenny! Glad I caught you." Gordon sounded more than usually brisk. "I've been on the phone for the past two hours, and I'm hoping I've persuaded a few people to come to your *Hamlet* auditions. Though of course, it wasn't easy, you being a total unknown." He cleared his throat, meaningfully. "You didn't send me that CV, you bad girl. That would have helped. Can you ping it across this morning?"

Damn. He wasn't going to give up on this. I needed to divert his mind. Before I realised what I was doing, I'd told him about Mr Norwich's email.

"*Titus*? But that's an absurd idea!" he spluttered. "Jenny, no one in their right senses will want to audition for that play, let alone come and see it! You need a proper bums-on-seats production for your first one. This guy patently hasn't a clue! You must get him to change his mind."

"I've already messaged him." I sprang across to my laptop as another email pinged up. "Hold on, Gordon. He's just come back to me."

Mr Norwich's reply was brief to the point of brusqueness.

Jenny

Your comments and recommendations have been noted. However, I must insist we proceed with Titus. I'm familiar with the play and don't believe the violence is a problem. Please let me know how the auditions go.

Best,

Leo Norwich

His brevity winded me. No 'Dear Jenny'; not even an opening for discussion. Only a brutal 'get on with it'.

"Well?" Gordon said.

"I'm so sorry, Gordon." I got up to spoon some coffee into Mags's cafetière. I had to have something to help me think. "I'm afraid he's insisting on *Titus*."

"Oh, for heaven's sake!" snapped Gordon. "Look, I've spent hours on the bloody phone. I can hardly ring them all back and say we're doing a different play. It gives totally the wrong impression!"

I didn't reply; my head was beginning to ache. *No stress.* I couldn't afford it. I'd simply have to deal with this and get over my abhorrence of the play. It would be fine.

"You must be able to change his mind."

"I don't think so," I said. And after the tone of that email, I was a bit afraid to try. I didn't want to get fired on my first week. "Look, I'm really sorry you've wasted your time."

"Yes. So am I, to be honest. It's a pity you hadn't checked sooner, Jenny." And the line went dead. *Great*. Now he was pissed off with me, too.

Then the kitchen shimmered around me, and I felt quickly for the bench, dropping my spoon. *Shit. Shit. Shit!* This wasn't supposed to happen. I closed my eyes tightly. *Breathe.*

Inch by inch, I fought back the swelling mass of panic, blotting everything out except each slow exhalation. When I opened my eyes and looked cautiously around, the kitchen had returned to normal.

Oh, thank God.

My phone buzzed, again. *Ben Whitaker.*

Hi, Jenny. Just wanted to say you can have access to the museum records any time you like, without me. I've squared it with Sarah. See you Thursday. All the best, Ben.

The tension in my forehead eased. Yes, that's exactly what I needed – a few hours of quiet research at the museum. I'd walk into the village, the long way round this time. George had given me careful directions. And I could have breakfast at the café; maybe then I'd be able to get my head around doing *Titus*. I got up to fetch my coat.

The museum was shrouded in its usual hush. Sarah Lander's face quivered when I approached her, but she led me without comment into the little room we'd used the previous day and set the metal chest of papers before me. I decided to focus my search on the year the play was supposedly performed: 1592–3. It was a long shot, but someone may have mentioned the performance in this strange mix of household accounts and notes.

After about forty minutes of patient scrolling, my eye landed on an entry dated 13th July, 1593.

'For the performance of an excellent, bloodie and tragicall Roman historie: 30 shillings.'

"That's it!" I was so excited that I exclaimed aloud, my finger hovering over the line. *Titus*. It had to be. So it *was* performed there – at the manor, by the looks of all those expenses. I made a note of the page reference on my phone and bent my head back over it. There wasn't likely to be anything else – but you never knew.

Five minutes before I was due to pack up, my eye fell on another entry. It wasn't linked to the *Titus* performance, but it was such a cryptic comment that it warranted further attention.

Under 'monies paid for A Poecie, to be read aloude', the writer had commented:

'For a sad and sweet lament of the love and tragedie of our owne.'

I pored over the words. 'Poecie' could be an alternative spelling of 'poesy' – an old word for poetry. I'd read somewhere that there were no regular spelling rules in those days, and I'd often seen words ending with 'ie' rather than 'y'.

A 'lament' could easily be a poem or a ballad, so that

fitted with the 'poesy' idea. But what about the expression 'of our owne'? What did that mean? Unfortunately, there were a few words before it that were illegible, and the rest of the page contained the costs of food and drink for guests.

I glanced hurriedly at the clock as hollow footsteps sounded on the stairs. One o'clock; the museum would be shutting at any moment, but I really needed to note this entry. Ben had said that it was okay to take photos as long as we didn't use flash, so I took two hasty snaps and threw my phone into my bag as Sarah appeared. No doubt Ben would want to come along and see both entries for himself anyway; he was going to be as excited about them as I was.

As I packed up, my phone buzzed with a text from an unknown number. I hesitated. Mags had told me a dozen times to delete anything I was unsure of, but curiosity was one of my weaknesses. I clicked on it.

Did you like the flowers?

I stood immobile while the dry clack of the museum timepiece marked the passing silence. An image of dried rosemary bound with narrow black ribbon flittered through my mind. Could that be what this unknown caller meant?

Delete the text, whispered the voice in my head. But I had to know.

Who is this? I typed.

Another minute passed, before the answer came.

Sorry. Wrong number.

FOURTEEN

'I'll speak a prophecie 'ere I go…'
(King Lear)

"Are you into local history, then?"

I looked up from my phone as Glenys set my coffee and cake down before me on the café table.

She nodded her dark head towards *The Witches of Wethershall-End*. I'd brought it with me to flick through, as *Titus* didn't really go with lemon drizzle.

"Well, history in general," I said, "but particularly Early Modern."

"I wanted to study history at university, but I was worried about not being able to get a job at the end of it." She wiped her hands on her checked apron and settled into a chair opposite. "And then my Dad offered to set me up with the café when Mum died, so here I am." She nodded again at the book. "What do you think of our great claim to fame, then? It's not every village that has its own three witches."

"It's fascinating," I said.

"The kids get told the story every Hallowe'en. I know people say it's a pack of old wives' tales, but we do still have a 'Hangman's Lane' that's said to mark the spot where they died. It runs from the river bridge back through the woods."

I put my fork down. *Hangman's Lane?* Mags was going to love this.

"The writer of that book claims the story's based on truth, you know, and that the witchcraft charge was completely made up. Have you read it?"

I shook my head and her face glowed like a shiny red apple.

"Well, there was this young woman: a maid who worked at a local inn, so the story goes. She caught the eye of a visiting gentleman – if you'll pardon the term, because he was anything but. Apparently, he raped her, then, when she complained to the authorities, he got out of the charge by accusing her and her two sisters of bewitching him, then stealing his money. They were all hanged, along with a young chap who tried to help them."

Apparently. It was such a comfortable word. I pushed my lemon drizzle further away, unable to share Glenys's relish in the story; the details made it uncomfortably real. No doubt the writer had added them to hype the old legend up a bit. And yet… did the hanging of three witches really *need* any more hype? A rape seemed an odd event to link to a witchcraft story. The 'theft' accusation, too. Could there be any truth in it?

I took a swallow of coffee, my interest piqued. "Does the writer have any proof?"

Glenys settled her bottom further into her seat. I was virtually the only customer in the place, and she seemed as eager for company as I was.

"Well, only bits and pieces she's fitted together, to back the story up. Of course, she had to turn it into a romance; she claims the young man and the maid were engaged. Ah, well. Even a so-called history book has to be a page-turner these days."

"These old folktales sometimes have a smattering of truth, though," I said, echoing Ben. "Does it give any names of the people involved?"

"No. Which is strange, because the writer was a historian. She's long gone now, mind."

"Mmm. The names could have been kept secret for fear of reprisals, of course," I mused. "If this gentleman was a man of high standing, he'd want to preserve his reputation."

"Good point!" Glenys's olive-green eyes gleamed. "What a bastard, though! I mean, he was making sure, wasn't he? Even if the witchcraft accusation couldn't be proved – and I did wonder about that, because, I mean, why weren't they burned, as witches usually were? – he'd got them for theft, anyway."

"Excuse me. Could I please get a couple of lattes and some carrot cake?" called an exasperated voice, and Glenys and I both jumped. A scant-haired businessman in a dark suit was hovering halfway between us and the counter. Glenys rolled her eyes as she got up.

"No peace for the wicked," she whispered, and hurried off, leaving me to my book. I drew my cake towards me again, and scanned through the introduction. Yes, it seemed that the writer had pieced together a number of clues from various other stories and factual reports, to suggest one common thread running through them – the tale of the inn maid. Fascinating. I turned to the author's biography: Dr Jane Elliott. She only seemed to have one other book to her name: *The Persecution of Witches in Early Modern England*, but when I Googled it, I found it out of print. *The Witches of Wethershall-End* was apparently a 'departure' from her academic writing: more an exploration of local folklore, and the truth that could be found within it. For my part, I preferred to think of the witches' hanging as fiction, but, either way, I'd definitely not be walking home past 'Hangman's Lane' in future. It had just occurred to me that my jogger had probably come from there.

As I stepped outside into the dull March afternoon, I glanced across the road to find a pair of dark eyes, framed by a grey woollen hat and scarf, staring back at me. The puffer-jacket man was hunched up by the museum wall, scarf pulled across the bottom half of his face, hands deep in his pockets, as though waiting for someone. My mind jumped back to the other times I'd seen him: outside the bakery; on his phone; bumping into me outside the café… like the jogger had on the river path. And I wondered: could he be the same man?

As I watched, he dropped his eyes as though bored with our encounter, and turned to look in the library window. Well, it was a village, I told myself, firmly. I was bound to see the same people; he had a right to live here. I buttoned up my coat and set off for the Co-op to buy some milk before my imagination went into overdrive.

As I walked back home, I pondered over my discoveries at the museum – particularly that last, mysterious entry.

'For a sad and sweet lament of the love and tragedie of our owne.'

'Our owne.' What a strange thing to say. Perhaps the writer was talking about a poem especially written for the Bennington family? If so, I could do some research: see if there were any poems on record that mentioned the Bennington name.

I stopped to study the screenshot on my phone, enlarging each word with my fingers. As with the first fragment I'd found in the museum cabinet, letters and words had worn or been rubbed away, making the whole difficult to read. There was a slight shadow before 'owne', for example, where one or more letters could be missing. I sat down on a low wall for a moment, a suspicion forming in my mind. What if the word *was* incomplete?

I hardly dared to think it, but... could *'owne'* actually be *'clowne'*? Maybe *'our clowne'*, as in the first fragment? Or maybe I was becoming obsessed with the whole idea of Henry and seeing clowns wherever I looked. But if I was right, where did I start looking for poems with clowns in? Another idea dropped into my head. On one of my open-learning courses, we'd used the British Library website. As far as I remembered, it stored information on just about every known publication in our nation's history. Perhaps if I keyed in some of the words from that second fragment – along with the word 'clowne', it might bring something to light. It was worth a shot. I hurried home and fired up my laptop.

The minute I'd slung my groceries in the fridge and got a fire going in the bar, I settled down beside it and typed the key words 'clowne', 'lament', 'love' and 'tragedie' into the British Library's search engine.

Within seconds, a stream of results melted onto the screen.

> The Clowne's Lament. *Part of a collection of songs and ballads, circa 1600.*
>
> *O ye, in times to come, who read my rime*
> *And wonder of the truth within its lines;*
> *Take pitie on the fool found here within,*
> *Unjustly hanged for love, his only sin.*
> *His only crime, to save his love from shame;*
> *And publish he who would besmirch her name;*
> *But Justice sleeps; the villain doth walk free;*
> *The Fool stares down into eternitie.*

I scanned it again, not daring to believe it might actually be the poem Edward Bennington had mentioned in his accounts. But how many poems could there be about a clown lamenting a lost love?

"'Take pity on the fool found here within,'" I murmured. "Fool was another word for 'clown' – and one unjustly hanged for *love*. So maybe the clown had a lover, whose reputation was ruined by another man." This was the witchcraft story from Jane Elliott's book, surely? It didn't mention a clown, but the basic story was the same.

I carefully scoured the other ballads and poems in the collection. All were incomplete, and none bore any similarity to *The Clowne's Lament*. Then a further thought struck me; what if I entered the words 'fool', 'love' and 'tragedie' into the library search engine? I did so, and another poem appeared on the screen. The *same* poem, but this time it was titled *The Fool's Prophecy*, circa 1593–4. And there were two additional verses:

> *Alack the day, this clowne who only sought*
> *To make folk smile, to such an end was brought.*
> *And he who dreamed to play a tragedie*
> *Was hanged for nought, with love his companie.*
> *There is no silence greater than the grave;*
> *But truth will speak out, from another age;*
> *And tell the story of the clowne and maid*
> *Who neither rest, until their debt be paid.*

And he who dreamed to play a tragedie. But this was Henry's story, too – the old folktale, according to George! And then there were the first two lines: '*... this clowne who only sought / To make folk smile, to such an end was brought.*' What was it George had said? *'He were hanged, poor beggar... a poor end for a man who gave his life to making people laugh.'*

Could the poem be connected to Henry – or was that a stretch too far? It was more likely that it had inspired Henry's story in the first place. Someone had found the skull in the cellar, recalled the old ballad, and the folktale had grown up from there. My eye fell on the last line: *'The Fool stares down into eternitie'.* What did that mean? Into my mind seeped the image of Henry staring blankly into the darkness. Oh, I needed to talk to Ben.

I seized my phone and texted him.

> *Hi Ben, Please call me. Have found something more about Henry. Jenny.*

Then I headed to the kitchen for a glass of Mags's white wine, and settled back at my laptop, huddled into my coat for warmth. All thoughts of working on *Titus* had evaporated; I could think only of Henry and *The Fool's Prophecy*. Eagerly, I added every word I could think of into my search criteria, hoping one of them would bring up similar writings. It was the word 'maid' that struck gold. I stared as another string of results rolled up onto the screen.

> *Fragment of a flyleaf, with the inscription: The Unhappy Youth who Died for Love. A straynge and terrible tale in which a young maid hath tried to bring a slander upon an honest gent, and he hath accused her of bewitching him.*

A *youth* this time, as in the Jane Elliott book; and it mentioned witchcraft! Bubbling with nerves, I clicked on the ballad, but apparently 'fragment' in this case, as in most of them, meant that only the title and description had been recorded. *Damn.* My eye travelled to the next item. Same problem.

> *Portion of a flyleaf, with remnants. The inscription reading: The Youth who Died for Love. A complete historie of a young man hanged in HertFord, his wife accused of witchcraft, and with her sisters, put to death.*

Sisters. I swept up Miss Elliott's book to scan the story again. She'd dated the witchcraft hanging loosely as 'the early 1590s'... and the year given for this new fragment was 1593: the same year as the local performance of

Titus! It was also the year Shakespeare was 'likely' to have penned the play, according to the introduction in Jake's copy. Only one detail didn't tie up. This young man was hanged in Hertford, which was a fair distance from Northampton in those days, in terms of travel. But otherwise, the story sketched on the flyleaf was uncannily similar to the one in the witchcraft book. I scrolled eagerly to the last example.

> *A miscellany of plays and ballads, 21 listed but only 9 surviving.*

Sifting quickly through the nine complete ones, I found nothing akin to *The Fool's Prophecy*, but one of the fragments of description was interesting:

> *The tragicall historie of a clowne, hanged for love, including the discourse of his new wife, abused by malice and unjustly accused...*

It was dated 1610; nearly twenty years later – but the same date as *The Clowne's Lament*.

I sat very still, trying to map out how all these details fitted together. It was undeniable – *The Fool's Prophecy* and all the fragments contained elements of the folktales I'd heard or read: the witches' hangings; the young man who died trying to clear his love's name; and the clown who longed to play in a tragedy and was hanged for stealing. Could the youth and clown be the same person? *Wait;* I needed to go slowly here. I pinned my eyes to the screen as though it would self-destruct if I looked away. Apart from

The Fool's Prophecy, these were only fragments, I reminded myself. The ballads themselves no longer existed.

And yet. And yet.

Something slid into place in my mind, and I snatched my phone to call up the museum screenshot. The first two words of the entry sprang out at me: '*A Poecie*'. Again, there were shadows where odd letters might have been worn away, but the writing was so compressed that it was less obvious at first glance. Then I realised: not 'poecie' – but '*prophecie*'. Surely, surely I was right, and this was the final clue. True, the spelling was different – but I was certain I'd seen 'prophecy' written with an 'ie' at the end, somewhere.

Mouth dry, I went back to my laptop and called up a facsimile of Shakespeare's *First Folio:* the collection of plays his actor/partners had published after his death. The great book looked so real on screen, even to the leakages of ink through the backs of pages. Feverishly, I searched for *King Lear,* and found the Fool's last speech. And there it was, in the line above: *'I'll speak a prophecie ere I go.'*

I read and reread my findings until my eyes ached, and still there was no text from Ben. I called Mags, but her phone just rang out. She was probably with a client. She'd be excited, of course, but it would mean so much more to Ben. He was a historian, after all. I'd sensed the same rush of adrenalin in him that I'd felt when we made those first finds at the museum.

It was past five when I decided to stop, stretch and visit the bathroom. Ben still hadn't come back to me; maybe he was working late. My hair was a messy tangle, so I spent some time tidying myself up, then headed back along the landing, feeling better. But halfway across I stopped, surprise gluing me to the spot. Ben was standing in the middle of the little lounge, looking up at me, a bottle of red wine in his hand.

No text, no call; yet he was here. And the oddest thing was, all the doors were locked.

So how had he got in?

For a moment, neither of us spoke. Then he gave me a nervous smile, and to my relief, he looked as anxious as I felt.

"Hi. I, um, didn't want to shout, or anything, in case I startled you. I got your text, and thought I'd come over and surprise you. But your front door was open. I did knock on it a couple of times but got no answer… so I came in to check you were okay." A waft of his sea and sun body spray drifted up towards me; but this time, instead of evoking a sense of comfort and pleasure, it felt oddly discordant. It was stronger than before, as though he'd just put it on, and mingled with it was a hint of something else I couldn't quite fathom.

I gazed at him, my confusion growing. "No, that's not possible. I'm sure I shut it properly when I came back from the village."

He shrugged awkwardly. "Well, maybe you just thought you had, and the wind blew it open. As you're on your own, though, you should be doubly careful. I closed it behind me as I came in."

I didn't say a word. He assumed I'd been careless, and I could see why. No one could walk through a locked door. Perhaps I'd been so wrapped up in my museum discoveries, I really had forgotten to check.

"Anyway, I'm sorry if I startled you, but I was a bit

worried, to be honest. Are you still up for some wine? If it's too early, we could always drink it later, with a take-away, if you fancy it?"

He sounded so calm that I gathered myself together and went downstairs, accepting the bottle he held out, though my face was probably about the same colour as its contents.

"To be honest, I could probably do with a glass," I said, attempting a laugh. Another wash of his body spray hit my senses, and my eyes wandered to his chest. The neck of his cream shirt was open, showing an enticing glimpse of smooth skin. "And yes, a take-away would be great," I added, quickly averting my gaze. I was more than happy to have some company, though my stomach bubbled with nerves at the thought of spending the evening with him. "I hope you didn't mind me texting you, but I made a real find at the museum and couldn't wait to show… someone."

His brows rose at that self-conscious last word.

"Lead on, Ms Watson," he said, with his easy smile. "I'm all yours for the rest of the evening."

FIFTEEN

'Full of scorpions is my mind…'
(Macbeth)

"So you don't think I'm imagining all these connections." It was half an hour later and I was totally absorbed in my museum finds again. There was a wind getting up outside; a few fronds of ivy gently patted the casement windows. But I was getting used to the old pub's sounds and sighs, and the wind was the answer, of course, to that open door. I must have left it ajar, and a sharp gust had done the rest.

"No; not at all," Ben said, his eyes still fixed on *The Fool's Prophecy*. "You're fitting together a story that was quite possibly based on truth and handed down in the form of folktales and ballads. Stories were passed on that way, long before they were written. There are so many shreds of detail here, Jenny. You have a keen mind."

I couldn't help glowing; it was a rare compliment.

"Well, I got the idea from this book, really." I handed him *The Witches of Wethershall-End*, and he scanned the back cover with interest. "You haven't read it?" I asked, surprised. It seemed an odd omission, for a historian. He reddened slightly.

"I should have, I know; just one of those things I never got round to."

"But you do think the youth and the clown in those fragments could be one person? And *The Fool's Prophecy* the poem Edward Bennington commissioned a reading of?"

He nodded slowly. "It's very possible. Private poetry readings weren't unheard of among the social elite, and if this poet was writing about local events that were politically sensitive, then a closed reading at the manor makes sense."

I perched on a stool beside him. "But what about that last line of the prophecy: the fool staring down into eternity? It's such a strange thing to say."

"Yes." He tapped his front teeth with his forefinger. He had nice hands; long-fingered and smooth, with neat nails. "You know, that comment may be our biggest clue that Henry *was* the clown in this story. I know it sounds a bit gruesome, but heads of criminals were often publicly displayed as a warning to others to toe the line. That may be why Henry's skull ended up here, and not buried with his body."

I imagined a head stuck on a spike, displayed on a wall or bridge, and felt sick. "I see. That would be why he's—"

"Looking down, not up, into the hereafter," said Ben, grimly. "Yes. It wouldn't happen to a common thief, but if Henry attacked some important official, well... that might explain why his head was severed. Sounds as though the stealing charge *could* have been a cover, to protect our gentleman rapist. Pity we don't know who he was."

"A justice?" I murmured.

"What makes you say that?"

"Shakespeare's *King Lear* mentions the debauchery of a justice, so we know it went on. And the play *Measure for Measure* is based on that idea."

He nodded. "Mmm. Well, we may never know. But Jenny, I think you really have something here. It's time you started writing this research down; keeping track of all the details. It's important."

I let this idea sink in. I was feeling warm and comfortable from the wine, and Ben was sitting very close to me. I drank in a mixture of the nautical body spray and his own scent, and felt a prickle of exhilaration.

As I raised my eyes, I found him looking intently into mine with a heat that made my stomach flip, and in that moment, I yearned to respond. To have him encircle me in his arms; shut out everything else but our closeness. But closeness led to intimacy, and as he leaned closer, fear lanced through me; I was up on my feet, the alcohol-induced fuzziness dissipating.

"Um… listen, I'm sorry, Ben; I know we said we'd have dinner, but actually I've just remembered I've got some work I really must get done." The words almost fell over themselves in my panic.

His eyes widened a little, then scanned my face as though trying to read my mind. "Sure, of course," he said, pushing his mop of hair back from his face. "I didn't realise. I'll get off and leave you to it, shall I?"

I looked away, fighting my usual surge of colour. "Look, I'm sorry, it's not that I don't…" I met his eyes again briefly, expecting to see annoyance or exasperation. But I read only bewildered kindness there. "I really do have a load of work to do." I spied the small plastic bag with Henry's bone samples in, still lying on the bar where George had left it, and seized it. "Oh, but I did get this for you, for the carbon dating."

His face relaxed. "That is so good. Thank you! So I'll see you on Thursday, for the auditions? Some of our students are quite keen; their drama teacher's off sick at the moment, and they could do with a bit of help. But they'll have to bring a parent, if that's all right with you."

"Of course. But I ought to tell you: I'm doing *Titus* now, not *Hamlet*."

"Ah. Right. That makes sense. Send me over the details; I'm sure they'll love it. Don't worry, I'll see myself out – but don't forget to lock the door!"

A few more minutes and he was gone.

I was left alone, wrung with embarrassment. What must he have thought? Probably that he'd be better off without someone who leapt like a grasshopper at the slightest hint of intimacy. And he'd be right, wouldn't he? I went off to bolt the front door.

The pub dropped back into its thick, centuries-old silence as I curled up on the rug by the fire, with a copy of *Titus*. Another two glasses of wine had made the room feel distant. My eyes were on the play, but my mind kept going back to Ben, and the shock on his face when I'd shied away from him. But I'd seen a certain look in his eye before that: the glint of desire that promised only one end. And once it began, I may not be able to stop it. Fear, cold and thick, uncoiled in my belly. As much as I yearned to be held and caressed, I never again wanted to cede that kind of control.

A memory of my last evening with Ross seared through my alcohol-weakened mind: of his voice spitting in my ear, while I cowered, face-down and naked on our satin quilt.

"For Christ's sake, Jenny! What's wrong with you?"

Instinctively, I screwed my eyes shut against the memory, but it spread through my helpless mind and senses, enveloping me. In an instant, I was back in our almond-and-white bedroom, yelping as Ross tore himself away from me.

"It's not as though I'm asking you to do anything terrible, is it?" He raked his nails across his scalp, dark hair spilling through his fingers. *"Just to be a bit more adventurous, for pity's sake. And you promised you would, in those bloody marriage guidance sessions* you *insisted on. Well, look what a waste of time they were!"*

"Please," I begged. *"You know I can't. Not like this. Not this way."* It was the same every time he coaxed, persuaded or bullied me into doing what he wanted. It had been the same for years – but when he had a drink, he always forgot and thought that, this time, it might be okay.

"Christ!" There was a series of thumps and breaking glass as Ross sent everything on my dressing table shooting across the room. My hairbrush and comb, perfume and a scattering of make-up hit the wall beyond me and I hunched lower on our bed, sobbing as the dressing table went over with a splintering crash. *"And you wonder why I had an affair? Can you bloody well blame me?"* He was panting now; trying to get a hold on his temper as he pulled on his jeans. *"My God; you need help, Jenny."*

"It's not my fault," I choked, into the quilt.

"Oh, I suppose it's all mine then, is it? Like us not having kids?" He glared at me as I rose upright, gasping. *"Oh, yes; I know what you think. What's more, I had to find out from my best mate, because you told HIS WIFE, and not your own sodding husband."*

I curled up in misery. So that was it. I'd only talked to Sonia because I so desperately needed someone to confide in. I had no idea she'd go and blab everything out to Graham. She was my *friend.* Well, not any more. There was no way I'd trust anyone with a secret like that again. Ever.

Ross yanked his T-shirt off the back of his bedside chair. *"Well, you need to be sure of your facts, before you go making a laughing stock out of me. It's more likely to be your bloody fault than mine."*

That was too much.

"You wouldn't even hear of either of us going for tests!" I burst out. *"So how will we ever know?"*

He took a step towards me, hand raised, and I quailed; but as our eyes locked, the anger died in his, leaving only an ugly disgust.

"Look at you." His gaze travelled slowly over my unclothed body. *"God, you've really let yourself go. How much weight did you actually put on?"*

I scrambled, trembling, to cover myself.

"Do you know something, Jen?" he said, quietly now. *"When we started out, I never thought our marriage would turn out to be such a shitty disappointment."*

Then he was gone, feet thudding on the stairs, little shards of plaster showering the hardwood floor in the hall as the front door shuddered behind him.

That was the night I'd left, because I knew there was no coming back from those words. I still carried them like a spear that had broken off inside me, and twisted when I moved the wrong way.

A log cracked in the hearth, bringing me back to the present. I sat before the flames, my arms wrapped around my chest. Thank God I'd got out of my relationship with Steve, too, the moment I'd recognised it was going wrong. I couldn't risk that happening again, and another man looking at me the way Ross had; I was better off alone.

Pushing myself to my feet, I double-checked that both doors were locked and bolted, then went back to *Titus*, dry-eyed and determined. I had a one-shot chance on a lifetime dream; one that wouldn't let me down. And I was going to tackle this play if it killed me.

SIXTEEN

'…but man, proud man,
Drest in a little brief authority…'
(Measure for Measure)

"Have you had any replies to those emails you sent about the auditions?" asked Mags the next morning, when we 'met' over the phone for coffee.

"Not a thing, actually. But Diana's put a notice on the village Facebook, so hopefully that will help. She says Gordon will come around eventually."

"That's big of him," snorted Mags. "How are you feeling about *Titus* now?"

"Actually, not quite so bad," I said. It wasn't a lie; the play had surprised me. In fact, there were moments where the writing was heart-stopping.

An email pinged up on my phone from Mr Norwich, and I stiffened as I read its title: 'Unacceptable Situation'.

What? What did that mean?

Shaking slightly, I clicked on it, as Mags chattered on at the other end of the line.

"Sorry, hang on a sec, Mags," I said. "This really weird email's come in from my boss, and I need to read it."

"Weird? In what way, weird?"

"I can't talk now," I said. "I'll call you back." And I cut off her protests mid-flow. *Now* what was going on?

Jenny,

We agreed that you would start work on Monday. Since then, the premises have been left unattended for hours at a time.

I am aware of this because after your nervous reaction to your 'visitor', the other night, I asked a security firm to call round and take a look at the premises. I had thought I'd sent an email to forewarn you, but now realise I'd forgotten – for which I apologise. The security firm, however, tell me that they rang the mobile number you gave me a number of times, and when they got no answer, called round in person on two occasions. There was apparently no sign of life on either.

I must say that this raises some doubts in my mind as to your work ethic, and I would appreciate your reassurance that it won't happen again. Although the premises are not yet officially open, I need to be confident that once they are, you will not leave them unattended during opening hours. Your unexplained absences, so early on in our arrangement, raise the question of exactly what kind of 'work' you have been engaged in, outside of the premises. I await your explanation.

Regards,
Leo Norwich.

I sat bolt upright, trembling. How dare he be so obnoxiously rude? He was making me sound like a layabout! After all, he himself had told me to concentrate on the festival, and not worry about the pub for the moment. And all I'd done was go out to the museum a couple of times... plus the café, I remembered, feeling my face go hot. But then, how was I to know he'd contacted a security firm? And certainly, no one had phoned me.

Then realisation dawned. *The unknown numbers.* Because of the two weird texts I'd received, I'd stopped answering calls from any number I didn't recognise. But that wasn't my fault; he should have said.

My mobile burst into Beethoven again and, in my fury, I almost hurled it across the room. It was Mags, of course; but I couldn't speak to her now. I ended the call, but tapped out a hasty text, saying I was fine and would get back to her soon. Then I looked up, and stilled. Little black holes were seeping into my vision, slowly but surely devouring it. I sank down on a bench, gripping its rounded edges. If this kept happening... the internet site I'd looked at flashed into my mind. *Repeated attacks may cause long-term damage.* I grabbed my phone and held it tightly; at least I had Mags on speed dial. But I didn't call her.

I was just tired, I told myself, gritting my teeth. Exhausted from a bad night, listening for every noise. And I wasn't going to lose my sight; not because of some stupid misunderstanding. Not when I'd been handed the chance of a lifetime. What was wrong with people, that a little authority made them into uncivil bullies? Tears pricked at my eyes, and I let them come. I felt weak and stupid and afraid, as I had whenever I'd wept as a child, after my mother had chastised me; she loathed tears. *"I'll give you something to cry about, you little swine!"* My toes curled as her voice pierced my head, lifting the skin on my arms.

No! She was gone, I told myself, savagely. And crying, however weak it felt, eased the pressure in my head.

My tears eventually dried. I sat very still, taking slow breaths and counting them, and gradually, the black spots were absorbed into my normal vision, until only two faint patches hovered in the corners.

Getting carefully to my feet, I went to the sink for some water. This was ridiculous. One reprimand from my boss, and my world started falling apart – but I couldn't bear that his criticism was so undeserved. It reduced me to the cowering child who, so many times, had had no idea what she'd done wrong.

Sipping a few mouthfuls of water made me much calmer. Mr Norwich didn't know about my research, so perhaps his annoyance was understandable. And yes, I might have let time fritter by a little... though not that much. Uncertainty flickered. Was this my fault? I'd gone along in a haze of enjoyment, and my new boss had seemed a disconnected figurehead who was content to let me decide my own working schedule. Now he loomed, uncomfortably real, at the edges of my day-to-day life. A dull, familiar ache grew up from my neck, over my ears. I boiled the kettle and made myself some tea, gathered up two paracetamol and my laptop and headed into the bar lounge, to a chair by the fire. If I sat very still, the headache would go. *It must.* Because if I messed this up, I had no job, no home, no future.

After half an hour or so, I tentatively opened my eyes to find that my vision was clear, and my headache easing.

Okay. The bottom line was, I wanted this job, so I had to try to put this right. I reached for my laptop and began typing a response.

Dear Mr Norwich,

I am very sorry you feel you've had cause to complain. I was in fact out doing some research on the pub's history, to use in our festival publicity. I also met with some actors and a director from a local drama group, who are helping to spread the word about our auditions in the right quarters. They are from the group I mentioned in my last email who are hiring the costumes. I will be going over to fit them on Saturday, and hopefully make some more contacts. The hire fee for the costumes has been agreed, and if you could give me your bank details, their group secretary will transfer payment after the fitting. I would also like to mention that I worked late last night on the play, and did extra hours over the weekend, cleaning the premises in readiness for our opening.

(I decided not to mention Mags's part in all this; he might take exception to her staying on, and I'd be in more trouble.)

Having said all this, I now realise I should have apprised you of the times I would be out, and will do so now whenever I have to be away from the premises. Naturally, once the pub is open, I will ensure there is always someone here. Please accept my apologies for any inconvenience caused. In future I will keep a detailed worksheet of my hours and tasks achieved, and email it to you on a weekly basis. I am keen to make a success of the project and assure you that I will do everything in my power to achieve it.

I hope you find my explanation satisfactory.
Kind regards
Jenny Watson

"There," I said, clicking on 'send' with a flourish. "Let's hope that makes you feel better, you authoritative little man." Then I sat back, stomach percolating, and waited for his reply.

By the time I called Mags, I'd reread my contract and found that Mr Norwich was within his rights: there was a clause stating that the pub must be attended at all times, and if I had to take time out, I should inform him.

"That's ridiculous!" snapped Mags when she'd stopped berating me for cutting her off. "It sounds like he wrote that contract himself. He can't go putting random stuff like that in. What are your official working hours?"

"Er, we haven't really established any yet," I said. "But we will, once the pub opens."

"Not good enough!" said Mags. "Get back to him and insist your hours are laid out properly."

I sighed. "But that would tie me down completely. What if I need to go out during those hours?"

"You're going round in circles, Jen," she said. "I think we should find out more about this guy, and have that contract properly looked at."

"Look, he probably just overreacted," I said, unable to believe I was defending him again. "This is new to both of us."

She snorted. "Well, I'm glad you mentioned all that cleaning we did. What a cheek, implying you've been gallivanting about enjoying yourself!"

I didn't answer. I was feeling a tad guilty that I'd let myself be carried away by the research on Henry.

"Listen, Mags, I need to get on with some work," I said. "I'll call you later."

I'd managed about two hours of audition prep when my mobile rang again.

"Jenny. Gordon."

God, he was curt. "Hi, Gordon."

"I'm calling about these auditions," he said, oblivious to my cool tone. "I'm afraid I've tried everyone I can think of, and the response was as I predicted; no one wants to do a production of *Titus*. You should have stuck to *Hamlet*."

The day wasn't getting any better.

"What about the Facebook post?" I asked.

"That's had some views, but not much response."

I now wished heartily that I'd learned how to set up my own account, as Diana had suggested.

"Can't you put a reminder up?" I asked. "I've made some more discoveries about this local actor, who was in *Titus* in 1593. Perhaps if we write something about that? Tell you what, can I speak to Diana?"

"She's out for the day."

Shit. I was running out of time. I must have been mad to let Diana talk me into holding the auditions tomorrow evening.

"What sort of proof have you got to back up these 'discoveries'?" he asked.

I hesitated. "Well, it's all pretty circumstantial, but—"

"Mmm. As I suspected. Well, send something over, and I'll do my best. But don't say I didn't warn you."

I ended the call, barely able to thank him, and my phone blared into life again.

"Hi, George," I said, trying to keep the weariness I felt out of my voice.

"Hello, my dear. Thought I'd better check: is it seven you want picking up, like before?"

Damn! It was Wednesday: the Speak Out meeting. This was going to cost me a fortune in taxi fares.

"Everything all right, my dear?" came George's voice.

"Oh, yes. Sorry, George. Seven is great, thanks."

Putting my phone firmly aside, I returned to work, though it was impossible to resist checking my email every ten minutes. But Mr Norwich remained ominously silent. Was the bastard ever going to put me out of my misery? I needed to know if I still had a job.

At ten to seven, as I was scraping my uneaten dinner into the bin, a 'ping' sounded from my inbox. *Thank God;* it was from my boss. I scanned it quickly.

Dear Jenny,

Thank you for your email. I appreciate your concern, and your swift response. Under the circumstances, I can see that you were acting in the business's interest; however, I do feel that a working schedule would be useful, as you suggest. Please make sure you inform me whenever you need to leave the premises unattended. Thank you. I look forward to reading your report at the end of the week. Best wishes,

Leo Norwich

I let out a huge sigh. I'd pulled it round. My job was safe. Now all I had to do was get through tonight.

SEVENTEEN

'Boldness be my friend...'
(Cymbeline)

"Right, ladies." Louise smiled round at the circle of Speak Out women, most still sipping their teas and coffees. "We've had a very productive first half of our meeting. Now I hope we're going to hear from a few of our newer members." She smiled at me. "Jenny tells me she's happy to tell us a bit about the play she's directing. Shakespeare, am I right?"

I nodded, and one or two people's eyes rolled upwards. *Great.* Clutching my notes as though they were a swimming float, I got to my feet.

"Okay. I know Shakespeare isn't everybody's bag," I said. "So I'll keep it brief."

"Thank Christ for that," muttered someone, and Louise frowned. The inside of my mouth shrivelled.

"Which play are you directing, Jenny?" Louise asked, with an encouraging smile.

My heart sank. *"Titus Andronicus."* And that said it all, really. The few who recognised the play looked aghast; the rest gazed blankly.

Then a pale girl called Beth spoke up. "I read some of the reviews about that, when it was on in Stratford. It's pretty violent, isn't it?"

"It's a Roman play," huffed Monica, before I could reply. "That sort of thing was normal then."

She was the older woman I'd seen last week, so broken; yet today, her face was chipped and hard, business-like beneath its windswept blow-dry.

"Rape and mutilation, you mean?" Beth looked pointedly at her. "And you think that doesn't go on today?"

There was a flicker of interest around the group.

"Mutilated, how?" said Isla.

I shifted, uneasily. This conversation was running away from me.

"They cut off the heroine Lavinia's hands and her tongue, to silence her."

"Shit." Isla's face paled. "Why her hands, for God's sake?"

"So she can't write down what's happened to her." A young girl who'd sat for most of the session with her head down now raised it, her sheet of onyx-black hair falling away from her face. I glimpsed a livid, white mass of overlapping scars on one cheek: burn marks, probably. I wondered what her story was. Seeing her eyes on me, she quickly retreated behind her hair, and I looked away, cursing my own insensitivity. "It's about power, isn't it?" the girl added, head down. "If you can't communicate, for whatever reason, you're no longer a threat."

I nodded. "And yet, she finds a way: by using someone

else's story. And that's one reason this play is important, I think – however unpalatable it seems. Because storytelling, whether in books or through songs, folktales or theatre, gives us a means of expressing those things we can't or daren't say in our own voices."

The room dropped into silence. Out of the corner of my eye, I caught Louise's smile.

Isla wriggled forward in her seat. "Okay, so tell us, then. How she did it."

"Well, Shakespeare based Lavinia's story on Ovid's tale of Philomela," I explained. "Philomela was also raped, but managed to sew the names of her attackers into a piece of embroidery. Lavinia finds a copy of Ovid's book and points to Philomela's story with her arms. Then she scrapes her attackers' names in the sand using a pole, which she holds in her mouth and guides with her forearms, and writes '*Stuprum*', the Latin word for rape, underneath."

"My God," said Kath. "That must be hard to watch on stage."

"I saw the play in London, once," remarked Monica, and all heads turned in her direction. "It was pretty shocking. People fainted at the rape scene."

I studied her face. "There was a rape scene?"

And she hesitated. "Well, no, actually. Now I come to think of it, you only saw the bits before and after. But it was the sight of that poor girl, standing there, with all the blood bubbling out of her mouth that really affected me. I had to look away."

"That's what you saw?" I asked. "The blood, bubbling?"

Her head tilted to one side. "I must have. But then, I was quite a way from the stage."

"I'm sure there was plenty of blood, if it's the one I'm thinking of," I said, "but you saw the exact movement in your mind because Shakespeare's words put it there."

There was a ripple of laughter, and I stopped, cringing inside. *I always had to go too far.* I'd never found a heart-to-mouth filter, as far as Shakespeare was concerned, though I managed it effectively with everything else, as Mags was always pointing out. But if I was going to be a director, I had to get through moments like this. Some people bungee-jumped or scaled mountains; this was my Everest.

"Seriously." My voice shook. "Listen to this." Pulling my copy of *Titus* out of my bag, I riffled through until I found the scene. "This is the point when Lavinia's uncle first sees her after her attack:

> *"Why dost not speak to me? Alas, a crimson river of warm blood, like to a bubbling fountain stirr'd with wind, doth rise and fall between thy rosèd lips, coming and going with thy honey breath."*

Shakespeare's words soothed me, as they always did. I looked around the circle of faces. "The blood is a river, then a fountain. A river, because rivers are arteries to the sea. A fountain, because it's aerated... stirred with her breath. He tells us it's warm, and it smells sweet, like honey. So we've got smell, temperature, colour and movement, all in one package."

I chanced another look around, and at least no one had run for the door, except – Louise's seat was empty. Then I became aware of her standing behind Isla, looking at her phone, and disappointment shrank my spirits. But I'd come this far; I wasn't going to let it do the same to my voice, when I was talking about the one thing I loved.

"The description of movement is really important, because our brains are wired to mimic the movements we see others make," I went on. "And it works the same way when we read about or hear descriptions of action. The better the description, the more finely tuned our own response. For example, we all know what it feels like to breathe. So if we were told Lavinia was breathing heavily, or slowly, we'd easily get the picture. But this is so much more subtle. Lavinia is breathing 'a river of crimson', 'coming and going' through her lips. So that movement tells us not only what colour the blood is, but what texture. For example, if it was thin, would it cling to her lips, and move in and out with her breath?"

"Christ. It's thick," said Isla, her pupils widening.

"Yes: syrupy, viscous." My voice shook again, with relief this time. "And it 'comes and goes' as she inhales and exhales: moving in and out with a rhythm that's linked to her pulse and carried by the words. They bring her in so close that we're breathing with her."

"Wow," whispered Kath. I looked sharply at her, but there was no hint of sarcasm in her face or tone.

"And the colour's specific. Crimson, not rosy, this time, because—"

"You can see them separately, the lips and the blood?" The girl with the long, dark hair broke in, her eyes alight. I gasped.

"Yes. That is so good. Tara, isn't it?"

She nodded, disappearing again behind her hair, but I caught her smile.

"So it makes a sort of multi-dimensional experience, then?" suggested Sam.

I nodded, expanding inside at the interest in her face. "Yes. That's a great observation. Vision is the most powerful sense, but people can still choose to close their eyes or look away. But you can't look away from spoken words. They're all around you, sharing the same air, as sounds and rhythms and meanings that get inside your mind and body, and your senses. They say a picture paints a thousand words. But sound can switch on a million, in my book."

The room settled again into a ruminative hush.

"Um, well, that's it. Thanks for listening," I said, and bobbed back onto my seat.

"Well, that was f... bloody brilliant!" breathed Isla. "When did you say this play was on? Because I, for one, am up for seeing it."

"Me, too," said Sam.

I gazed at them in surprise.

"Really?" Within minutes, I was telling them about the festival, answering questions on the auditions, and handing out my email address. I could hardly believe it.

"Your talk went well," said Louise, as I helped to stack away chairs at the end of the meeting. "See, you can do it, when you try."

I gave her a small smile. "I can always talk about Shakespeare. Don't ask me to do anything else."

She studied me, her head on one side. "Yes, you're more comfortable telling other people's stories, aren't you?"

The memory of lying on my father's bed, regaling him with my made-up tales while he stroked my hair, lit my mind. I hadn't made up a story of my own since that awful day at school, when I'd watched a thousand pieces of my 'writing' drift into the depths of our dustbin. But my love for storytelling hadn't been extinguished, I realised; it had latched onto theatre instead, and been nourished by it.

"I've sent you a video file," she said, and my head shot up in surprise. "Don't worry; it's for your eyes only. I just wanted you to see yourself as others see you, when you're really confident."

"But… I'm not," I stuttered.

She smiled. "Watch it. And not just once. Keep going back to it and telling yourself that the person speaking so eloquently there is the same one standing here now, stumbling over her words and blushing." She tapped her head with a finger. "She is in there, Jenny. Somewhere in your head and your heart, bursting to shout up at the hilltops, when it's something you care about. It's just a process of discovery. See you next time."

I was silent on the journey back to the pub, Louise's comments revolving in my mind as I played the video she'd taken on her phone. She was right; although I cringed at my appearance, I could hardly believe it was my voice I was hearing. Louise had filmed the circle of listening women, too, and caught a few of their faces, alive with interest. Yet at the time it had felt like such a battle between the part of me that wanted to lose herself in the wash and relish of words, and the other that shrank with shame and self-doubt at the slightest hint of criticism. Still, I'd won though – at least on the surface. Louise was right: I was happier championing someone else's story.

I was home. As George's taxi rumbled away again into the night, I waved and headed for the front door. Now would be a good time to work on the play.

But a footstep from the porch, I stopped. Skittering gently against the door was a muddied sheet of paper, clearly visible in the shimmying light of the security lamp. No doubt some rubbish, blown here by the wind, I told myself, bending to pick it up. As I flipped it over, four words met my gaze, written large in a thick, blue felt-pen that looked as though it was running out of ink:

Now might do it.

I frowned. Was it some kind of message? No, it made no sense. It wasn't even complete. I took it inside, snapping on the light to have a closer look.

The arctic chill of the pub's interior hit me. Dumping my stuff on a table, I scraped some kindling up and got a fire going. If the auditions went well, I was definitely asking Mr Norwich for permission to sort out this heating. Meanwhile, perhaps some of Mags's brandy would warm me; she'd left a bottle on the bar. I poured myself a glass and added the muddy note to the grate, then made myself comfortable, enjoying the cheerful light as well as the warmth, watching the flames melt the blue words as the paper curled around them.

As I stared, however, an idea sprouted in my mind. There had been an odd gap between two of the words on that page. No, not a gap. A long, straight impression between 'might' and 'do', where a letter had been traced with a parched nib. I'd barely noticed it at the time, but now it seemed so obvious. The missing letter was an 'I'.

I was up and rushing to the fire in a second, pulling the

charred paper free and blowing on it, nearly singeing my fingers in my haste. But it was too late; blackened strips corkscrewed from the scorching page as I dropped it on the hearth.

Could I be right? Who, in modern society, would ever say 'Now might I do it'? It was an uncomfortable thought, yet there was only one place I'd seen that phrase written: in a scene where Shakespeare's Hamlet debates whether or not he should murder his uncle.

'Now might I do it pat. Now he is a-praying.'

But why on earth would someone write a quote from *Hamlet*, and leave it by my door, where it could easily blow away? None of it made sense. I picked up my phone to call Mags, and then paused. I could hear her in my head: "Only you could turn a few chance words into a quote from *Hamlet*, Jenny." Ross would have had a field day at my expense, had he been here.

No. I wasn't going to do this anymore – frighten myself stupid at every shadow. It must be a scrappy note from some child's homework that had blown out of a dustbin. There was no other explanation.

EIGHTEEN

'If I do dream, would all my wealth would wake me!'
(Titus Andronicus)

I woke to the sound of crackling and spitting and the smell of burning paper. Leaping from my bed, I ran to the sill and clambered up onto the wicker basket beneath so I could see out. The little top window was open a crack, and smoke was coming in. I could see giant flames at the bottom of our garden, where my father used to burn the rubbish, and there was my mother, throwing armfuls of paper into the fire like the picture of the woman scattering seeds in my little blue Bible. What would Mr Roberts and his wife next door say about such a big fire? Mr Roberts had come round to complain once before about my mother burning rubbish in the garden. But wait; it was the school holidays, and the people next door on both sides were away.

My arms hurt as I stretched to shut the window; my mother had dug her fingers into them when she'd dragged me to my room after the visitor went. *Oh, yes.* The strange woman in a navy-blue suit, who'd come to our house after tea that day, and screamed back at my mother as much as my mother screamed at her, so that I had to put my hands over my ears. I'd never known anyone shout at my mother; it made my legs shake. So I got under the table while they were fighting, hiding my eyes with my hands. When I heard the front door bang, I peeped out and saw Mummy on her knees, crying. And then I saw that Daddy's picture was gone, and that made me cry, too. It was the only one we had of Daddy that was in a frame, and it had stood on the little table in our big room ever since he went to the hospital.

I didn't know who the woman was, and I daren't ask, because soon after she'd gone, Mummy had started running around the house, opening cupboards and pulling everything out onto the floor. She was looking for pictures – photos of Daddy and her and me – and when she found them, she threw them into a pile in the middle of our big room, screaming things I didn't understand. She found me, too; that's when she dragged me out and bumped me all the way up the stairs, to my room, and banged the door shut. I'd run straight to my bed where my picture was hidden under the mattress. Daddy had given it to me himself when he got ill, and told me that as long as I had it, I would always remember him. I'd fallen asleep clutching it.

Now I trembled as I climbed down from the sill. *She mustn't find my picture.* As soon as my toes found the floor, I grabbed it from my bed and tucked it back in its hiding place. *There.* I looked at my bedroom door with its thick white paint. It was probably locked. She always locked it when I was being punished. But what if the flames spread up the garden and burned the house? I didn't know how quickly that might happen, and my mother was so close to the flames. What if she was burned up in the fire? What if I couldn't get out – and no one could get in? I had to make sure she didn't die, because I'd promised Daddy. And if she died, I would have to go into a home, where I wouldn't know anybody. She'd said so. That was why I needed to be extra good. I did try to behave myself, but it was hard, because sometimes I didn't know what I'd done wrong and I couldn't ask, because Mummy said that was answering back.

I went back to the door and tried the round knob with both hands. It turned and clicked. She hadn't locked it! Feeling sick at what she'd do if she saw me, I crept downstairs, stepping over papers and letters on the floor. It was cold in the big room; the door into the garden was open, and smoke and bits of burning paper were flying up in the air like fireworks.

The big front room looked different. All the cupboards were open, drawers hanging down like big empty mouths, handfuls of papers sticking out like tongues. In the middle of the room was a pile of pictures and letters, and a heavy white book lying open. Oh, I remembered that book! Daddy had shown it to me. It was full of photos of Mummy and Daddy's wedding day. I knelt down and opened it, and ran my finger over my Daddy's smiling face, though I knew I shouldn't touch. I wasn't allowed to look at these pictures since Daddy went away in the ambulance. Mummy wouldn't talk about him, but my teacher said he was in a place better than here. Perhaps I could take a picture; just one, to remember him. This one, because he was smiling with his eyes. She wouldn't miss it if I was very, very careful.

I peeled the shiny plastic cover back with my fingers and reached for the photo's white corner, but couldn't pull it free.

Then something sharp dug into my neck.

"Leave it!" Mummy screamed, and she lifted me and shook me until I dropped the photo. "Now get upstairs!"

I ran as fast as I could, falling over my feet and hurting my knees; wanting the toilet but knowing I daren't ask. I felt the wet on my legs as I pushed my bedroom door shut and got into bed, wiping myself with the bottom of the sheet and hoping it would dry before she saw. I rubbed and rubbed the wet patch with my hands, trying to make it sink in. It would be all right as long as she didn't send me away... and I still had my own picture of Daddy. I dug my fingers under the mattress, just to be sure.

My bedroom door hit the wall with a crash, and Mummy was in my room, staring at my hand. I shoved the photo underneath me and laid very still, trying to pretend I was asleep. But she bent over me, and I could feel her breath on my face, and my legs started to shiver.

"You took one, you disobedient little swine. Didn't you? Give it to me!"

I always did everything my mother said, straightaway. But not this time.

"Please, no, Mummy. Daddy gave it me. It's mine. Please, don't take it!"

I yelled as she dragged my arm out and bent back my fingers, but it hurt much more that the only thing I had of my Daddy was gone.

Then a much bigger fear was in me, squeezing my insides so hard that I started to cry as my mother picked me up and turned me onto my face.

"I'll give you something to cry about!" she said, and she pulled up my nightie so I felt the cold air on my legs and bottom. Then she went quiet and I waited and waited, pushing my eyes closed and curling my toes, and the ache in my belly got worse. I pressed my legs together to make it stop. "You've done it again, haven't you?" she said, and her voice was soft. I hated it when she spoke like that, because it meant she'd seen the yellow on the sheet. "My God; what did I ever do to deserve you?"

"I'm sorry, Mummy." I tried hard not to cry. "I couldn't help it. Please." But she never believed me; never listened, no matter how hard I begged. It was done, and there were only consequences.

"Stay here," she said, and went out of the room, and I was now shivering all over; my teeth, too. I screwed myself up into a ball, thinking about what she'd gone to fetch. She'd given away all Daddy's clothes to the charity shop, but she'd kept his best brown leather belt – for me, she said. So I could remember what he would do to me, if he were here, and realised how naughty I was. But I didn't think my Daddy would ever be angry, like her. He was always kind, even when I did something wrong. And now the crying wouldn't stop, because I knew how much this was going to hurt. Once it had stung so badly that I was sick, and everything had to be washed, so I'd had to sleep on the floor.

Then I heard it: the clink of Daddy's belt in her hand, as she walked along the landing; and I buried my face in my quilt, as she stood over me.

"Lie still," she said.

Lie still, and soon it will be over. I said the words again and again in my head, and bit my arm to stop myself from crying, because if I did, she would hit me harder. The belt stung so badly, it made my breath stop. As long as I wasn't sick. *I mustn't be sick.*

Then it was quiet, and there was only the throbbing, burning ache. I screamed in my head, my mouth closed. *Lie still, and soon it will be over.*

"That'll teach you not to lie to me. Or wet the bed. Now lie down in the dry bit, and go to sleep."

She was gone, and I was alone, sobbing face-down on my quilt. Outside, the flames crackled, and I could hear my mother howling in her room, like our neighbour's dog when they left him alone and went to work. I wrapped my quilt round my head, so I couldn't hear her anymore, and waited for the stinging to stop, trying over and over to draw a picture of Daddy's face in my head – one that no one could ever take away from me.

In the middle of the night, she came to my room and woke me up, and made me kneel and say a prayer, so that God would forgive me. And though I was tired, and it hurt when I moved, I wanted to do it, because she always laid a hand on my head while I prayed, so I knew I was good again. Sometimes she'd put on my bedside light and read to me before I fell asleep, and that was the best, though it was only a story from my Bible.

"You can never tell anyone about this, Jenny," she said, and her voice was soft in a way I liked. "Because if you do, people will know how badly you've behaved, and they'll take you into a home, with lots of children and adults you don't know. And you wouldn't want that, would you?"

I shook my head, and the squeezing feeling was back in

my stomach. The one that made me want to get under the bed and hide.

"Then you must swear, Jenny. Swear on your Bible, that you won't tell anyone else you've been this naughty, and I've had to correct you."

I sat up, and put my hand on the Bible, and promised. I wanted so badly to be good. Then I laid down and she stroked my head, until I went to sleep. And the words went round in my head: words that kept me safe from a life with strangers. *Lie still. Keep safe. Never tell.*

With barely a second's pause I was in that same bedroom, but the colours on the walls and bed had changed from white to pale pink, and Ross was with me. Now I could see easily out of my window, for the sill only came up to my middle. I was twenty-four, and soon to be married: packing up my things to leave for ever... and my mother was gone. I knew where she was. I'd seen her yesterday, and she looked so peaceful after her long illness. Perhaps she really had gone to meet the God she loved and believed in. But it wasn't any God I wanted to know.

All my books were boxed up, except for one. Ross picked up the little blue Bible that was sitting on the table, beside my bed.

"Do you want this, darling?" he asked. I looked at it for a moment, my insides twisting. *Burn it,* hissed a voice in my heart, hoarse like the flames in the bonfire, where she'd thrown my father's picture. *Burn it till there's not a microscopic charred shred of it.*

But my mouth wouldn't utter the words. It was a Bible, after all.

"Let's take it to the chapel," I whispered. "Perhaps we can ask them to put it in with… with…"

"With your mother's body?" he asked, gently.

"Yes." It had always been more of a comfort to her than I had.

And I'd kept its secrets, for seventeen long years. Now I wanted it buried, drowned, *'deeper than e'er did plummet sound'*, where I never had to see or hear from it again.

NINETEEN

'Sorrow concealed, like an oven stopped
Doth burn the heart to cinders where it is.'
(Titus Andronicus)

The noise was thrumming through my quilt. Music, again. Shaking, I surfaced and sat up, head thudding. The bed sheet was wound around me, my hair drenched with perspiration. And Beethoven's Fifth was blaring from my phone on the bedside table.

I was awake – and my vision was clear.

Glancing at my screen, I saw Diana's name flashing. What was she phoning me this early for? Then my memory kicked in. It was Thursday: the auditions.

"Diana?" I said, groping for my coat as the cold hit me.

"Hi, Jenny!" she sang out. "Sorry, I've not caught you in the middle of exercising, or something?"

I glanced at the time. Half past eight.

"It's fine." I headed downstairs to light the fire.

"Look, I'll come straight to the point," Diana said. "I

called to tell you I haven't had much luck persuading people to come tonight."

The temperature in the pub plunged a few more degrees.

"I know Gordon's had problems, too," she added. "I'm so sorry, Jenny; my husband and I don't agree on much, but I have to say I think he's right about this. Can't you get your boss to see that *Hamlet* would be a better choice? I could do a quick ring-round."

It was like listening to a satnav stuck in a loop.

"No. I've asked, I'm afraid. He's insisting on *Titus.*"

"Ah, that's rough. But don't worry," said Diana. "Perhaps we'll have some last-minute interest on Facebook. Listen, I've got to go. Meeting a friend for lunch."

I sat back on my haunches, watching the fire spatter into life, wondering bleakly what to do if I couldn't cast the play. If no one turned up, surely Mr Norwich would have to compromise?

But deep down, I knew that wasn't going to happen. I went over to the windowsill to dig out Jake Reeve's copy of *Titus* and get to work. I'd put the plays in alphabetical order, so they were easy to locate. But as my fingers reached the 'T' section, I paused. It wasn't there. And yet I was certain I'd put it back. I was a bit obsessive about having things in order; another by-product of my mother's training.

Running my eye over the collection, I noticed one book protruding slightly, under 'H', next to *Hamlet*, as though someone had shoved it back in a hurry. I hooked it out and scanned its spine: *The Taming of the Shrew.*

How had I missed this? Maybe Mags had slipped it back in the wrong place after dusting? Turning the dense volume over in my hands, I noticed a bulge between its pages, and flipped it open. Along the spine lay a thin spike of dried herbs, their tiny flowers long drained of colour. But there was no mistaking their faint aroma: *rosemary*. A whisper of unease ran down the hollow of my back, as though someone had breathed along it. My eyes turned involuntarily towards the front door; then I remembered my new resolution – not to turn every tiny coincidence into a Miss Marple mystery. Maybe Jake Reeve had been fond of rosemary. I should ask George. My eye rested on the top right-hand corner of the page, which was turned down – something Mags or I would never have done. A few words were underlined in pencil, from one of Katherine's speeches: '*best beware my sting*'.

Another smell prickled my nose. I lifted the pages to it and sniffed; apart from general mustiness and a trace of herb, surely that was… a hint of stale nicotine? Well, perhaps Jake Reeve had been a smoker, too. But would smoke taint a book to that extent, months or years afterwards? Possibly. I slid the book carefully back in the 'T' section.

A burst of Beethoven scattered my thoughts, and I looked quickly around for my phone. It was next to my laptop – under which lay the copy of *Titus* I'd been searching for! Maybe my 'condition' had affected my memory, too. I stared in surprise at my phone screen, wavering before I answered. *An international code.* Had my boss decided to talk to me 'in the flesh' about *Titus*? The idea was unpalatable. I had no idea what the code for Germany was, but I'd better answer.

"Hello."

"Jenny?"

"Aunt Clare?" This was the last person I'd ever expected to hear, particularly after the way we'd parted. *New*

Zealand. That's where the code was from: Auckland. It must be late there; nine or ten o'clock, maybe? Perhaps it was bad news.

"How are you? How's Uncle Peter? I can't believe you've called," I added, barely above a whisper.

"Well, to be honest, I wasn't sure if I should." Her voice was tight. Controlled. "Peter's okay – a bit frail, these days. He's not the man he was."

Frail. I couldn't imagine that. In my mind's eye, I still saw him, dwarfing every room in my mother's little house on the two occasions he and Aunt Clare had come to visit: once when my father died, and again when my mother was first diagnosed with cancer. The third time, when her illness returned, Aunt Clare came alone.

Uncle Peter, with his muscular frame and open stride, and his chest as solid as our wooden breadboard, was always the dominant one; the decision-maker. But when Aunt Clare visited without him, she'd caused a rift between my mother and me that never healed. Perhaps she was calling to build bridges. But why now?

"Are you, um, still at the bungalow?" I asked.

Now I was making small talk, to put off whatever revelation lay ahead.

"Oh, yes. We didn't see the point of moving, as there's only the two of us. It's nice to think you remember it. What about you? Are you still in office work?"

I understood why she was asking. I'd done my office training course in Auckland when I lived with them for a year. I shook my head at the memory. *I was sixteen.*

"Not at the moment." I hesitated. "Aunt Clare, I'm so sorry."

I meant about Uncle Peter, but Aunt Clare assumed I was apologising for the crowning misdemeanour that had led to my New Zealand 'gap' year.

"It was a long time ago," she said, comfortably. "Best not think too much. It all worked out for the best, anyway."

The best? I choked back the bitterness that crowded my throat.

"Did it? Do you know that for sure?"

She sighed. "Jenny, you were sixteen. You were hardly ready to bring up a child. And when you wouldn't have… the procedure, the children's home seemed the kindest thing."

The 'procedure'. Why couldn't she just say the real word?

"And he's been happy and well cared for," she added. "At least I've always known that."

I stopped breathing.

"You kept in touch? But you made me promise—"

"That's why I'm ringing you, Jenny. You see, at the time we believed that a clean break was better for everyone, especially the child. And I swore to Peter that I'd never say anything. The only reason I'm calling now is because…" she paused. "Well, we're all getting older, and Peter and I have both had health problems. It makes you realise you shouldn't leave things. You know. Loose ends."

I pulled my phone away from my ear and stared at it in disbelief. My child was a *loose end?*

"Jenny?" I heard her say.

"I'm here."

"The other thing is… I thought you should know; Mark is in England."

Mark? My son had a name. It sounded strange as I tried

it out in my mind, and my throat swelled. I'd wanted to call him James, after my father.

"He's here? Where?"

"He started a design course at Birmingham University last September. I've been wondering for a while whether to warn you, because he…" she paused, as though searching for a way to couch her words. "In fact, I rang your old landline number a few weeks ago. Your ex-husband said you'd moved on, but he gave me your mobile. I was sorry to hear about your divorce, Jenny."

I brushed her sympathy aside. I could think only of *him*.

"Do you have a surname for Mark?" I asked. The silence thickened while I waited.

"Radford," she said at last. "Mark Radford."

I shook my head, trying to understand.

"How do you know all this?"

"I was friends with a woman who worked at the home. And so when he was placed with the Radford family, she let me know. It wasn't difficult to keep track of him via the internet as he got older. He's on Facebook and LinkedIn, and so are we; but we've never contacted him. Peter wouldn't have it."

All this time, she knew.

"Does… Uncle Peter know you've called?"

"Peter has dementia," she said, quietly. "He doesn't really follow what's going on these days. But even so, I wouldn't say anything. He never forgave me for telling your mother, that time."

And now we'd reached it. That last poisonous argument.

"You had no right," I whispered. "You and Uncle Peter both swore you never would."

"I had every right!" she snapped. "I kept that secret for seven years. And I wouldn't have told her then, except… she was my sister, for God's sake, and she'd just been told she wouldn't live the year out!" I flinched at the dry whip of a voice that was so like my mother's. "You weren't a child anymore, Jenny. At twenty-three, you were old enough to face up to things. And I didn't want my sister going to her grave with a secret like that on my conscience. Or yours."

The words I'd fought back came flooding. "She might have got better! She did the first time, when I nursed her. If you hadn't told her about the baby, I would have stayed at home. She would have let me help her. I hope *that's* on your conscience!"

I heard her sharp intake of breath, and closed my eyes; felt my cheek against our rough, wooden door, as my mother crashed it shut on me, its flaking green paint under my clawed fingernails. I winced at her voice as it screamed through my head. *"Get out of my house, you filthy little whore! You lied to me; it's what you always do, though God knows I've done my best to knock it out of you. It breaks my heart to think what your father would have said."*

And I sobbed inside, as I had then, because I'd had no idea where I was to live; if I'd be able to get my clothes; or how she would manage – because God help me, I'd promised my father I'd look after her.

None of this had taken place in front of my aunt, of course. My mother didn't make scenes in front of other people.

"She threw me out," I said, my voice trembling. "Did you know that? You didn't even ask what happened afterwards, did you? Oh, no. You waited till the day you were leaving, so you didn't have to live with the mess you caused."

"You said you never wanted to speak to me again, if you remember," she spat. I curled inside as the things I'd said thronged my mind; but I'd hated her for betraying me. And if it wasn't for Ross, I would have ended up homeless. We'd only just met up again, for the first time since leaving school, and the row precipitated our fledgling relationship into the intimacy of living together. I'd often wondered: if things had worked out differently, would we have married?

"Anyway, I didn't phone to have another argument," said Aunt Clare, cutting through my thoughts. "But I will say this: you've a short memory. I remember how grateful you were that your Uncle Peter and I were in England when you found out you were pregnant. God knows what you would have done without your uncle to sort everything out. I mean, what does a sixteen-year-old know about work permits?"

The memory subdued me. Yes, they had both been kind after the first shock of the news: taking all the responsibility off my shoulders. Uncle Peter had found me a course – and persuaded my mother to let me have a 'gap' year with them. And when it came to it, she'd seemed only too glad to be rid of me.

"Do you think he ever believed me?" I asked now in a small voice. I'd never admitted to myself how important Uncle Peter's opinion was; how I'd looked up to him after my father died. "About… what happened?"

"What, when you told us you were raped?" She snorted. "Of course he didn't. First, you made it sound as though you'd led the boy on. Then you said the opposite. What were we supposed to believe?"

I laid my aching forehead in my hand. That was why he'd been so angry with me initially. I could still see his florid face. *Just some boy from school? For Pete's sake, Jenny. He's got the same equipment as a man twice his age, and probably in better working order. Where does he live, this boy? I'll be paying him a visit, before he's any older!* It had taken all Aunt Clare's efforts and my pleas to persuade him that we needed to keep this secret, for my mother's sake; she'd been so tired and run-down over the past few months. None of us realised at the time that she was entering round one of the fight for her life. Nor did she tell me, until I came home.

The silence grew, with neither of us willing to end the call, until Aunt Clare decided that 'enough was enough'.

"Anyway, what are you doing with yourself these days?" she asked, with determined brightness. "You said you'd moved on from office work?"

I hesitated; the pretence cloying my throat. But I'd already decided that I was going to try to contact Mark – and I might need her help. So I swallowed down my nausea, and told her about my directing job, missing out the bit about the pub. She and my mother had always been strictly teetotal.

"Oh!" she said, with a small laugh. "Well, I must say I'm surprised, though I shouldn't be. You were keen on all that stuff at school, I remember. Your mother told me once about that play you were involved in."

For the second time, my heart stopped. *My mother remembered?*

"Really? What did she say?"

"Oh, only that you got a lot of inflated ideas about working in the theatre. She said some woman in the audience told you how good you were, and that started you off. I don't expect you remember now."

I shrank and breathed; and wondered why I had always hoped, in our dry little life, to find the drop of an oasis.

"That's why she was so determined you should train for a proper job; the theatre's far too precarious." Aunt Clare treated herself to another laugh. "She said the woman *actually* came up and spoke to her, while you were getting your things: had the nerve to tell her that you should apply for some drama school. She was an actress at one time, apparently. Your mother soon gave her short shrift. The last thing she wanted was you getting silly, impractical ideas in your head."

And that was it; the reason I'd responded to the words in that photo frame, back in the agency. *Children are what you tell them.*

"Anyway, I'd best get back to your uncle. Listen; I know you'll probably think about contacting Mark. Consider carefully, Jenny. He does know he was adopted, but he's probably happier not knowing why."

I could bear no more.

"Goodbye, Aunt Clare," I said, stiffly, and ended the call. Then I walked, robot-like, into the kitchen to make myself a drink, her last words reverberating in my mind. As much as I longed to see him, how could I ever explain to Mark the reason he'd come into the world?

The answer was simple. I couldn't.

I sat curled up by the fire until my legs were stiff, mulling over Aunt Clare's call and thinking about my mother and that terrible row. I'd trudged back and forth for almost a year afterwards, always to be turned away; each time wondering if this would be my last hope of seeing her.

I was only admitted to her stark little room on the day she died. It had a single cross of dark wood on one wall that reminded me of the Quiet Room at my junior school, where I'd spent so many hours on my knees.

"So you're back." I was shocked at her strand of a voice. *"About time."*

The carers around her bed lowered their eyes; I think they saw me as the ultimate neglectful daughter and my mother a saint. And yet time after time they'd opened the door to me, only to snap out the same answer: *"She doesn't want to see you."*

Her cheeks were sunken, but her eyes still held a faint glimmer of light.

"Stay with me."

And the world stopped.

"Stay, Jenny," she whispered. *"You're all I have now."*

Shock held me silent, but a storm of longing broke inside, conjured by this bitter woman who held perpetual sway over my heart. Not even Ross or my father had wielded that power. Only her. All I'd ever wanted was her love.

Moving like a shadow, I went to the bed and took her fingers in mine. They felt as though they might crumble like white communion wafers. She tugged slightly, drawing me down towards her mouth, and I prayed that now she would tell me why: what I'd done to make her so unhappy. And then perhaps we could part in peace. I knelt by her bed, laying her hand on my hair, asking for her blessing.

She was too weak to lift her arm, so I moved my head,

coaxing her fingers to stroke my hair, as they'd done when I was a child, after she'd punished me.

"Come here," she whispered, and I knew a reflex thrill of fear. So many times those words had terrified me when she was young and strong. I moved my ear to her lips: needing; dreading.

"I never wanted you, you know," she panted. *"He was so… happy when I got pregnant. And I loved him, you see. Never thought he would let me down; ruin my life. Leave me with nothing… but you."*

Her body shed its breath and her eyes closed; her grip slackened on my hand. I didn't move or speak, or even cry, but waited till the nurse confirmed she'd gone, then made my way blindly out into the street, trying to find a way to process her words. But all I could feel was a crossing so vast, there would never be a way back.

I sat for two hours on the church wall after the ambulance had left, blindly picking at the mortar between the bricks, and then made my way home. I could only do what I'd always done: anaesthetise the memory as best I could; lock it away, get on with my life.

As long as I never spoke the words that would reconstitute reality, I could remain outwardly whole.

The crackle and spit of the fire brought me back to the old pub lounge, and Jake's copy of *Titus*, still open on my lap. I had so much to do to prepare for the auditions, and yet Aunt Clare's words had withered my spirit. I looked around the room, almost cosy in the leaping light. I had my job; a future, at last. So what was the point in dwelling on a past that contained little beyond darkness and pain?

But what about Mark? Was it best not to disturb him, potentially hurt him?

I thought of the chasm left by my mother's death. Not because I missed her, but because death was where all hope of conversation ended. And inside I ached for those I'd never had with Mark: his first words. First 'I love you, Mummy.' First day at school. A million moments we would never share.

My eye fell on my copy of *Titus*, to a speech I'd been working on earlier.

'Sorrow concealed, like an oven stopped / Doth burn the heart to cinders where it is.'

There was so much more to *Titus* than I'd ever realised.

The image of my mother's cavernous eyes came into my mind. It was what she had done, wasn't it? Shut in the rage of her grief until it had consumed everything but the blame she kept for me, glowing fitfully through its embers.

And yet… if I never opened up a conversation with Mark, wasn't I doing the same?

Something Mags had once said to me ran through my head: "You mustn't see yourself the way others do. Make your own self-image." And she was right; I didn't want to be the person my mother had seen, in her charred heart, when she'd looked at me.

I picked up *Titus*, and sat down in front of my laptop with new determination. I would go on with this play, however difficult it was – because theatre fed and washed my soul as nothing else ever had. And I would contact Mark. If I wasn't to turn into another version of my mother, it was time I faced up to that part of my own history.

TWENTY

'That skull had a tongue in it, and could sing, once...'
(Hamlet)

It took ten minutes to find Mark's email address, but over an hour to write to him. I'd no idea what kind of person I was talking to, though I'd seen a photo of him on Facebook.

Blond hair. I never expected that; he was so dark when he was born. I traced the square jaw and one-sided smile of the stranger onscreen with my finger, not knowing how to feel; trying to reconcile this handsome young man with the baby I'd brought wriggling into the world. Yet that smile stirred a memory I couldn't quite pin down.

I didn't have a single childhood photo of Mark: part of the agreement I'd made with my aunt and uncle that I would never try to contact him. I realised now that they had no right to extract such a promise from me, but at the time I'd been so overwhelmed with pain and guilt, I'd accepted the 'clean break' as the best option: for my baby, anyway. And later on, the gap of time had made it easier to convince myself that I'd done the right thing. There were only a few photos on the Facebook page of him with university friends and one with a girl on a beach. I raked my mind for a suitable opening.

Dear Mark,

Should I put 'dear'? Was it too much? I deleted and reinstated it, then cursed myself for being stupid. It was a standard form of address.

I have no idea how to start this conversation, but if you can find it in yourself to forgive me, I would love to meet you. Though when I've explained who I am, I'll understand if you prefer not to. My name is Jenny Watson, and I'm your natural mother.

It sounded clumsy and crassly insensitive, and yet it was all I had at the end of countless attempts – and if I didn't send it now, I'd bottle out. So I suggested a coffee shop in Northampton where we could meet, if he was willing, though my courage failed every time I imagined facing him. He'd be twenty-four now, and I hadn't shared one of his birthdays: a young man who'd lived a life I would never know. I couldn't blame him for judging me, but I dreaded him doing so.

Feeling as though I'd run a marathon, I made myself a sandwich and poured a glass of wine before people began to arrive for the auditions. *You should call Mags,* a little voice nagged in my head. *Tell her about this.* But that was a step too far; until I'd met with Mark, I couldn't talk about him.

It was eight-thirty: an hour after the advertised audition time, and the front door was quiet. Upstairs, a dozen of Ben's students and a few parents were feasting on the biscuits I'd laid out, but the only adults besides Ben and George were Isla and Tara from Speak Out – and Gordon and Diana. The latter made their way towards me.

"I think we'll be off, Jenny," Gordon said. "It's pretty clear you won't be able to run the auditions – unless you're planning a youth production."

Diana narrowed her eyes at him. "Listen, don't panic," she murmured in my ear. "Change the play, and we can set up a second audition for next week."

As though it was that easy.

"What's the plan, then?" Ben materialised at my side, with a mug of tea for me. I sighed; at some point I had to face things. Not only had I failed to cast *Titus*, but the youngsters and their parents were unaccountably under the impression we were doing *Hamlet*.

"I don't think they read the second lot of stuff I sent out," I told Ben, rubbing my hot forehead.

"Oh, shit." He clapped a hand to his head. "That was my fault; I meant to pass it on. I'm so sorry, Jenny. *Now* what do we do?"

I hesitated. "Well, I guess we'd better tell everyone it's off. Unless…"

His eyebrows rose.

"From what I've gathered, the youngsters are working towards a performance of *Hamlet*, but their tutor's ill, so they're struggling a bit," I said. "They were hoping that watching the auditions would help. What if I did a bit of an acting workshop for them?"

"Would you?" His eyes lit up. "I think they'd love that."

I then wished I'd kept my mouth shut. I'd never done a workshop in my life, but I had watched and attended a few. An idea glimmered in my mind.

"You go and tell everyone," I said, glancing towards the cellar door. "There's someone – thing – I need to fetch."

We were all seated in a big circle, the students on the floor with me, the parents on the bar stools George and I had brought up earlier. He'd turned up at seven to help, and I was beginning to wonder what I'd do without him.

I'd gone through the plot with the youngsters and watched some of their scenes, but the problem seemed to be one of understanding *Hamlet's* deeper themes: its exploration of life – and death.

"I'd like to concentrate on a single scene," I said to the listening group. "To give you a chance to really connect with what's driving this play. Act 5, Scene 1: where Hamlet encounters a gravedigger who is preparing an old grave for a new tenant." A boy with a shock of blond hair and gentian blue eyes grinned up at me in delight from his seat on the floor.

"My scene," he said.

"Yes." I smiled back. Luke had a talent for humour, and delivered his darkly comic lines well, easily drawing laughs from his fellows; but none of them had glimpsed the stark reality of death that the writer unfolded.

"Look, there's a particular reason this character was played by a clown," I said. "The comical way he talks about how long it takes a body to decompose; the way he tosses the other skulls out of the grave, without a thought – no matter who they belonged to – reduces life and death to something of a joke."

"Some joke," muttered Tara. I nodded.

"Exactly. And that's the point. Initially, we all have a laugh at Hamlet's witty interchange with the gravedigger. But then what does that do for us, the audience, when that same good-humoured young man finds the skull he's holding is not just a filthy piece of anonymous old bone? It once housed the mind of a very dear friend, who was loving and kind to him in his childhood; who took him for rides on his back and, above all, made him laugh. A comedian."

"Like me," offered Luke.

I placed a cardboard box in front of the listening group, dipped my hands in and closed them around the dry bone that was Henry. George's words rippled through my head. *"Local legend has it he were once a clown, desperate to play in one of Shakespeare's tragedies."*

"Yes. Very much like you," I said. "Meet Henry. He was once like all of us."

There was a shocked silence as I lifted Henry out.

One of the girls shrank back. "You don't mean… that's real? Oh, that's gross." She clamped a hand to her mouth, and one or two more of the students shuffled to the edge of the group.

"Isn't it?" I held Henry out to the boy who was playing Hamlet. "Take it. Hold it. Tell us what it feels like."

He recoiled. There was some nervous laughter; a few fellow students thought it was funny to egg him on. But under my unbroken gaze, he lowered his eyes and stretched out his hands for the skull.

"Wow. It's really light," he said.

"Yes. Run your fingers over it. Focus on the object – nothing but that. Explore it, bit by bit. Smell it. Stroke it. Everybody else: close your eyes and listen. It's Hamlet's job to make us feel, smell and visualise this skull."

He wriggled uncomfortably, then realised I was deadly serious, and bent his concentration on the skull.

"It's so cold. And it smells… urgh." A few suppressed giggles. "It feels… really rough. All covered with little bumps here, but here, it's smooth. I can put my finger inside the holes… oh… that were its eyes…"

"It's a him," I said, quietly. "Yorick. Henry. Someone you know. Not an 'it', any longer."

And I tried not to think of that head on a spike on a wall somewhere, with people staring at it.

"*His* eyes," he corrected. "They feel all… full of ridges, round the edge. But it's the space that makes it so awful. The space where the… his… eyes were."

"And what you are holding had real eyes," I said. "Looked on the world, as you do, as all your friends do. Think about all you see, every day. All you love looking at." The hairs lifted on my neck as I glanced around the pub. "He once did that, too. Had dreams and ambitions, as you do."

I looked up and found George staring at Henry. *"It were a dream he never got to fulfil."* And my mind flew back to those moments in Stevenage town square, when I saw my own dreams slipping away from me forever.

"I can't handle this," said young Hamlet, his voice trembling. "To touch where actual eyes have been… and look, here, I can feel its jaw."

"*His* jaw," I corrected gently. *"Here hung those lips that I have kissed I know not how oft.* Listen: the words are starting to clothe the bare skeleton. That repeated 'S' – the sibilants – and the light vowels make the words themselves a caress. The writer is fleshing the bone with sweet and tender memories. But they don't sit well, because we're getting two conflicting images at once: Yorick as a living, feeling being – and then the reality of this skull: the overwhelming evidence of death. Tell us how it feels, Hamlet. But this time, use Shakespeare's words."

And he began, tentatively, still running his fingers over the skull, bringing it to life in his mind.

"Alas, poor Yorick. I knew him, Horatio." The young man playing Horatio instinctively slid an arm around Hamlet's shoulders, to support him. The students who had opened their eyes watched them silently, in a mixture of horror and fascination.

"A fellow of infinite jest, of most excellent fancy." He glanced fleetingly at Luke, who gave him a small smile. *"He hath borne me on his back a thousand times, and now... how abhorrèd in my imagination 'tis!"* He paused, struggling to finish the speech. *"My gorge rises at it."* All eyes were open now, every student totally engaged by his words. *"Here hung those lips that I have kissed I know not how oft. Where be your gibes now?"* He looked again at Luke, whose expression was quenched of all mirth. *"Your gambols? Your songs? Your flashes of merriment that were wont to set the table on a roar?"*

Every eye in the room was focused intently on the skull. It was as though Henry was giving the performance of his life. *"Not one now to mock your own grinning? Quite... chop-*

fallen?" Here, young Hamlet manipulated Henry's jaw with his fingers, so that the grinning mouth fell open, and I closed my eyes involuntarily, dreading the laughter. But none came. I silently beckoned Katie, who was playing Gertrude, Hamlet's mother, to join him; she did so, kneeling opposite. He fixed his eyes on her for the final lines. *"Now get you to your lady's chamber and tell her, let her paint an inch thick..."* he ran his finger under her glossy lips, and she shuddered, *"to this favour she must come."* He was unable to deliver his last line. The silence was total, as though time itself had stopped within the walls of the old building.

"Let her laugh... at that," said a soft voice, and Tara stretched out her finger to run it along the skull's jaw, where his mouth would have been. As she moved, her hair fell back from the scar on her cheek. I caught a gleam of wet on its riven skin; and one or two others were similarly affected. She ducked her head down again, as though unable to bear the intrusion of my eyes.

"Bloody hell," said Luke. There was a murmur of laughter, but many of the students didn't join in.

Ben came up to me as the parents' applause died down and chatter broke out. "Jenny, I've recorded some of this on my phone, and if we can put it on social media, it will make fantastic PR for your auditions. See if you can get the parents' consent to use it. If this gets around, you won't have any trouble casting your play, I promise you."

"All done," said Ben, as the last of the parents and their offspring left. "They're all emailing you about the permissions thing. Now I'm going to take George home – but I just wanted to ask. Would you like to meet on Friday morning, at the museum? My classes are all away on a trip, so I've a few hours free."

My mouth swept up into a smile. "I'd love to. And thank you so much." I turned to find George carefully mounting the stairs towards us. "Oh, George. You're a real star."

Before I could stop myself, I'd rushed over and enfolded him in a hug. He was so soft and warm that a long-ago memory stirred, of how it had felt to hug my father and burrow my face into his chest.

I pulled away, embarrassed, and found George grinning at me.

"Well, now, that's the nicest thank you I've had in a long time," he said. "And the best evening for years, I can tell you. You're the one who's the star, my dear."

"I'd better get on and wash these cups," I said hastily, gathering a couple up, as my cheeks started to simmer.

"Oh, no need." Ben took them off me. "Mags is doing that."

"You... what?"

"Your friend, Mags. She's been here a while, but didn't want you to know until everyone had gone. She's in the kitchen, washing up."

Without a word, I flew down the stairs towards the sound of clinking crockery. She'd said over and over again on the phone that she hated 'letting me down' – but she did have a business to run. And yet here she was. She turned as I erupted through the doorway.

"You came," I said, and brushed the back of my hand over my damp eyes and nose.

Mags's face crumpled. "I couldn't stay away. And oh, good grief, Jenny; I'm glad I didn't. I watched the last bit, and you're absolutely doing the right thing, taking this job. You're a born director. I've never felt so sure of anything in the whole of my life, and... I'm so proud of you."

I rushed into her arms, both of us crying like children.

Before I settled down in bed that night, full of hope and a brandy nightcap I'd shared with Mags, I decided to check my laptop one more time – and there, waiting for me, was an email from Mark. With fingers that didn't seem attached to the rest of me, I clicked on it.

Hi Jenny,

A meeting would be good. As it happens, I have no lectures tomorrow, so would be happy to meet at the café you suggest at 2pm.

Best

Mark Radford

TWENTY-ONE

'Poor harmless fly, that with his pretty buzzing melody,
Came here to make us merry. And thou hast killed him.'
(Titus Andronicus)

"What are you going to do about *Titus*?" Mags asked
over breakfast in the kitchen next morning, with one of
her fan heaters on full blast. "You know, much as I hate to
admit it, Diana could be right. Why don't you email this
Mr Norwich of yours, and say what a great response you
got to your *Hamlet* workshop?"

"I did, last night," I said, shortly. "After…" *After I read
Mark's message* – the one I hadn't told her about. "He sent
me a reply half an hour ago."

"And?"

"He still won't hear of it. It's *Titus*, or nothing."

"What?" She lowered the piece of toast at her lips. "That's
ridiculous! When he knows you won't be able to cast it?"

"He says he's confident I'll find a way, and that *Titus* is
the best possible fit to open the festival."

"Then you must persuade him he's wrong!" I wished I might. But there was a certain implacability in my new boss's tone, and his official rebuke had shaken me. Mags sighed. "Look, why don't you give it a rest today, then tomorrow we'll sit down together and work out a response. I'm sure we can sort this out."

I wasn't. His reply still stung whenever it flashed through my head. *'You patently need to think about the way you advertise, as it's obvious your current methods aren't working.'*

And this was the man Denise had described as 'a real sweetie', desperate to employ me. Still, I'd taken the job, and had to work with what I'd got.

"The only thing I can do is set up a second audition and try harder to get people to it," I said. Mags's mouth dropped open.

"Why you're so afraid to challenge this man beats me."

"I'm not afraid." I wished she'd just let this go. "I know he'll never agree, that's all."

"But… don't you think it's a bit odd, Jenny, that he's so stuck on a play no one else thinks is a good idea? Even though, if it fails, it'll cost him money – employing you, for a start?"

A twinge of uneasiness made me shift in my chair. She had a point.

"I imagine it's because of the history. He knows that *Titus* once played here." There I went, defending him again.

"I wonder." She swept up my empty mug, still frowning. "Well, you'd better get off, if you're meeting Ben." She lowered her lashes. "Why don't you ask him if he'd like to come along to Mile-End with us tomorrow evening? We could do with an extra car, to carry some of this stuff."

Ah. Ever since she'd seen for herself that Ben wasn't a greying academic, she'd started asking questions about him. Still, we did need help. Everywhere I looked, there were costumes, draped and hung.

As though reading my mind, my phone burst into Beethoven.

"Where are you?" demanded Ben.

"I'm on the way in five—"

"Good. Listen." His voice shook. "I had to call; I've some news about Henry!"

"Hold on!" I hastily put him on speaker, as Mags started towards me. "Okay. Go ahead!"

"Well, I mentioned to Sarah at the museum about Henry, and our plan to get him carbon dated. And Mr Clarkson – he's retired but used to be the curator, apparently – just happened to be there. He remembers Jake Reeve bringing a sample of a skull into the museum years ago, and it was actually sent off for dating. Unfortunately, they can't find a record of the results – Sarah's going to have a further search, but it'll take time. The thing is, though, Mr Clarkson remembers them coming through."

"And?" hissed Mags.

"It's as Aaron suspected; they couldn't accurately pinpoint a year of death. But they did say we're looking at a male, probably in his early twenties. And – this is the real stunner, Jenny – they estimated that death occurred in the first half of the 1590s."

"Good Lord," whispered Mags.

"So it looks like your theory could be right, and we have a real Shakespearean actor in our midst," said Ben. "Okay, maybe not one of the known London players, but he could have acted with the man himself at one time; who's to say? Jenny, if this doesn't bring the pub back from the brink, I don't know what will. I got that video clip of the workshop edited and ready, by the way. It looks terrific, although I say it myself!"

"And I got all the consent emails," I said, my insides fizzing. If we could get all this out on social media, surely it would draw people to the auditions? "Do you think we can tell people what Mr Clarkson said?"

"No; better not until we see the evidence. However, Sarah did say that Jake Reeve must have had a copy of the dating results, so it could still be somewhere in the pub."

Mags's eyes rounded with horror, and with good cause.

"Well, all the other rooms have been cleared of paperwork. So the only place would be the cellar," I said. "And that could take weeks to go through."

"Ah." There was a brief silence. "The new owner might have them, of course."

"I could ask," I said, doubtfully. "And perhaps George could phone Mr Reeve's solicitors in case they've come across it."

Mags got up. "You talk to George, Jenny, and I'll start sorting through the old boxes of paperwork in the cellar." I cast her a grateful look.

"That's great," Ben said. "I'll ask Aaron to go ahead with his investigation, to be on the safe side, and I'll get the video clip across to you today, so we can get it on social media. We can start on those parish records this morning, Jenny."

"I'll come straight down." I ended the call and enveloped Mags in a hug, a guilty blush stealing over my cheeks. "Listen, I might not be back for lunch. I've got one of these therapy things booked in Northampton this afternoon, and Ben's taking me in." I hated lying to her, but I had to see Mark, and I didn't want her offering to drive me.

"That's fine," she said. "It's not as if I've nothing to do."

I rushed to get my coat, guilt and nerves warring with anticipation.

The parish registers were locked in a large safe in a small back room. We waited outside while Sarah dialled in the code, then followed her to a heavy mahogany desk, onto which she lowered several weighty tomes.

"I must tell you that these are copies," she said, stroking the top one with a reverent hand. "Made in the nineteenth century, to preserve the originals. But still very valuable, of course – and perfectly suitable for your needs."

As she disappeared, we donned our cotton gloves.

"Where do we start?" I asked.

"Well, we know Henry was in his early twenties," said Ben. "And that he probably died in the first half of the 1590s. So on the assumption that he is Coates the innkeeper's son, we could look through the early 1570s for a date of birth. The ledgers cover ten years apiece."

"I'll tackle that," I offered. "You work backwards from 1595, to see if you can find a date of death."

We bent our heads over the books, but some of the writing was tiny, and it was tedious work. After an hour, Ben went across to the café for take-away coffees, which we drank outside on the step. Ben checked his phone for messages and choked over his cup.

"What is it?" I asked, taking it from him as he raked his pockets for a hanky.

"Village Facebook. One of the parents has beaten me to it with a video clip from your workshop."

I peered at his screen and recoiled at the sight of myself on camera. "Oh! I look awful."

Ben burst out laughing. "You women, honestly. Believe you me, this will do more for your PR campaign than anything. Anyway, you look very nice," he added.

Very nice. My hair was sticking up, and my face was puce. What was it with men?

"Well, someone here thinks you do." I peered to where he was pointing. *Nice coat,* said one comment. They had to be joking. I'd put my black quilted coat on for the last half hour, because it was more than chilly upstairs. Why would someone bother to comment about something so trivial?

"Let's hope it doesn't reduce the impact of the full-length version," Ben said. "I'll upload it as soon as I get home. Come on, we need to press on with our research."

After an hour and a half or so, my eye halted at a ledger entry dated 15th May 1570. I had to read the same line three times before I dared to believe what I'd found.

"Ben. Look." My voice came out in a croak. "'To William and Mary Coates. A son, John *Henry.*' George said that the owner of our skull was called Henry *or* John. This really can't be a coincidence, can it?"

Ben bent over the entry. "No, I think it's him, all right." He whipped out his phone and photographed the page. "Now, how about helping me with the 1590s? There's an unprecedented number of deaths, no doubt because of the plague."

It was painstaking work, and after an hour we could barely straighten up. I drooped over the desk in disappointment.

"This could take forever," I said. "And it could be he wasn't even hanged here. Deaths are only recorded where they occur, aren't they?"

Ben clicked his fingers. "Damn! Of course. Henry didn't die naturally, did he? Perhaps hangings weren't recorded in these registers. Criminals may not have been allowed burial in consecrated ground, particularly if there was any association with witchcraft."

I groaned. "You're right, of course. So perhaps it's not worth carrying on the search." I pondered for a moment. "I wonder if he even got married here? If he did, it would show up, wouldn't it? We might find *her* name and then we could trace her."

Ben's face lit up. "Yes, that is an idea. Let's go forward about twenty years from Henry's birth and start there."

But again we turned up nothing, and our shoulders and backs grew stiffer each time we stopped for a break. We stood outside on the steps in the sun and Ben laid his hands on my neck. I jumped at the unexpected contact.

"Wow; you're pretty tense. Here. Let me loosen you up." He began kneading my knotted muscles, and I couldn't help feeling that this was way over our 'friendship' line. But it felt so good, I couldn't resist lingering for a moment, before stepping away.

"Er... yes, maybe we should get back to work; it's getting late," Ben said. I hoped I hadn't offended him, but he was getting closer by stealth and I wasn't quite sure how to manage the situation. *But then, you don't want to manage it*, whispered a voice that had nothing to do with my head. I ignored it.

"Let's have a last look at those 1590s again," he suggested. "We could have missed something."

Back at our desk, we scanned line by line down the musty-smelling ledger, until Ben gave an exclamation.

"Yes! My God, Jenny – here, in the summer of 1593. Look."

I got to my feet, my eyes following his forefinger as it traced a series of entries. "The same year as the *Titus* performance!"

"I know. It makes the hairs stand up on the back of your neck, doesn't it? Coates isn't the first name listed, so I almost missed it. Three mentions, from the end of June to the middle of July. Bray, Elizabeth Molly, and Coates, John Henry."

"Banns," I murmured, my finger hovering above the wiry scrawl.

"Well, now we know the name of his lady," said Ben. "Elizabeth. But there's no mention of a wedding."

We exchanged glances. "I think we know why," he added, "if there *is* any truth in the ballads. If only we could find out where he was hanged."

A thought dropped into my mind. "Ben! Can you remember what date Edward Bennington wrote about the disappearance of that boy actor?"

"1581," he said, his eyes brightening.

"So, if he was born in 1570…"

"He'd be eleven. The perfect age to be useful to a boys' acting troupe. You know, I can't believe all this. I do think we've found him, Jenny."

"I'd really like to tell his story," I said, looking down at the dry words that recorded Henry's and Elizabeth's promise. If the ballads were based on truth, then *The Fool's Prophecy* was Henry's last attempt to be heard. *'And truth will speak out, from another age.'*

My phone vibrated in my bag and I pulled it out, thinking it could be Mags. But it was a text from another withheld number.

Settling in, Jenny Grogan Watson?

I stepped back, confused, and my legs bumped against my chair. I hadn't used that name in years. Who was this?

"What's up?" asked Ben, concerned. "Bad news?"

"No. Just… a bit of a weird message." *Grogan was my mother's name.* She'd given it to me so that her family surname wouldn't die out, and I'd dropped it because it had too many memories of Ross. His affectionate name for me was Jenny GW: a tag the kids at school had labelled me with in our last year.

Could this be Ross? Maybe he'd found out about my job; he was the only person I could think of who would use that name. But I hadn't spoken to him since the night I left – except through a solicitor. And anyway, why would he be interested in me now?

"Time to pack up, I think," said Ben. "Perhaps we can do a bit more next weekend."

I nodded, absent-mindedly. I could think only of my weird message.

TWENTY-TWO

'I cannot heave my heart into my mouth...'
(King Lear)

The cream and brown walled café brimmed with chatter and the clatter of spoons and cups. I clutched the *Shakespeare's Globe* bag I'd promised to carry, and among the bobbing heads and dark-wood tables, glimpsed a waving hand with slender fingers, an amber-blond head and a flash of a grey sweatshirt with 'London' in black block print. He was here even earlier than me, and I'd spent ten minutes outside, fighting to keep down the coffee I'd drunk with Ben.

Mark. He was a man; I could only tell myself he was my son. I'd dreamed of and dreaded this moment. But now it was here, I felt strangely anaesthetised.

"Hi." He flashed me a nervous smile – the one-sided quirk of a grin I'd seen on Facebook. That at least was familiar. And we both scraped into seats, looking everywhere but at each other, while the mill and zing of coffee-makers cut above the babble of voices.

"What'll you have? Coffee?"

It sounded strange, that New Zealand accent, removing him still further from everything I knew. I nursed my bag and watched him as he queued, my mind still struggling to match the slender young man digging in his jeans' pocket for change with the flurry of skin and blood and limbs hoisted into the air as my body gave him up to the fierce tug of forceps. I'd held him close, his sweetness under my nose; watched his scrunched-up, navy-blue eyes rimmed with pouches of skin; followed the contours of his blotched little body. I couldn't look away until they took him. Now I could only snatch prying glances, and I felt like an intruder when he caught me.

They'd said it would pass, the grief; the early separation was best for him, as it was for me. And I'd agreed. But now I had no words to fill this void; only bitter coffee and broken smiles.

"Did you find the place okay? How long are you staying?"

And so it began: the stilted enquiries, the long pauses, until I was brave enough to go off script.

"Were they kind to you? Your adoptive parents?" I said in a rush.

Those blue eyes came up very quickly. His answer was measured. "My *parents* were incredible."

I don't know what I'd expected. But I was unprepared for the lash of his words.

My smile wavered. "I'm glad. Did you tell them you were... coming to see me?"

"No." His head dipped. "They've both gone, now. They died. In an accident, eighteen months ago, while they were on holiday." He looked away over the sea of heads around us, his eyes hollow.

"I'm so sorry." *Oh, God.* Could I think of nothing better to say?

"Thanks." He gave me a perfunctory smile, and I was cowed by it. We sipped our coffee as though it was all that mattered in the world.

I remembered what I'd told Ben's students: that the unspoken words between scripted lines can say so much more than those we utter aloud. But I didn't know whether I could deal with what was lodged between these cut-and-pasted platitudes.

"That's what made me decide to come over here, in a way," he said, after another pull at his mug. "Losing my parents."

"Oh?" My pulse speeded up. I sensed we were over the cliché stage.

"I'd always wondered, you see." He met my eyes. "What kind of a mother walks off and leaves her newborn kid in a home?"

I'd accepted he might be angry; bitter, even. And I had no defence. I'd fiercely told myself 'no tears', but they seeped out like blood from an open cut. I brushed them away with my hand, and he shifted in his chair. Tears were such an easy way to make someone feel guilty. And I'd never meant to do that.

"Oh, look," he said, awkwardly. "That was a bit—"

"No, no. Understandable. Of course." I kept my head down, fighting for control, my throat wrenched with effort. "I'm so sorry," I said, brokenly. "I don't know what to say."

He handed me a serviette. "Here. I guess it must have been pretty awful; you were only a girl yourself."

That was generous, I wanted to say. But didn't.

"How long are you staying?" Now I sounded like Aunt Clare.

"I'm doing a three-year course at Birmingham. Started last September. Then when the holidays come, I thought I'd tour around a bit, as the UK's part of my heritage. Get a feel for the place."

"If you'd like to see a really old English pub, you should come and have a look at where I work," I offered, cheeks heating at my own daring.

"Sounds interesting," he said, with a polite smile that silenced me. "Um, can I ask, how did you find me?"

I hesitated. It was just easier not to bring Aunt Clare into the conversation. "The children's home put me on the right track, and then I searched online."

He looked at me very much like Ben did sometimes. As though he could see straight behind my eyes.

"Right. I wondered if it was through your aunt. If she's still alive, that is?"

I spluttered a mouthful of coffee, and his eyebrows arched as he passed me another napkin.

"How did you know about her?"

"Oh, hell, did she never tell you?" He faltered. "Christ, I'm sorry if I've put my foot in it. But my mother…" he flicked me a quick, defiant look. "My *mother* once told me that she went to meet your aunt in Auckland when the adoption started going forward. She said that at first, your aunt and uncle were totally against the idea. But my mother kept pushing, and eventually they agreed. That's how

I found you. Thank God for your middle name, because there are a few hundred Jenny Watsons listed on Google. It wasn't on my birth certificate, but my mother had it written down in an old diary – from when she visited your aunt. I found it among her things."

What?

My head flew up as I remembered that strange text. *Settling in, Jenny Grogan Watson?*

"If you key it into Google, it comes up on your old school's Facebook page," he went on. "There are a few pictures of you up there with your classmates, and one of you and your husband that he'd posted way back, I think. But no contact details. It put me off for a while, because I started looking for Jenny Grogan Williams, until I went back and had another look, and saw a comment about your divorce."

I shook my head in confusion. I didn't even know there was a Facebook page for my old school. The building had been closed for years. "What did the comment say?" I asked, then regretted it as he lowered his eyes. "Don't worry," I added, hurriedly. "I'm not bothered." If it was Ross who'd put the post up, it wouldn't be complimentary. Not if the vitriolic messages he'd sent me after I left were anything to go by.

"I went back to Google and eventually up came this box-office form for a drama group, with Jenny Grogan Watson as the contact, and your email address."

"My God!" I said. "I'd forgotten all about that. I only did the box office for one play, to help out, and in those days, it was all handled by post and email." I was babbling, now. "It's amazing to think that form's still out there." Then a thought struck me. "How long ago did you find it?"

He took a sip of coffee, avoiding my eyes. "Oh, a few weeks ago, I reckon. I did mean to get in touch, but somehow, well… you know."

I should understand. I was the world's worst at avoiding confrontation. He kept his gaze fixed on something outside the café window.

"To be honest, my mother tried to talk to me about you a number of times, but till just recently, I had no interest whatsoever. As far as I was concerned, they were my parents."

And that was it. I folded inside, knowing that he'd ultimately come here to hurt me.

He shrugged, his lids hooding his eyes. "I can't apologise for that," he said. "You wanted to come, and you must have known this meeting was going to be a bit shitty, at some point."

I nodded. There were no tears this time; I could barely breathe, let alone cry.

"I don't blame you," I said. "It's fine."

The simmer of voices intensified around us, and he looked at me as though expecting me to leave, but I sat still. I'd left him once; I wouldn't do so again unless he asked me to.

"So, what are you up to for the rest of the day, then?"

His question was a blessing; work was always safe ground, for me.

We talked for half an hour longer, now firmly established as two strangers. I told him about my job, and discovered that he loved cricket and wanted to be an illustrator.

"That's what brought me to Birmingham," he said. "They do a brilliant course. I love film and theatre, too. My parents used to say I must come from artistic stock. Meeting you, I can see why. So... Shakespeare, then? What's all that about?"

I managed a smile.

"For me? It's about finding ways of understanding life in words that no other writer has ever matched. I'm looking forward to directing the festival play, though I'm a bit nervous about it. But I've waited all my life to do something like this."

"So what's the deal with this old pub? Tell me about it," he said.

I found myself regaling him with the story of The Old Bell and Henry's history.

"That sounds quite a legacy," he said.

"Yes." But I'd talked enough. I changed tack, asking about his course and where he lived and, for a while, he chatted about a life I would never know, while the café hummed around us like a nest of happy bees. And anyone looking on would have assumed it was an ordinary meeting, on an ordinary day; never knowing that beneath the surface, I was bleeding out.

At three we stood outside, waiting to part, not making the move. He was playing with a miniature Swiss army knife he'd pulled from his pocket, twisting the little blade in and out of its scarlet sheath, while I cudgelled my mind for something to say.

"Did you know he'd died?" he asked. And although his tone was careless, the words felt loaded.

I blinked. "Who?"

"Scott Sutton. The man who fathered me."

He may as well have twisted the little blade into my flesh. I struggled for calm while he watched me carefully, still flicking his knife.

"A few weeks ago," he added. "He was alive when I looked him up. In fact, I actually found him before I found you."

"How did you know his name?" I whispered. "I never told the people who ran the home."

He looked incredulous. "Your aunt told my mother."

My mind flew back to the day I'd plucked up the courage to tell my aunt and uncle that I'd done a pregnancy test. It was the first and last time Uncle Peter was ever unkind to me, and I was broken by it. After all, I had nowhere else to turn. So he hadn't found it difficult to terrify Scott's name out of me. I shook my head, despising myself now for my cowardice; hating Aunt Clare for her dishonesty.

"As I got older, my mother felt I had a right to know," Mark went on, still watching me. "We had no other family, you see. No one we're close to. So she wrote to your aunt and asked her outright. And your aunt came back with a few details. His name; the school you both went to; the fact that he originally came from Leeds, in the north, but moved to Hertfordshire to live with an aunt when his mother died."

Of course. They were all the things Scott had told me at the party, over our drink downstairs; and I'd stumbled them out in a panic to my furious uncle. *But he and my aunt had sworn to me that no one would ever know.* What right did they have to make decisions that could so radically affect my child's life? I choked down the thought of Mark finding out how and why he'd come into this world. How could I ever protect him from that?

"Mark…"

"Yeah?"

I shrank in the silence. "No. She never told me."

"Right." He shot me another glance. "Well, I phoned him, but he didn't say much – he was real shocked, poor guy. It was a pretty stupid thing to do, I guess, out of the blue – but as his brother said, I wasn't to know he'd been ill." He lowered his lids, but I knew he was watching me. "Or that he never knew I existed."

I dragged my own gaze away from his face, feeling faint. "And did you… did he agree to see you?"

"He did say he'd call me back the next day, but apparently he had a massive heart attack in the night, and died the following week. His brother – my uncle, I guess – called me back and invited me to the funeral."

I stared at him, bleakly, not knowing what I was supposed to feel, except horror. "Did you go?"

He shook his head. "Now I wish I had. But at the time, I felt a bit shitty about the whole business, as if it was my fault that he… you know."

"You weren't to blame!" I said, quickly. *And neither was I,* I screamed in my head. *How was I ever to blame for this?* And yet on cue, my face burned, stained by a shame that was as integral as breathing.

Mark nodded, a shade of relief in his eyes. "Yeah; that's what Len said – my uncle. He asked me over there one day after the funeral, and I went and had a beer with him." He paused, as though wondering how to put his unpalatable thoughts into words. "It was plain he was pretty torn up. And he didn't seem very keen on you, either. To be honest, that's why I decided not to look you up. He asked me not to."

"*What?* What did he say?" I could barely whisper the words.

He shrugged. "That you were…"

The dusk was gathering around us, so I couldn't see his eyes clearly, and his voice was light and casual, giving nothing away. But his fingers went on flicking the little blade back and forth. Back and forth. I wished he wouldn't.

"That you couldn't have wanted me, if you left me in a children's home and never even told his brother I existed."

He looked away, back towards the café, and I knew there was more he wasn't saying.

"It wasn't that I didn't want you. I stupidly thought…" I turned away, my throat bursting. "It's not an excuse. Please believe that. But I thought I was doing the right thing. It's what everybody said. Better for you, I mean. I can never blame you, if you feel bitter. But please, try to forgive me. Though I know I shouldn't ask," I said, my voice disappearing.

"Don't beat yourself up about it," he said, in a softer tone. "Like I say, you were young."

Here was my chance. But I couldn't do it; I couldn't tell him what had happened. What child needed that, to carry for the rest of his life?

I shook my head. "I'm a fool. I wanted to come back for you. But they said it would uproot your life once you were settled."

He nodded. "It would have. And, well, you made two lovely people very happy – and I had a wonderful childhood. It is as it is. So you be happy, Jenny Grogan Watson. You know, that's a great name."

But hearing it on his lips, it sounded like a scientific label: cold. Distancing. He was using it to categorise me as the stranger I deserved to be.

"Take care now." He shoved his hands in his coat pockets, and I watched helplessly as he turned to go. Then he swung back towards me, as though changing his mind, and my heart skipped in hope.

"Oh, by the way. You're probably going to know all this stuff, but I did some research on Ancestry, for your side of the family. My mother was really into that sort of stuff."

His mother. The word jolted me, yet again; but I had so much to be grateful for. She'd loved him. And he, her.

"Again, we had a few details from that aunt of yours to go on. Your parents' names, at least."

"Oh?" I kept my voice casual, but the feeling that I was walking through a nightmare began to spread through me. Aunt Clare and her 'promises'. She'd lied and lied. *And you haven't?* whispered the voice in my head. *Isn't not telling the truth the same as lying? After all, it may even have caused Scott Sutton's death.*

"Yeah. We found the orphanage my grandmother – your mother – was at, in Ireland. It made me feel I had some sort of link with her, to be honest."

For the second time, I found myself struggling for oxygen.

He looked at me. "You didn't know that either, did you?"

"Oh, yes; yes, of course," I lied. I couldn't bear to admit that he knew more about my mother than I did.

"Might go and take a look at it, some time. Do you have any snapshots of her – and your father?"

I shook my head. "They were all destroyed in a fire."

"Ah. That's a shame. Listen, I have to go. Important date tonight. But thanks for the chat. Look after yourself."

And he gave me a backward wave as he strode off.

I'm never going to see you again, am I? I thought, and panic spiralled up into my throat.

"Mark?" I called. And he spun round, and walked a few steps back, his face a question, his hands in his pockets, splaying out the sides of his coat.

"Someone once said to me, 'don't let yesterday's regrets ruin tomorrow's hopes'." It was Mr Roberts, our old neighbour, as he left my mother's funeral; and I'd never understood those words as I did now. "I have far too many regrets; but I'm learning to believe in hope for the future. I should never have given you up, and I'm sorrier and more ashamed than I can say. But now you're here, it's a doorway I don't want to close." I waited as the silence bred between us in reply.

The glow from a streetlamp lit his slow smile – it was the sort I couldn't read – and I pulled my padded coat closer around me as the wind bit.

"Nice coat, by the way," he said, and walked away. I watched him till he was a speck on the horizon.

TWENTY-THREE

'Mine eye hath play'd the painter and hath stell'd
     Thy beauty's form in table of my heart;
     My body is the frame wherein 'tis held;
     And perspective it is the painter's art.'

(Sonnet 24)

Mags was still in the green room of the little theatre in Mile-End at quarter to ten on the following evening, a row of pins with coloured heads protruding from her lips as she fitted an olive-green gown to the actress playing Desdemona. I could hear Helen, the group's director, still working with one of the leads in the hall, though most of the cast had gone.

"Ben and I were thinking of having a drink at the pub with the others, Mags," I said. "Are you up for that? Shall I give you a hand packing up the rest of these costumes?"

She sat back on her knees and removed the pins.

"No, that's fine. Helen's taking them home to try in the peace and quiet. She's had to take on a minor role that she couldn't cast."

Helen. I was curious to get a closer look at this friend of Diana's who'd consistently ignored my messages about the *Titus* auditions. She flitted into the room at that moment: slim, auburn-haired and late thirty-something, with an oval face, large brown eyes and a sunset orange scarf billowing out behind her like a flag.

"How's it going?" she asked, her smile showing a flash of even white teeth. I studied her with a pang of envy. She was so attractive; so poised.

"I've got a bit to do yet," said Mags. "Then I think I'll get off, Jenny. I'm dead tired, and I've got a bit of a headache."

"You spent too many hours bent over all that paperwork," I said. "A drink would probably relax you."

She didn't look at me. "No, I don't think so. You can get a lift home with Ben, can't you?"

Ah. Phase two of her matchmaking efforts, I presumed. But I really did want to go to the pub and do some networking. At least, that's what I told myself.

"Of course. If you're sure."

"Fantastic. I'll start packing up." Helen wafted out with the grace of a dancer. I found myself wishing I could move like that. *'You're a fairy elephant, Jenny,'* my mother had said as I'd tripped up to her after my first ballet show, at the age of six. I'd avoided dancing ever since, and the one time I was forced to take part in a 'dance interlude' at junior school, I'd imagined myself prancing heavily across the stage like one of the pink elephants from *Dumbo.*

"Penny for them," Mags said to me as the young 'Desdemona' swept off to get changed.

I sighed. "Oh, I was only thinking how attractive Helen is."

Mags huffed in exasperation as she struggled to her feet.

"What?" I asked.

"You don't see it, do you, Jenny?" She grasped me by the shoulders and turned me to face the wall-length mirror. "Look there. The first thing that struck me when I saw Helen tonight is how alike you are."

"What?" I laughed. Maybe Mags was suffering from temporary blindness, too.

"Okay, her hair is auburn and yours is chestnut, and hers is not as curly as yours. But your faces are the same shape, your eyes glow like hers. You've both got good skin and attractive figures. You just use your body differently, Jenny. You haven't been taught to be as graceful, and you're far too self-conscious."

I pulled away, not wanting to look in the mirror a moment longer than necessary.

"That's ridiculous, Mags. Helen's perfect. And I'm... well, full of lumps and bumps. You just can't see them under this sweater."

Mags snorted. "I've told you, before. You should try seeing yourself as others do. I mean, take Ben. He looks as though he could eat you for breakfast, but you never seem to notice." She flicked me a wicked little smile.

I grabbed my coat. "Right. I'll see you at home, then."

"Not that coat," said Mags. "Yours is in the hall. That's Helen's."

I glanced at it. It was a black padded one, exactly like mine; they were popular at the moment. Then as I shook it out I noticed that Helen's had fur round the hood, and was far more substantial – and expensive.

"Did you ring George, to see if he'll contact Jake Reeve's solicitor?" she asked.

"Yes, and I sent an email to Mr Norwich, and he's already come back to me to say he doesn't have any of Mr Reeve's old papers. You sure you're okay on your own?"

Mags nodded vigorously, the row of pins back in her mouth, their brightly coloured heads making her look like some sort of exotic bird. I went to find Ben, faintly disturbed, in a pleasurable way, at the memory of her words.

"So, did you manage to get your boss to agree to *Hamlet*?" Gordon eased his way onto the pub bench beside Diana.

"Where's the wine?" she demanded.

"Ben's got it." He started chatting happily to Steve, the sound technician for *Othello*, while Diana fixed her eyes on Ben, who was still at the bar. He had a tray of drinks balanced on one hand and his phone in the other, and was surrounded by a group of people.

"Oh, for goodness' sake. He'll be there all night." She squeezed herself free and marched off towards him. The knot of people around him grew as I watched; they were all gazing at his phone. Even Diana was now bent over, her eyes straining to see the screen.

Then she pointed in our direction, and a dozen people looked up and surged towards us, like a many-headed hydra. I instinctively moved back in my seat.

"The *Hamlet* video clip's been shared faster than we anticipated, Jenny," Ben said, and my insides wriggled with nerves.

"Gordon, you've got to see this!" Diana whipped Ben's phone from his hand and thrust it into her husband's. "For heaven's sake, Jenny, why didn't you show us this earlier?"

I shrugged. "It just sort of… happened."

"What's up with you?" Diana demanded. "Don't you see what this means? Now we've really got something to work with. Have you fixed that second audition date? Because I've a feeling you're going to be packed to the gunnels when this gets around the drama groups. It's brilliant. Look at what people are saying."

I caught sight of myself on Ben's phone as Gordon tilted it for a better view, and groaned inwardly at the image of me, awkwardly bundled up in my coat. Facebook comments were sprouting beneath the video like mushrooms at dawn. I peered at them upside down, while Gordon gazed at the phone in stupefaction. Diana plucked it free and it was eagerly seized and passed around the group. A young man with lank, blond hair and oily skin pulled up a stool next to me.

"I can't believe you're reviving the festival," he said, eagerly. "So, when are the production and audition dates?"

I looked desperately up at Ben, wishing I'd done some re-planning.

"There's an email coming round." Diana whisked a notebook and pen out of her bag and slapped them down on the table, while I gawped. "Write your details down here if you want to be on the mailing list," she boomed to the pub at large.

"My wife comes from a highly successful family of business people," murmured Gordon. There was a mix of pride and envy in his tone. "No slouch, is Diana."

I could believe it. Is that where all her confidence came from? Her family? For a moment, I wondered what it would have been like to have that kind of support.

"Wake up, Jenny." Diana muscled in beside me, and the nucleus around Ben split and reformed as people dragged up stools and seats and looked at me expectantly. "So, for those of you who didn't get the second email, the play is now *Titus*."

"Oh no, really? Why? I do think *Hamlet*'s a better choice," piped an older woman, with long white hair that would have looked very much at home in *Lord of the Rings*. "That rape scene in *Titus* – you know, when what's-her-name comes on stage, dripping blood. It's really off-putting."

Gordon held up his hands. "And there's our problem. You're absolutely sure you can't change it, Jenny?"

"You know," I said, curling my nails into my palms beneath the pub table, "there's so much more to *Titus* than its violence."

"So you're really not doing *Hamlet*?" asked a bull-shaped man with a pale and patchy bald pate that reminded me of Henry.

"No. Sorry." I cast Diana a desperate look. "It's… not my decision, I'm afraid."

"Mmm," said the older woman, pushing Diana's notepad away. "Sorry. Not my thing." The bald man sighed and sank his nose into his pint, with a mutter of 'pity', and the conversation and the group melted away from us. Gordon shrugged.

"QED," he said.

Diana raised her eyes to the ceiling.

"Never admit you're not in control, Jenny," she said. "But don't worry. I like your earlier comment; let's work with that. So, if there's more to *Titus*, how do we get everyone else excited about it?" She glanced at Ben's phone, which was still playing the *Hamlet* clip. "What we need is the same as that, but using *Titus*. Gordon and I will make sure it's circulated – and Bob's your uncle. How quickly could you organise that?"

I stared at her. "Well…"

The odd feeling that fate was once more taking a hand in my life ran down my back, like an escaping spider. Gathering up my phone, I located the clip Louise had taken at the Speak Out group.

"There is this," I said, passing it to her. "If it's any good."

"We'll go for auditions on Wednesday evening this time, shall we?" said Diana, half an hour and another glass of wine later. The video clip was already on her phone, and she'd started a Facebook post before I'd even checked with Louise whether it was okay to publish it. "Thursday clashed with quite a few other drama group rehearsals," she added.

I gulped. Why did that seem like no time at all? "Can I let you know tomorrow?"

Gordon looked pained, but for once he kept his mouth shut.

"Of course!" Diana smiled. "Now, I know this lot aren't on board yet, but they will be. So let me introduce you to the Mile-End Players."

Helen drifted in as another round of drinks arrived. She was wearing her hat and coat and had the costumes Mags had put out for her draped over her arm. She blinked a little at the gathering around Ben and me, but didn't comment.

"I'm beat, Gordon," she said. "I'm off home to bed." Ben looked up briefly from his phone, where he was absorbed in a long text.

"Do you want a hand putting anything in the car?" Gordon asked. "I can walk you back to the car park, if you like. It's a bit of a stretch, if you've got stuff to carry."

"No, no; that's fine. You stay and finish your drinks. I hope you lot aren't driving," she added, eyeing the cluster of glasses.

"We've got a lift arranged. But we'll see you tomorrow for coffee, okay?" Diana waved her glass at Helen, and Gordon ducked.

"You'll be getting a lift to casualty, if you have any more," he muttered.

Helen laughed, as Diana scowled at him. "Have fun, guys. Nice to meet you, Jenny." She flashed me a cool smile.

"You, too," I said, politely. Ben looked up from his phone, his face anxious.

"Oh, damn!" he said. "I'm so sorry, Jenny, but I've got a bit of a problem, and I'm going to have to dash up to Janie's uni. She's okay," he added, seeing my look of concern, "but she needs me to sort something out, and it can't wait. Can you get someone to drive you home?"

"Er, right… hold on a minute." I seized my phone. "I'll see if Mags has left yet."

She hadn't. "I'm just putting stuff in the car," she said. "I'll come straight over – and maybe I'll have that drink after all. Order me a dry white, will you? I won't be long."

I turned to relay the message to Ben, but to my surprise he was already disappearing out of the door, without a backward glance. Something pretty urgent must have happened to Janie, to take him off in such a rush. I'd been a bit anxious about going home alone with him anyway, so I told myself I should feel relieved. Yet all I felt was a flat sense of disappointment.

TWENTY-FOUR

'Fire that's closest kept burns most of all.'
(Two Gentlemen of Verona)

"Have you heard any more from Ben?" asked Mags, as I came into the kitchen on Sunday morning. She was still working on the *Othello* costumes.

"Not a word," I said. My phone blared out, making us both jump.

"Perhaps that's him," said Mags, nursing the finger she'd impaled on a needle. I glanced at my screen: *Louise.* Good. I'd left a message last night for her to ring me.

"Jenny," she said, brightly. "Sorry I missed you. Yes, I've checked with the group and it's fine to use the video clip."

That was a relief, because it was already rife on social media.

"Thank you. And you got my message that I can't make Wednesday, because we have auditions?" I asked.

"Yes, I wanted to talk to you about that."

"O-kay." I braced myself for an argument.

"In fact, we've had to postpone the meeting, because there's a problem with the heating in the hall. I'll email you the new schedule. But actually, I wondered if you'd consider running some drama workshops for us, in addition to our normal sessions?"

Mags looked up as I gasped.

"I think you've really got something," she added. "I've never seen the group respond as they did to your talk. I wish I could pay you – but I'm afraid it would have to be voluntary, for the moment."

My pulse was leaping. *Validation*. That's what this was, after so many years.

"Um, payment isn't a problem," I stuttered. Then I remembered Mr Norwich, and how upset he'd been about me leaving the pub unattended. "I'll need to check with my boss, though."

"That's fine. Anyway, let me know. And send me your audition details, will you? I'll email them to the group."

I agreed in a daze, as Mags mouthed *'Who is it?'* in her usual goldfish mode.

"Good. Have you got round to writing anything in that diary of yours yet?" Louise asked.

"I haven't had time." I was glad she couldn't see my face.

"Ah, well, maybe keep trying. You might find it helps."

"I will. Um, sorry, Louise, I have to pick up another call." To Mags's frustration, I went from call to call without filling her in on my news.

"Jenny?" Diana's voice sounded so unlike its usual bouncy self that I prickled with apprehension.

"Diana, what is it?"

She didn't answer, but I thought I could hear a tissue rustling.

"Diana?" I asked, tentatively. "Is it Gordon?" Mags sprang up, abandoning her sewing, and I quickly switched my phone to speaker mode as she bore down on me.

"No; no, Gordon's fine. It's Helen. She was attacked last night in the woods next to the car park."

"What?"

"My God." Mags sat back down, her hand to her mouth. I joined her. "Is she all right?"

"I think so," Diana said, her voice trembling. "She looked awful, though."

"You saw her?" I swallowed, trying to block the images that were crowding into my mind.

"Yes, when we went back to get our car, there was an ambulance just pulling up, and Helen was sitting on the seat near the toilet block, with some guy we don't know. He said he'd been out running and found her pretty much crawling out of that wooded area, behind the car park. He called the emergency services straightaway."

A jogger. I almost blurted out the details of my own encounter with the hooded runner on the riverbank, but then thought better of it. Mags would want to know why on earth I hadn't mentioned it.

"Of course, we ran straight over to see what was wrong," Diana went on. "Helen managed to say that a guy had jumped her from behind, when she was loading her car, but then the paramedics took over, so we don't know any more. Gordon went to have a look at her car, and the boot was still up, with half the costumes on the ground, but we thought we'd better not touch anything until the police got there. The attacker was obviously long gone, though."

"Did he… Had she…?" I had to ask, though I could hardly bear to hear the answer.

"I don't know." Diana's voice was thick, as though she hadn't slept. "God, I hope not. She was obviously in shock though, shaking like a leaf; they were taking her to hospital when we left. Gordon called her Mum for her, as Rob and Helen have just split up, so she's on her own. Sheila said she'd get straight up to the hospital, and that she'd let us know how Helen is." There was the sound of tissue rustling again. "But apart from a quick text to tell us that Helen was staying in overnight, I've no more news."

"But…" Mags frowned. "Wait a minute, what time did all this happen? I passed Helen on my way to the pub, and Jenny and I only left about half an hour later. And we didn't see a thing."

"Well, we didn't leave the pub until about half eleven, and it was clearly all over by then," Diana said.

Mags looked at me. "Maybe Ben saw something, then? He left just after Helen."

"No, I thought of that, and messaged him this morning to ask if he saw anything. He said no; nothing. Still, I expect the police will want to talk to him anyway. They asked us and the jogger guy a few questions and took our contact details, just in case they need us."

I could see that Mags was wondering why Ben hadn't called us, but I couldn't go there right now.

"Poor Helen." Mags slid her arm around me. "Jenny, are you okay? You're freezing. I'm so glad I didn't let you walk to that car park on your own."

"Yes," said Diana, soberly. "That's why I rang. We'd better all be careful from now on, until they catch whoever did this."

"Thanks, Diana." I managed. "If you speak to Helen…" I was aware I hardly knew the woman, but the thought of what she might have been through paralysed me.

"Yes, of course. I'll tell her you're thinking of her. We'll be in touch."

And she was gone. Mags's eyes stayed on my face.

"Perhaps you should come back with me for a few days, Jen. Just till the police sort this out. I can't say I've ever felt comfortable about leaving you here on your own."

I set my jaw. "Mags, you know I have to stay. I'll lose my job otherwise."

Her lips tightened. "Well, at the very least, we ought to think about having the place properly secured."

"You're right," I said. "I'll have a look online at burglar alarms."

Mags didn't go home on Monday; she said she'd arranged for a friend to 'business-sit' for her, and I was secretly relieved. Neither of us could settle, even though Diana rang to say that Helen was home and recovering, and the police already had a lead.

Mags kept nagging at me to email my boss about security, but I was reluctant. He was already annoyed with me, and I didn't want to start making demands before I'd produced any results. In the end she dropped the argument, but kept glancing sharply at me every time I put a hand to my head, or went quiet for a while.

"Headache?" she asked, so many times that in the end I snapped at her.

"Sorry," I muttered, as we sorted through yet another box of paperwork from the cellar. "But please, believe me. I'm fine." She snorted.

The only text I had from Ben was a brief one, saying that Janie was okay, but he was having a few problems on the home front and would catch up with me as soon as he could. Aside from Helen's attack, my meeting with Mark was gnawing at me, and sorting paperwork left far too much time to think. While Mags went off to heat up some soup, I abandoned my work and typed him a brief email, giving him my mobile number and telling him I'd love to see him again, any time. There was little chance he'd respond, but it was worth a try.

After lunch, George dropped by and relieved our minds a little by securing the windows for us and checking the locks.

"I heard the news about that poor girl from Mile-End," he said, "and I thought you might be worrying. Now, these doors are solid and no one's going to get in that way, without an axe. The windows are a different matter – these metal handles are easily forced." Mags went pale. "But all I have to do is fix a screw above them, so they can't lift. You won't be able to open them from the inside, either, but at this time of year that won't be a problem. It'll keep you safe until you can get something more permanent done. And if you've got the money, you could get yourselves one of those little security camera systems; some of them are quite reasonable. I'd be more than willing to fit it for you."

"There's already one on order," Mags said.

"George, you're a treasure!" I kissed his cheek. He grinned, and offered Mags the other, as she got up.

"And thank you for that lovely Victoria sponge from your wife," she added. "Do bring her round for a visit."

"Oh, she's not a great socialiser, my Vera; but I'll see if I can persuade her. So, have you recovered from last night?" he asked, as he set to work on the windows in the lounge bar. "I thought you must have had a late one. I saw Ben coming back into the village about midnight. I were just bringing Vera home from a visit to her sister's."

I stared at him. "That couldn't have been Ben. He went flying off up to Leicester at about half ten, to his daughter's uni. I came back with Mags."

He gave me an odd look, then stood back to try the casement handle. "There. No one will be able to budge that."

"Are you sure it was Ben, George?" I asked.

"Aye, it was him, sure enough. I'd know that car of his anywhere. He always has that daft fluorescent sign on the boot – *If you can read this, you're too bloody close!* Maybe he changed his mind."

He moved off towards the kitchen, drill in hand, leaving me with a prickle of uneasiness. Perhaps Ben had come back for something. Yes, that would be it. Otherwise, why would he tell me he was in Leicester, when he was at home all along?

TWENTY-FIVE

'All our yesterdays…'
(Macbeth)

I persuaded Mags to get off home after breakfast on Tuesday morning, then went upstairs to return a few costumes that she had left in the little lounge. The chairs were still up there from the *Hamlet* workshop; hopefully we'd need them for the *Titus* audition. I scooped up a forgotten coffee mug from the table and then paused.

Where had Henry gone? I'd left him right here after the workshop. I ran my hand over the space where he'd sat. Then I remembered Mags dusting in this room yesterday morning. She must have put him back in the cellar; she said he always made her uncomfortable 'hanging about'. I shivered. The last thing I wanted was to go down into that cellar alone to check – with or without new bulbs and a torch. I could ask her when she phoned.

Downstairs in the kitchen, I settled down to my phone and laptop, warmed by the little fan heater Mags had brought. Ben and Diana had both left texts while I was asleep, and I clicked eagerly on Ben's first.

Hi, Jenny. Sorry I've been a bit quiet – things are pretty hectic. But glad to see the Titus video clip is doing well! Talk soon x Ben.

And that was it. No more explanations; nothing. With a lurking trace of unease, I opened Diana's message.

Hi, Jenny! I've had a visit from Sheila, Helen's mother. Helen is a lot better; the police have someone in custody, so all very relieved. Helen's now having counselling. It was a frightening attack, but thank God, not a sexual one. Helen thinks the jogger scared him off. So lucky he came past at that moment! We've sent the Titus video out to everyone we can think of, and there's loads of interest already on FB. Eight people have already signed up. Well done, you. xx D.

My spirits lifted with relief at the news about Helen, then shot into panic mode when I thought about the auditions. I quickly keyed in a message of thanks to Diana, and a brief reply to Ben, though I resisted asking him how his visit to Leicester had gone. It was his business, I told myself. But George's remark still niggled.

There were no less than nine replies to my own e-shot; and, oh joy, an email from Gordon, formally advising me that his 'efforts this time had met with greater success'. As I was reading it, George called to say he'd rung Jake Reeve's solicitors.

"I only spoke to the office secretary, I'm afraid," he said. "Everyone was out or in meetings. But she had a check through all their records, and there's nothing about any carbon dating of a skull. I am sorry, my dear. It's probably somewhere in the pub, knowing Jake. He were a devil for squirrelling things away."

I assured him we'd keep looking, though another weekend of scrubbing and sorting was a gruelling prospect. "But thank you so much, George."

"That's my pleasure."

I headed to the kitchen for some strong coffee. In the light of all the positive responses, I needed to make some progress on the play.

Darkness was gathering when my phone went off with a call from Ben. I seized it eagerly.

"Jenny!" Ben's voice was full of excitement. "I've got some news. Simon has come up trumps with his research on the trial records at Kew; he'll be emailing the results over later. And I wondered, if you felt like it, could we view them together?"

"*What?* Oh, that's fantastic!" I said, almost knocking my chair over as I got up. "This evening?"

"If that's okay. I've asked him to send the email direct to you. Shall I bring a Chinese take-away over? I've just finished work."

"Sounds lovely." I glimpsed my reflection in the bar mirror as he rang off and hurried to straighten my tangle of hair.

Within forty-five minutes, we were settled in front of the fire with my laptop, a bottle of red wine and loaded plates of food.

"If this goes right, we may need champagne," Ben said, scooping up a forkful of chow mein. "Open your email. Simon's should come through any minute."

"I'm trying. Blast this slow connection." I watched the little cog on my screen revolve so arthritically that I could have screamed.

"My God. It's there, look." Ben thrust a forefinger at the screen as my inbox materialised. "*Hertford Assizes, July 1593.*"

I clicked on the message.

Hi Ben,

See below summary of the indictment you're researching. I wasn't sure how good your Latin is, so I've done you a translation. Hope it helps. Simon.

"Latin?" I said.

He grinned. "He knows I'm crap at it."

I gripped my hands together. "Oh, my God. This really is it, Ben." We both bent forward, meal forgotten, and raked the lists of headings with our eyes.

Name of defendant: Coates, John Henry
Occupation: Actor (Clown; lately apprenticed to [name missing])
Parish of Residence: W-E, near the town of Northampton

"Bloody hell," said Ben. "You were right, all along. Wethershall-End! But what was he doing in Hertford in that case?"

My eyes were already searching below.

"Damn. The 'date of alleged offence' and 'list of prosecution witnesses' are missing. Isn't that a bit strange?"

"Not necessarily." Ben scooped up a forkful of congealing sweet and sour chicken. "It could be that the record was partly destroyed, or the ink's too faded to read. Or that the prosecutors were protecting someone, as we suspected."

"The gentleman at the inn?" I turned back to my own food, but my appetite had faded.

"Yes. He might have been someone important – like your justice."

My hand flew to my mouth. "Oh. But look at this."

Below, under 'Details of the Alleged Offence', Simon had typed:

On this date, the accused did follow [name scratched out] to his home in the town of Hertford and there did attack him and steal a purse containing the sum of two shillings.

"George's story," I whispered, transfixed. Ben tapped his lip with his fork.

"So it looks like it *was* a cover-up: the charge of theft would ensure John Henry was silenced about the rape. It also suggests why he was in Hertford. Our elusive gentleman came from there."

"And there *is* a date – look, further down." I pointed. "See, 14th July 1593: the date of the 'incident'. They must have forgotten to expunge that one."

I pushed my food aside.

"Ben, don't you remember? That's the day after the

performance – the one mentioned in Bennington's expense accounts. John Henry followed this man to Hertford because of something that happened on the thirteenth."

Ben whistled through his teeth. "Yes. Because the man in question visited the nearby inn, before or after the performance."

"And while he was there, raped the woman Coates intended to marry – as the folktale goes."

"We're still assuming quite a lot," said Ben. "That the skull you have *is* John Henry Coates's, for one."

"Yes." I fell silent, picturing my hollow-eyed tenant below stairs. Or I assumed he was. "Yet there's so much that points to it being him."

We turned our attention back to the screen, this time a little more soberly.

Verdict: Guilty.
Sentence: Sus.

"What does that mean?" I asked.

"Hanged," he said, soberly. "Literally 'suspended'. Simon hasn't bothered to translate it from the Latin, but it's plain enough."

My gaze rested on the word, imagining the hand that had penned the original centuries ago. "That's… a bit unthinkable," I said.

"Another email's come through." Ben clicked on it quickly:

P.S. There were some notes, added later, about a related case.

We both leaned forward almost into the screen, as we took in what we had never hoped to find.

> *Indictments for Jane, Ann and Elizabeth Bray on various charges related to Witchcraft, were referred to Northampton Assizes. Further searches have failed to turn up anything more, as the relevant records are nonextant. Would you still like a facsimile of the Coates indictment?*

"The three sisters," I whispered. It was like watching Jane Elliott's book come to life before my eyes.

"What a shame the Northampton records no longer exist," said Ben, as he typed a brief reply to Simon. "But we know they did. That's so important and will only add to their story. Are you feeling okay?" he added, giving me a sidelong glance.

"Yes, of course. It's only that – it seems such a waste. All those young lives, their potential, unfulfilled."

"Hey." Without warning, Ben leaned forward, brought my face up towards his with his hand and kissed me, so gently that all thinking stopped. Then he drew away, searching my eyes; and at that moment I wanted the comfort of his touch so much, my body ached.

A ping from my inbox announced the arrival of another email from Simon, but neither of us moved.

"That will be the facsimile," I said, at last. Ben stifled a sigh.

"Always at the wrong moment," he muttered. But his face straightened as he clicked on the attachment. We watched it materialise as if by magic, through the pixelating dust of centuries. And there it was: *Sus*. The word that had condemned John Henry's life in the space of a breath was in itself curtailed, scrawled across the document like an 'etcetera'. I thought of all those who had trudged to the scaffold after receiving that casual sentence. A line from *Macbeth* slipped into my consciousness. *'And all our yesterdays have lighted fools the way to dusty death.'* It was as though the writer's mind perceived with prism-like clarity what we only glimpsed as single pinpricks of light.

"Perhaps not the time for bubbly," said Ben. "Funny, I thought we'd be dancing round the room." He reached out a hand to stroke my cheek, and a tremor ran through me as he moved in for another kiss, his other hand sliding along my thigh.

And I was on my feet, my wine glass spinning to the floor, shattering around me.

"No!"

I stared, trembling, at the ruby drops spattering the floor and table. Then my body shrank inwards, taking my voice with it. "*Shit*. I'm so sorry," I whispered.

Ben blanched. "My God. Jenny, what the hell just happened?"

All I could do was shake my head. I didn't even know. Perhaps it was hearing about the needless slaughter of a family; talking to Aunt Clare about Mark; or Helen's attack. My head was full of the past, and in some disturbing way it was converging on the present. I could feel it.

"Jesus. I'm really getting this wrong, aren't I?" Ben looked at me in confusion. "I mean, forgive me, but I thought you were… well, giving me the right signals. And then you react as if I'm a bloody rapist, or something. What's going on?"

I couldn't move; couldn't speak. It was happening again – just as it had with Ross and Steve. I would never be free of the fear.

"I'm sorry," I said, at last. "It's… not your fault. Honestly. But I think you'd better go."

"You're serious?" His eyes were troubled. "Listen, tell me what I've done. If I've upset you, I really didn't mean to."

I turned away. Bursting into tears wouldn't help anything.

"Please," I said.

"Look, are you sure you're okay?" And his gentle tone nearly undid me.

"Absolutely."

The fire crackled in the silence. And then he gathered his keys, and when he spoke, his tone was light and studied.

"Okay. Perhaps I have got this wrong; but don't worry, I won't be making the same mistake again. Anyway, good luck with the auditions tomorrow. I really hope it all goes well for you."

And he was gone. Any chance of intimacy was over. I sank down by my laptop, laid my head in my hands and sobbed. I was like some inverted, twisted Midas, who burned every offer of love or friendship to embers at a single touch. The only thing I could be grateful for was that my vision was still whole.

For more than an hour I crouched over the small pub table till my body was wracked and emptied, and gradually everything calmed; then I got up and poured myself a brandy.

I couldn't let this ruin my one chance to succeed at doing what I loved. And Ben didn't need all the 'crap', as my mother would have called it, that I constantly towed around with me.

No. It was better this way. My phone buzzed with a text and I snatched it up eagerly, part of me hoping that it was Ben, asking if I was okay. But it was from Diana.

Jenny, just thought you should know. The police have released the man they had in custody for questioning, re Helen's attack. More later. D x

It seemed as though the day was destined to get worse.

I made my way to the front door to lock it, and paused. *That was odd.* It wasn't properly shut – which was unlike Ben, particularly as he knew I was alone in the pub. He'd obviously been more upset than I realised. A faint, acrid smell found my nose, and I sniffed the night air through the crack in the door. *Cigarette smoke.* It was unmistakable. Ben had never told me he was a smoker, and I hadn't smelt it on him. *Or had I?* I thought back, trying to recall the indefinable something I'd detected, in with his sun and sea body-splash, when I'd come downstairs and found him in the little lounge.

Pulling the door open a little more, I peered out into the night. Maybe he'd lingered outside and had a smoke to calm his mood. Just outside the porch, I spotted a used match and a cigarette butt: the tiniest spark of an ember still glowing on its rim like a tiny garnet. I felt heavy with exhausted defeat. He'd stood here while I was crying. And I hadn't even heard him drive away.

TWENTY-SIX

'Nothing is but what is not.'
(Macbeth)

"Where have you been?" complained Mags when she called late on Wednesday afternoon. "I've rung twice already."

I was busy collating photocopies of scenes and character breakdowns in the bar. George had had them copied for me while I was with Mark, and I was so grateful. He was even coming to help this evening.

"Sorry," I said, guiltily. "My phone was on silent, and I've only just noticed. Are you okay?"

"I am, but my Dad's had a fall," she said. "Veronica and I were at the hospital all afternoon. He hasn't broken anything, though, and he's a lot better now. Coming out on Saturday."

"Oh, thank goodness!" I breathed. "You must have been worried to death. Mags, I feel terrible; I should have made sure my phone was on."

"Not to worry; you weren't to know. But we've decided it's time Dad came to live with me, though he'll go to Veronica's at weekends, to give me a break. So I'll still be able to come up, but it'll have to be on Saturday. And I won't make the auditions, I'm afraid."

"Mags, it's fine," I said. "You worry about your Dad."

"Thanks, Jen. Any news your end?"

I realised that I hadn't brought her up to date with Diana's news about Helen, or Ben's and my latest findings on John Henry's indictment, so I filled her in – though I avoided talking in too much detail about Ben.

"We've had loads of interest in the auditions," I finished, brightly.

"That's wonderful! Well, look, I only rang to say 'break a leg' for tonight. Let me know how it goes. I'll be at the hospital tomorrow and Friday, and the signal's rubbish, so if you can't get me, leave a message."

We ended the call and I stood looking blankly at the piles of photocopies, guilt growing inside me. *Why did I keep lying to her?* Why couldn't I tell her about Ben, and Ross, my mother... and Mark.

Mark. The image of him walking away, his hands in his pockets, haunted my dreams, sleeping and waking. How could he feel so distant, and yet know more about my mother's life than I did? She'd been put into an orphanage. And yet when Aunt Clare had told her about Mark, she'd never suggested trying to find him. *She'd called me a whore. Thrown me out into the street.* This was the woman he acknowledged a link with – and yet there was nothing for me.

Resentment stabbed at me; why had Aunt Clare never told me about my mother's past? I had a right to know.

I headed for my laptop. It would be four o'clock in the morning in Auckland, but my email would be waiting for her when she woke.

> *Dear Aunt Clare,*
>
> *I have just found out that my mother was in an orphanage in Ireland. She'd always told me that you and she were brought up by an aunt, after my grandmother died. Please can you shed some light on this? Very best wishes, Jenny x*

It was brief, but at least I'd kept it light – and that was essential if I was to coax her into talking. Then I emailed Mark, repeating the essence of my parting words.

> *I don't want there to be a void between us that can only get wider and deeper the longer we don't speak. Please give me a chance and talk to me.*

That was enough. I needed to try to eat something to give me energy for the evening.

"I'll call everyone to order, shall I, Jenny? There's a lot to get through."

It was gone half past seven. Gordon detached himself from the chattering auditionees clustered around the refreshments upstairs and made a beeline for me. My God: how many people were here? So many men, too, of various shapes, sizes and ages – but none of them Ben, with his easy smile and crinkle-skinned eyes. He wasn't coming, and I couldn't blame anyone but myself.

The men milling around our costume area looked like wildebeest at a waterhole, grazing on the custard creams and sizing each other up. Some were perusing the scenes and character breakdowns carefully stacked on my 'audition table' nearby. A number of Louise's Speak Out ladies were hovering uncertainly, ready to bolt at the slightest provocation. I sympathised.

"It's fine, Gordon; I'll give everyone a shout when I'm ready." I hoped he wasn't going to be a problem. I was grateful for all he'd done, but I couldn't let him muscle in.

Diana sailed up to me. "Brilliant, isn't it?" she beamed. "What did I tell you?" She leaned to murmur in my ear as Gordon strode off to chat to some newcomers. "Something else to tell you, before we get started. The police have been questioning Helen's husband, Rob."

Despite my anxiety about the evening ahead, I was eager to hear more.

"What? But you said they were separated!"

"Yes," she breathed. "That was the point. Helen was having an affair, you see. Rob found out about it months ago, and they had a huge bust-up. They got over it and said they'd try again, but then Rob caught her sending texts to the other guy and realised it wasn't over. Another big row, Helen left, and Rob was heartbroken. He actually took an overdose; shocked everybody. His brother found him, and managed to get an ambulance just in time."

I gasped. "So, you mean the police think it was Rob who attacked her? Surely she would have recognised him?"

"No, Helen's told them it definitely wasn't Rob. But the thing is..." she lowered her voice, "the man they arrested was Rob's brother. I know he said some pretty threatening

229

things to Helen, while Rob was in hospital. She must have mentioned them to the police – because why else would they arrest him, and spend so much time questioning Rob?" She saw Gordon coming, and pursed her lips. "Anyway, I'd better not say any more."

"Wherever did you get all these men?" I said, changing the subject as her husband descended on us with his clipboard. "We hardly had any under sixty-five in my last drama group."

Gordon's chest swelled. I'd given him the job of recording everyone's details as they came in. "We have done rather well, haven't we? You've got some of the best male leads in the area, Jenny, so I shouldn't keep them waiting."

Before I could reply, Diana's authoritative voice rang around the room. "Take your seats, please, everyone!"

My mouth dried as about twenty people surged towards me – but my eyes honed in on just one: stocky, with coarse, brown hair; dressed in dark blue jeans stained with oil, and a black puffer jacket, over the shoulders of which flopped the hood of a grey sweatshirt. His face was sunk into his chest as he came to a stop, texting on his phone. Yet he was unmistakably the man I'd seen loitering outside the butcher's and the library. In fact, he seemed to appear everywhere I went. As though sensing my startled gaze, he lifted a pair of cedar-brown eyes to mine, and a soft, round beard in a matching hue unfurled from his collar. Then he looked away as though bored, and strolled to an empty seat.

"I'll go and round up the stragglers, shall I?" Gordon's voice pierced my trance.

"Um, yes. No, I mean." He frowned at me as I dithered. "Actually, Gordon, there's something more important.

Could you take a look at those scenes I've prepared, and organise the names on your list into suitable casts for each one, please?" It was a job I'd meant to do myself, but my time – and concentration – were both at a premium.

"A pleasure."

I sighed with relief as he headed off. George panted up the stairs towards me, clutching a set of keys. "I'm so sorry, my dear, but I need to pop home for a bit. The wife's locked herself out. Can you manage?"

"Of course!" I said. "Thank you so much – and don't worry about coming back; I've got Diana and Gordon."

"Oh, I'll be back, never fear," he said, skirting Diana as he hurried off as fast as his legs would allow.

"Ready to start, Jenny?" she asked.

"Yes. Yes, of course."

I faced my audience, remembering to make eye contact with as many as possible. But my gaze kept returning to the bearded man at the edge of the group; his attention was everywhere but on me. He kept glancing around, scanning the place as though he was looking for someone... or something. His eyes rested on the window, and the casement handles, lingering on the screws George had put above them. Was he checking the place out? A memory scudded through my mind. Didn't the man in the agency have a beard?

"I'll man the door, Jenny," murmured Diana in my ear, and slipped away. I looked up to see Gordon's eyes fixed expectantly on me from the back of the room, and rushed into speech.

"Good evening, everyone." To the side of me, Tara, Nadine, Sam and Isla from Speak Out were filing in, followed by Monica, Beth and Louise. Several Mile-End Players from the pub were gathered in front of Gordon, and a number of Ben's students from the *Hamlet* workshop. It was almost like having a family. "Welcome to the festival auditions." Puffer-Jacket's eyes lingered on the staircase, and I resolutely dragged my gaze away. At least his contact details would be on Gordon's list; I could check later.

"I'm going to start with a quick overview of *Titus*, in case some of you aren't familiar with the play." I wavered as Diana arrived with a couple more men I didn't know, and showed them to seats. "Then we'll divide up into groups, and each group will have a short scene to work on." From the back of the room, Gordon was mouthing *'Introduce yourself'*, with a lot of exaggerated face-pulling. *Shit!* The most obvious omission. "Oh, and in case you don't know me, I'm Jenny Watson, and I've been employed to direct the festival." Gordon nodded his approval, and I resisted rolling my eyes. "Please can you make sure you've added your details to the contact sheet, if you haven't already? Thank you."

Smiles from the people I recognised; bland stares from the others, including the two new arrivals, one of whom – a well-groomed individual with caramel highlights in his hair and dressed in a cream Aran sweater and jeans – crossed his arms and legs as he sat back, assessing me. The thin, pale-skinned man next to him with ink-black hair, glowing dark eyes and angular features was dressed as if by contrast in a well-pressed business suit in charcoal grey. He muttered a comment into his friend's ear, and they both tried not to smirk. The trouble was, I was aware that beneath all the cool stares were probably years of collective experience in auditioning, acting – even directing. Well, the only thing that had worked for me so far was pushing on regardless, so I launched into my five-minute 'tour' of *Titus*.

I'd just warmed to it when Puffer-Jacket got up, circled round the back of the seats and headed downstairs, phone in hand – with my eyes straining in their sockets to follow him. I faltered, amid a couple of audible sighs. *Whoever he was, I was not letting him scupper my auditions.* At last, I reached the end of my spiel, to see Gordon coming towards me with his list. I could only be thankful that my introduction was over.

Half an hour later we were well into the workshop; groups of actors were proclaiming lines all over the pub. But nowhere could I see puffer-jacket man. Perhaps he'd left.

Gordon strode over from the group he was watching.

"This is a bit different, Jenny; rather long-winded, though, if you ask me. You're going to run out of time."

I glanced at my phone. *Blast.* It was eight fifteen already. "It'll be fine, but we need to round everyone up," I said.

"And then what?"

"Each group performs their scene, and we all watch. Then we repeat the exercise, swapping the actors into different roles. That way, everyone gets to know the play, and each actor can audition for a number of parts. But I need some time to cast the next lot of scenes first."

Gordon nodded. "That's quite a clever plan, actually. Leave it to me." He bellowed like a ship's siren. "Five minutes, everyone, and then we're performing the scenes!"

I was torn between an irrational pleasure that I'd actually won Gordon's approval, and the fear that he'd be casting the play before the night was out – and judging by some of the looks cast in my direction, my credibility as festival director was already tenuous. Even so, I couldn't resist asking him if he recognised the puffer-jacketed stranger.

"The chap who left early?" he said in surprise. "No, I can't say I did. He didn't put his name on the list. But he's probably one of the printers; Dave takes on extra labour during his busy periods." He frowned at me. "Mind you, I think you put a few people off with that opening speech. Two others left before we even started rehearsing. I had a quick chat when I saw them going, but I couldn't change their minds – which was a great pity, because one was an ex-pro actor, and the other had drama school training. You could tell, of course, from the voices. Perfect annunciation, great tonal quality, and they both clearly knew the play inside out. So you've lost out there, I'm afraid." He strode off upstairs with my list.

I bit back a bitter retort. If my memory was correct, the men he was talking about – the caramel-haired man and his friend – hadn't taken their disdainful eyes off my face the whole time. I didn't think I wanted them in my cast anyway.

The second round of scene rehearsals was just coming to an end when Gordon and Diana pounced on me again.

"Jenny: here. We've written down a few casting suggestions." Gordon pushed a sheet of paper into my hand. "Now, Adam is a sure bet for Titus. He's a bit of a cherry-picker. He'll only take the parts he wants," he explained, as I raised my brows. "You'd be a fool not to take him. I also thought Janet for Lavinia?"

Diana nodded. "Oh, yes. She'd be brilliant."

I kept my voice light and pleasant. "Actually, Gordon, I have my own ideas about that." Tara's portrayal had been tentative, but I could see its honest potential; and while Adam was a fine actor, there were others who had stirred my interest more.

"Jenny, with all due respect, my love, you don't have the experience," Gordon said.

I stiffened. "Look, Gordon, I appreciate your concern, and your help. But I am the festival director, and I'll be the one to decide on my cast. Give me the list later, if you must."

And I left him standing open-mouthed, while Diana muffled a snort of laughter, but the triumph I should have felt didn't come. Instead, a slow, dull ache spread up from my neck, and with it, the murky patches I dreaded drifted in at the sides of my vision. I stopped, gripping the banister. *Oh, not now. Please, not now.*

Somehow I got back upstairs. If I could only reach the table, I could stay put until it passed. I managed it, stumbling a little as I found my chair. The clatter of feet sounded on the stairs, then Gordon called for the first scene to be performed before I'd had a chance to open my mouth. Shadows moved back and forth in front of me and I kept my eyes turned towards the performance space, assuming what I hoped was an expression of calm interest. The only thing I could do was live from moment to moment.

Diana's voice whispered in my right ear. "Are you all right? You've gone really white."

I nodded, not moving my gaze. "Bit of a headache," I said. I heard Diana rummaging in her bag.

"Wait, I've got some paracetamol here. I'll get you a drink. And look, if it's a migraine, sunglasses might help. They're not too dark, so you'll still be able to see clearly." *I wish.* But they would at least hide my eyes. Something pattered down on the table in front of me. "Here are the pills," Diana murmured. I reached out tentatively and grasped them.

"Diana! We're trying to listen," Gordon hissed from the other side of her. They'd both taken seats at my table, no doubt counting themselves as my audition panel. It was like some awful nightmare in which control was slipping away from me on all sides. A light hand touched my shoulder and Louise's voice spoke in my other ear.

"Would you like some help making notes, Jenny? Only I know how difficult it is to watch and write."

I felt slightly faint with relief. "Yes please. If you could note who's playing which character in each scene, it would really help."

And then what? Was I going to remember every performance, when I couldn't even see what they were wearing, let alone their expressions?

I felt Louise settle into the empty seat beside me. "Oh, my goodness, listen to Tara," she whispered. "I never realised she had all this in her."

I forced myself to listen to Tara's voice, and gradually concentration calmed me. And it was so strange; not seeing Tara somehow sharpened my appreciation of the energy in her voice; the changes and gentle nuances in tone and inflexion. She was feeling the words, as though they were a natural part of the flow of her emotions. As the minutes went by, my pulse steadied. I became lost in the words I was hearing, seeing the scene unfold in my mind.

And then Isla spoke as Tamora, pleading for her son's life. She was usually so confident, but this evening she sounded tentative and uncomfortable. Gordon muttered something to Diana under his breath and, unfortunately, Isla must have heard it, because she faltered.

"Jenny, I don't think I'm up to this, to be honest," she said, coming abruptly out of character. "Let's face it, you'll nae cast someone like me the way I speak. I have enough trouble getting people to understand me in shops!"

I got to my feet, my fingers knocking against a glass on the table. Thank God it didn't go over.

Gordon piped up, "Actually, I was about to suggest—"

Shit. I'd murder him, if he didn't shut up. "Isla, hold on." I wished I could see her face properly and read her eyes.

"Look, it's okay; I'm crap anyway," she said. "There's plenty of others can give this role what it deserves."

"No, listen for a minute." I forgot my own troubles in the overwhelming need to reassure her. "Is this because you have a regional accent? Isla, your character would have had one, too. She was a Goth: a German, speaking to Romans, remember."

Gordon sighed. "You say that, Jenny. But she was a queen. You'd normally play that kind of role in RP, surely?"

"What the bloody hell's RP?" I heard Isla mutter.

"Received Pronunciation," I said, wishing I could see to glare at Gordon. I riveted on a smile. "And I certainly don't have any such expectations. These plays weren't written to be spoken in any sort of 'Standard English' – because it didn't exist, back then. And besides, English would probably have sounded very different – a lot softer, with more of a West Country twang."

"Nonsense!" said Gordon, a smile in his voice, and my back went rigid.

"We can argue about that later. And by the way, Gordon, I'd like you to take part in the next round of auditions, please." In the silence, I thought I heard Diana gasp. "Meanwhile, my advice, Isla, is to forget about how you *think* it should sound, and focus on *why* Tamora's saying what she is. She's a mother, with a son who's about to lose his life in the most brutal way, unless she can save him. She has no weapons; no recourse to justice. All she has are words, and they are her last-ditch attempt – so she puts everything she has into her plea. How she sounds is part of her, as her son is part of her flesh, and the words that come from her heart and her body are her weapons. Use them. Use who you are and be proud of it. As long as the emotion behind them is honest, it'll work."

She didn't answer, and I could have cursed with frustration at not being able to see her face.

"Okay. I'm up for it, if you are," came her voice at last.

"Well *done*," murmured Louise as I sat down.

When the scene started again, it felt transformed: raw and full of emotional energy, and I swelled with gratitude and admiration for Isla as she gave herself up to it, edging Tamora's eloquent prayer with a rough desperation that was moving in its sincerity. Louise squeezed my shoulder as Diana whispered, "Bloody hell, Jenny. How did you know how to do that?"

"I didn't. She just needed a bit of faith in herself," I said.

The auditionees were buzzing as they left. When all was quiet, I caught the sound of George stiffly climbing the stairs. Poor man; God knew how many times he'd done that this evening. I only hoped he wasn't too exhausted.

"All right, my dear?" he asked. "I didn't miss much of it after all, I was up here for the last hour. I just went down to get you a hot chocolate."

I peered up at the shadow of his face. It nodded towards Diana's sunglasses, now abandoned on the table. "My Vera gets migraines, and it affects her vision. She looks at me just like you're doing now!"

I shook my head. There was no point in lying any more, not to George. "Not migraine. It's a form of temporary blindness, caused by stress. It comes and goes." *There.* I'd actually said the word.

"And you carried on." George sighed. "You're a rare one, aren't you?" I was so used to my 'stubbornness' being called stupid over the years – by my mother, teachers at school, Ross – that George's compliment took me by surprise. "What are you going to do about casting the play?" He placed the warm mug on the table in front of me, and his rough hand closed around my fingers as he gently guided them to it. He hadn't made my drink too full or too hot, and its milky sweetness was heaven.

"Do you know something, George? Not seeing properly gave me a totally different perspective."

"Aye," George said, scrubbing his stubble with his fingernails. "Well, they do say people went to hear a play in those days, rather than see one. But if you need help, I saw most of the auditions."

Relief swept over me, and with it, exhaustion. "Oh, yes, please," I said.

"Good. Well, I'm glad you've told me what's amiss. I'll

ring the missus, and tell her I'll stay for a while. Make sure you're all right."

"No, George, really. I'm fine."

"No arguments. You go and get some sleep. I'll see that everything's tidied away." I was too tired to protest.

As I undressed, I rejoiced in the fact that I now had a cast – quite possibly a brilliant one. Tomorrow, if my sight was okay, I'd make a full report to my boss.

TWENTY-SEVEN

'Let me have surgeons; I am cut to the brains.'
(King Lear)

When I cautiously opened my eyes on Thursday morning, my little blue and white room unfolded before me, unmarred by grey patches. I could have wept with relief. Then a clattering of dishes downstairs brought me bolt upright. What on earth…? Was Mags back? Maybe she'd got some time off after all. I flipped off my quilt then stopped, legs halfway out of the bed. But what if it wasn't Mags?

Thrusting my arms into my dressing gown, I crept to the top of the stairs. George appeared from the kitchen, the pedal bin in his hand, his eyes bright.

"Ah, you're awake! That's good timing. I've made a nice pot of tea. How are you this morning?"

I grasped the banister. "Er, good, thank you. Much better. But wait a minute, you've been here all night?"

"Yes, my dear. Vera insisted when I rang her. I stretched out on Jake's old bed. Hope you don't mind."

My heart squeezed. I barely knew the man, and he cared as though he was my own family. Better than my family.

"I'll be off in a few minutes," he said. "Unless you'd like to talk over the auditions while we have a bite of breakfast? There's some notes here, too, that your friend Louise left. She said they might help."

I couldn't contain my smile. "George, I would love to. Thank you. Give me a few minutes to wash and dress."

"I'll cut some toast," George said. "Oh, and by the way, did you cast that young electrician I told you about? I saw him come in, though I don't reckon he noticed me. He passed by the kitchen while I were phoning Vera."

I stared up at him. "Electrician? The one you showed around the pub?" A disturbing suspicion crept over me. "Was he stocky with a beard, by any chance?"

He scratched his chin with a ridged and slightly yellowed fingernail. "He were well-built all right, and he did have a bit of a beard, when I saw him first; but nothing to speak of."

I wondered how long it took beards to grow. "Did he tell you his name?"

"Well, he did tell me, but bless me if I can remember it. It were some foreign name; Greek, I think. Began with a 'D'." His eyes sparked with sudden memory. "Alexander! That was it. Did he get a part?"

"No," I said, slightly bewildered. "He left early." But if he'd been here before, maybe that's why he was taking such an interest in the place?

"Pity." George sighed. "Seemed like a nice lad: he were keenly interested in the local history, especially the old pub and the festival, so I'm not surprised he turned up."

I watched him head away to the kitchen, puzzling over his words.

Well, if the guy was so interested, why did he leave?

By half past ten, George was on his way home and I'd prepared the basic text for my casting emails and sent a report to Mr Norwich. Gordon hadn't called, which surprised me until a rap on the front door announced his and Diana's arrival in the flesh.

"Do you have time for a coffee?" asked Diana. "We've some news for you. But first, we're bursting to know. Did you cast Adam?"

I hid my smile. "Actually, I didn't, because I'm offering the part to Gordon." Gordon's mouth dropped open.

"Brilliant!" laughed Diana. Sometimes she was like a sixteen-year-old – and it was wonderful to watch. "Oh, well played, Jenny."

"Good Lord. I was convinced you'd ask Adam," Gordon said when he found his voice. He had the grace to redden. "Well, if you're sure; I'd be honoured, Jenny."

"You were by far the best fit," I said as I filled the kettle. Though privately, I suspected he'd be a nightmare to direct. Still, I'd proved now that I could hold my own with him. "But please don't tell anyone until I've had confirmations from the rest of the cast."

"Of course. Can I see the list?"

I handed it to him; and to my surprise, he nodded his approval.

"I think you've done really well with this, Jenny," he said.

"Thank you, Gordon." I suppressed the urge to curtsey as I set coffees down in front of them. "Now tell me your news."

"Sheila – you know, Helen's mother – came to see us," Diana said, her face becoming serious. "She thinks the police have found a new lead on Helen's attacker."

I set a packet of Jammie Dodgers down in front of her, which she immediately seized. "It's not her husband, is it?"

"No, I think they've given up on that one. But they've been doing a door-to-door enquiry in Mile-End, and Dave at the Black Bull happened to mention he'd had a guy renting a room there for the past couple of weeks. A businessman, apparently – very quiet and polite, according to Dave, and kept himself to himself. He was either in his room or off out in his car, on visits to customers. But Saturday evening, Dave said he was in a real mood; came down to the bar and just sat there, drinking one vodka after another, and kept checking his phone. He left a while before we all came in."

Gordon grimaced. "Look, we need to keep sensible heads about this. The man probably had nothing to do with Helen's attack."

"Well, in that case, why did he just up and leave, without any warning?" demanded Diana. "That's probably why the police are so interested." She turned to me. "The guy didn't come back till Sunday morning, then paid his bill, packed up and left. Dave's wife took the money. Cash."

I pushed my coffee away. It tasted of curdled milk. "How do you know all this?" I asked.

"Dave told us, of course. The pub's been our local for years." She took a biscuit, ignoring Gordon's pointed look. "But Sheila still thinks it's someone Rob knows. I mean, it's really weird that whoever it was dragged Helen all the way into that wooded area and then just let her go."

I gazed at her. "What do you mean? He got frightened away by the jogger – didn't he?"

She leaned towards me. "That's what I thought. But Helen's remembered a bit more about the attack, over the last couple of days. She hit her head on a tree root when he pushed her, you see, and got knocked out; we don't know how long for. Apparently the guy spoke to her – that's why she's so certain it wasn't Rob. He'd covered her head with some sort of blanket, to stop her screaming, but when he got her to the wooded area, he pulled it off."

I sucked in a breath. "So she *did* see him, then?"

"No, she said he had one of those black balaclava things on, with just his eyes showing. All she remembers is him swearing and letting her go, then nothing more until she came round and found him gone."

"I think that's enough, Diana," said Gordon, glancing at my face. "I know Sheila's your friend, and needs someone to talk to, but I don't think we should be discussing her affairs so openly. Besides, you're frightening Jenny, and she's on her own here." For once, I was grateful to him. "You've nothing to worry about," he assured me. "Whoever this is, the police will track him down pretty swiftly."

I was relieved when they went, Gordon reminding me to lock the pub door behind them. I checked Amazon to see when our burglar alarm was due. Another two days. Well, work was the only thing that could take my mind off this, though working on *Titus* wasn't something I relished.

An hour later, I'd sent all my cast emails. I checked my phone and inbox in case Mark or Ben had left messages, but there was nothing. The pub was dark and cheerless except for a patch of sunlight that had struggled through the window in the little lounge. I decided to make a sandwich and eat it there. I still hadn't heard from Mags; and as I washed up the mugs, a random thought slipped into my mind. How odd that Mags hadn't collected that dirty coffee cup from Henry's table. It had been sitting right beside him, after all, and Mags was even more careful than I was about tidying up. Then I gave myself a mental shake. I was doing it again: finding things to niggle my anxiety levels. Making a drama out of a bit of spilt milk, as my mother used to say. It took two hands to lift Henry; she'd probably meant to go back for the mug later, and forgot. I sighed; going to check the cellar wasn't an option. I'd already promised George I wouldn't risk it in case my sight went again, so I set about preparing my lunch instead. As I munched my way through a cheese and tomato sandwich, a faint, familiar scent caught at my nostrils. Surely that was cigarette smoke? Where was it coming from? It was so slight that I couldn't be sure whether I was imagining it. I picked up my copy of *Titus* and sniffed it cautiously. Yes, the same aroma of stale nicotine I'd detected in Jake's copy of *The Shrew*. Perhaps he'd been fond of *Titus*, too. Then my phone buzzed with a text and I snatched it up, hoping it was Mark. But no; it was a number I didn't recognise.

You do realise by now that I made a mistake?

I stared at it, wondering who on earth could have sent a message that made so little sense. It was clearly intended for someone else. I was debating whether to respond when my phone burst into Beethoven, making me jump.

"Hallo, my dear," said George's voice. "Everything all right?"

I summoned a smile. "Yes, fine, George. All the casting emails have gone."

"Wonderful. Well, listen, I'm only calling because I suddenly remembered who that man you mentioned might be: the one with the beard. There's a new printer who's just started going out with Tania, the young girl in the bakery. He's always hanging around, waiting to take her home, or to lunch. I was in there this morning, by the way, and she said she'd planned to come to the auditions, but when she got home, she found her mother unwell. So she wondered if she could still get involved."

So that was it. A simple explanation.

"Yes, yes, of course; I'll call in at the shop when I'm in the village," I said. "So, the guy with the beard wasn't your electrician, then?"

"Oh, no. I realised afterwards: he were wearing one of those cable sweaters when I saw him last night. Cream, it was."

"An Aran sweater? The guy who was really well spoken? Gordon loved him; said he'd spent three years at drama school." *He* was George's electrician?

George laughed. "Aye, he caught me out as well, but if he's an actor that explains a few things. He started off all well spoken with me the first time. But when I came up here to check on him, he was having a real argy-bargy with someone down the phone, and he sounded broad northern. Anyway, I'll get off and have my lunch. As long as you're all right."

We said our goodbyes, and I sat for a moment, nursing my phone. Broad *northern*?

Then the ping of an incoming email distracted me and hope flared; perhaps it was from Mr Norwich. But it was from my aunt, and looked the length of an epistle. Leaving my phone, I hurried into the lounge bar, to read it in comfort on my laptop.

Dear Jenny,

I was surprised to hear from you again so soon, and with such a question! I'd love to know where you got your 'information'. It's not been an easy one to answer, but here goes.

Your grandmother died in Ireland, having her third daughter, my sister Lydia. I was thirteen at the time; your mother was eight. Your Grandfather, unable to cope on his own, asked his sister if she would take all of us into her own family. She agreed to have baby Lydia and me, because I was old enough to be useful, she said. But she had no room for your mother, who was placed in an orphanage. It was very difficult. Your mother was extremely unhappy, and I'd always planned to send for her once I had my own home, and look after her myself. But she left the orphanage when she was sixteen, and went to England with some friends who had family there. Then she met your father, and you know the rest. Tragically, Lydia died when she was nine, and soon after that I met your uncle and we decided to emigrate here.

I did visit your mother a few times, but it was distressing for us both. She blamed baby Lydia for our mother's death, and for ruining her own life. She swore she would never get pregnant herself, so your uncle and I were surprised when you came along. But then she loved your father so much, she would have done anything for him. She wanted to be a photographer; did she ever tell you that? That's how she met your father. James had some work displayed at a gallery in Hertfordshire, where she was living, and they got talking. They'd planned for her to go on a training course, but then money was tight, and even your father gave up professional photography for a job with more money, when you came along.

I know your mother wasn't the easiest person, Jenny, but she always swore she would never put you in a home, as she had been. Anyway, I hope that helps. Take care of yourself.

Love, Aunt Clare

I sat in a daze, reading and rereading her message. My father was a photographer? And my mother – she'd had her own dream crushed. Perhaps that was why she was always so blighting about my aspirations; how unbearable to see her child grasp what she never could. And now I understood why she'd burned all those photographs. How bitter her sacrifice must have felt when my father betrayed her.

'And I loved him, you see. Never thought he would let me down; ruin my life. Leave me with nothing – but you.'

A bleak ache spread through me. The memory of that afternoon visitor was bad enough; and the thought that my father had led a secret life away from us both. But I realised now that my mother's bitterness went way beyond that. He'd left her with a life sentence: another little being to tie her down; one her conscience bade her keep and house. She'd hated me, as she'd hated baby Lydia, for ruining her life. Oh, she'd kept me 'safe', but she'd punished me mercilessly, because she couldn't get at those who had made her suffer.

My God; she'd needed help. We both had. And not one person had come to our rescue. Not my uncle, who'd questioned how she treated me; nor my aunt, who knew. They'd stood by while she lashed my bare behind with her hand, two days after my father's funeral, for spilling juice at the tea table. And afterwards I was made to sit on a hard kitchen stool alone in the dark till bedtime, when my uncle said enough was enough and came to get me. But I was still too terrified to move until my mother was persuaded to give her consent.

"Has your mother done this to you before, Jenny?" he'd asked as he knelt down beside me. And I shook my head, and looked at the floor, because I couldn't bear to be sent away. My mother had hissed that threat at me anew while they were upstairs packing. But my uncle kept his eyes on my face, and I stretched my little blue skirt as far as it would go to my knees, curling inside when I thought of what he'd already seen. It was the first time I remember blushing.

When my uncle went back into the sitting room, I heard him saying, *"I know it's tough, Bryony, but you can't take it out on an eight-year-old kid."* The next day they went home, and I didn't see them for another eight years.

Bile simmered in my throat at the memory of what followed. Whenever they phoned, or my mother wrote, everyone pretended it was all fine. *Keep it light.* They'd let me go on living a life of toxic shit that had got under my skin and into my bloodstream, in the same way my mother's past had poisoned her.

I sat up, quivering. *No.* Not the same way. Because I would *never* be her, whatever life did to me.

If I didn't get out of the pub, I felt like I'd burst, and all the years and hours and seconds of filthy humiliation and fear would spill out and infect the life I had left. I swept up my coat and keys and made for the door, slamming it shut behind me. And I ran. And ran. Across the bridge, along the riverbank, away from the village, meeting no one, thrusting through undergrowth and tearing my clothes on brambles, finding a twisted sanctuary in physical distress. When I'd outrun my lungs, and my chest ached, I wound my arms around the trunk of a tree and sobbed into its bark – because as much as my insides screamed for help, each time I opened my mouth or took up a pen to try to tell my secrets, fear unfurled, cold and deep and muscular, like some terrifying reptile: swelling inside me until there was no breath, no light left. I could barely remember a time before that threat of suffocation, except for odd, bright pinpricks of memories… moments with my father, when I was small and loved and praised, and those I spent immersed in books and plays.

So many people had offered help. Mags, Ben and Louise – the hospital doctor. But if I was too terrified to communicate, how could they help? My fear had become part of my being, like a dark life-blood; flush it out, and how much of me would be left?

And yet somehow I had to find a way. Because today I'd taken the biggest step of my life. For the first time, I'd admitted that the person I was running away from was me.

TWENTY-EIGHT

'O, it is good to have a giant's strength,
But it is tyrannous to use it like a giant.'
(Measure for Measure)

I got back to the pub, exhausted but determined to have one more try at what Louise had suggested. I would confront the memories that haunted me by writing them down. But first, I checked my laptop, then my phone. George had left a message on my answerphone, and I clicked on it, wondering if he was okay. He never left messages.

"Hallo, Jenny," came his cheerful voice. "I hope I get this message thing right. I just wanted to say that I remembered that electrician's name after all. Dmitri, he said it was. Dmitri Alexander. His mother was Greek or something. Anyway, I hope it helps."

I shook my head, too exhausted to think. I wasn't going to cast the guy anyway, so there was no point in worrying about him.

There was also a text from Diana, who I really wasn't in the mood to hear from – but the word 'Ben' at the beginning arrested my attention.

Jenny. Don't want to say this in front of Gordon, because he says it's none of our business. But the police have interviewed Ben, and I heard (don't ask how) that he admitted he didn't go up to Leicester last Saturday night. Just felt you ought to know.

A trickle of cool perspiration from my run squeezed down my back. I knew this, from George. But somehow, seeing it in writing made it worse. Why would Ben lie to me?

There was nothing from Mags, so I rang her phone again but it went to answerphone. She must still be dealing with the aftermath from her father's fall.

"Hi, Mags; hope your Dad's okay. Let me know when you get a minute," I said. "Oh, and by the way, did you move Henry down into the cellar? He wasn't upstairs when I checked. Talk soon."

I went to the kitchen for a drink and, as I got to the doorway, another faint odour drifted towards me. This was more oil than smoke. Maybe the problem with the heating was more serious than we realised. I'd have to ask George if he could have a look at the boiler when he came. Meanwhile, I'd make myself a coffee and settle down to work.

But after half an hour of starting and deleting the same sentence, I was cold and sweating simultaneously. I threw down my notebook and seized *Titus*. Other people's stories had a way of calming and clarifying the problems in my own life.

Other people's stories. I paused. Like the one Lavinia used in *Titus*, to name her attackers. An idea peeked from a dark little recess in my mind. What if I put my thoughts into someone else's mouth? Used their voice to tell my story? Would it work? Maybe it wasn't a diary I should be writing, but a play: a medium I was much more comfortable with.

The idea grew. I'd been writing someone else's story for some time, of course: Henry's. Opening my laptop, I called up the blog I'd started experimenting with. Here was a tale already formed, and one with which I had an instinctive bond. Henry's fiancée, Elizabeth, could be my mouthpiece. Opening up a new document, I typed the first title that flashed into my mind – one I hoped might speak for others who had gone through similar experiences: *Lost Voices*. And then I started work in earnest.

By two o'clock, I could hardly believe that a (very) rough draft of a one-act play was sitting on my screen, three-quarters done; I'd even ignored my inbox. It had seemed entirely natural to write Henry and Elizabeth's story, centring it on the supposed performance at the manor in 1593, and thus interweaving it with snippets from Shakespeare's *Titus*. With that framework in place, everything flowed beautifully – until the climax. And then I came unstuck.

I couldn't write Elizabeth's rape scene without making it stupidly over-dramatic or trivialising it. Either way, it didn't sound real – because how could you show something so horrific and life-changing in a few words? My mind went back over *Titus*; perhaps that was why Shakespeare had chosen to leave so much to his audience's imagination. But then his descriptive brilliance more than made up for the lack of onstage action. Without a pivotal rape scene, my own play felt empty.

I couldn't face any lunch, but perhaps a glass of white wine would ease the flow. I got up and poured one, and as I sipped it, recalled the exercise I'd played with Ben's students, where I'd encouraged them to write their characters' thoughts between the spoken lines. *'We all run a continuous dialogue in our heads,'* I'd told them. *'And often, what we think is so much more potent than what we allow ourselves to say.'*

Maybe I could try something similar with Elizabeth's character? Thoughts would be freer and easier to write than polished lines, and they could be erased afterwards. No one but me need ever see them.

Tentatively, I returned to my scene, at the point where the justice had trapped Elizabeth in his chamber. His first line was a threat: *'You will never speak of this.'* But it hardly evoked the terror I knew full well she must have felt, and I couldn't bear my play to be a shallow sketch of her fate. I flicked back through my copy of *Titus* to reread the scene just before the brothers, Chiron and Demetrius, rape Lavinia. And the first line I encountered made my stomach roll.

'Nay, then, I'll stop your mouth.'

I'd always skimmed over this section, and never realised how visceral the sounds were in that one line: the way they conjured the rough feel of a man's hand; the violent forcing back of breath. My own breath snagged in my throat at the thought.

And this was why I hadn't wanted to do Titus.

The words weren't quite the same as the ones I'd heard twenty-four years ago – but similar enough to make my skin lift.

'You stop still, or I'll bloody well make you.'

The present fell away like a landslip around me; I was back in a dimly lit box-room at an illicit school-leavers' party with that voice in my ear; hot moisture on my neck; slim fingers smelling of nicotine jammed across my mouth, making me retch. For once, I'd lied to my mother – told her I was at the cinema, or she'd never have let me go. But I was desperate to be at the party because Ross was going, and I wanted to try to impress him. I'd failed; he was sitting on the stairs, kissing another girl – and I was being pushed face-down on a bed among the guests' coats, by Scott Sutton: a boy who'd only joined our sixth form a few months ago. I'd never even spoken to him before tonight.

I couldn't yell, couldn't even breathe as his other hand yanked up my dress. *God, no.* I couldn't let this happen! But the more I struggled, the more he tightened the vice-like grip of his legs around mine.

"Now then." He pushed his wet mouth close to my ear. "You know you've been asking for this all night, or you'd never have come upstairs. Anyway, you're sixteen, aren't you? Old enough to know what you're about."

I choked, trying to speak… trying to explain. I'd only let him kiss me to make Ross jealous. When I came upstairs to the loo, I'd seen them: Ross and his girl, mouths locked together, his hands caressing her waist… her thighs. So, when I found Scott waiting for me on the landing, I'd let him press me against the wall and kiss me, too – because I was desperate for Ross to think of me as something other than the class geek. But I'd never agreed to go into a bedroom like this.

"No!" I managed to drag my mouth free. "Please! I didn't mean… you pushed me in here. I don't want this!" His hand was back over my mouth; I wailed against it, thrashing my head, trying to get enough purchase to bite him, so he'd let me go; but he was strong.

"No! Please! I don't want this!" I twisted free again, screaming for help, but the music from downstairs was thudding through the floor, drowning everything. *Please, please let someone hear.* Then Scott was on me, trapping me underneath his body, thrusting my head forward. His hasty fingers peeled my dress further up over my back, and my legs were pinioned to the bed by his.

I thrashed desperately, trying to get my mouth free, but his hand cupped my head and rammed my face hard into the bed. *Please, let me breathe.* Sounds receded into the distance: a door thudding shut; Scott panting in my ear. I was fading, wondering if he was going to smother me. The hand on my head loosened its hold and I freed my mouth, dragging in air, but too weak and dizzy to focus on the room around me, never mind fight back.

A zip rasped, and I bucked my head up, but it was plunged down again, and I was drowning, drowning in nausea.

Christ. I can't stop him. I was hauled backwards and bent over the edge of the bed, legs splayed, dread squeezing my belly.

"That's better, sweetheart," Scott murmured, in my ear. "You know this is what you want."

Never. I never wanted this!

Now I could feel him, hot and hard between my legs and my chest pounded against the mattress. I wailed in shock as he thrust inside me and it pierced and burned.

"That's it," he murmured, bending over me, his lips on my cheek. And I could hear him smirking. "You stay quiet, now, and enjoy." And then I sobbed as he rammed into me, over and over, faster and faster, his breathing hoarse, till I thought I was going to pass out.

"Shit!" He shuddered violently against me, gasping, and I stayed still, praying it was over. "Jesus. That was good." Then I felt him pull out of me, cursing. "Oh, Christ! The bloody condom's split." His hand twisted in my hair, yanking my head up, and I gasped in pain. "Are you on the pill? Answer me. And it had better be a sodding yes."

I nodded, terrified and shaking, not daring to do anything else. He shoved my head back down.

"That's all right, then."

There was an explosion of knocking at the bedroom door, but before I could scream out to whoever was there, his hand landed back over my mouth.

"Scott?" A girl called from outside. "Are you in there? Lennie says he's got to take Melanie home. So, you need to get downstairs, now."

Scott spat and swore into my ear, and I turned my head away, sobbing. "Tell him I'll be down in two minutes." I could hear someone pushing against the door, and squirmed beneath the hands pinning me down.

"He needs to go now," said the girl's voice. More expletives from Scott. He put his mouth right against my ear.

"Right. I'm going to stand you up, and you're going to get dressed. And if you scream, I'll hurt you. Understand?"

All I wanted was to get out of this alive. I nodded against his hand, and the smell of stale smoke overwhelmed me. For a moment I was terrified I'd vomit into his palm, and shut my eyes, fearful of what he'd do. I couldn't see his face, but I could feel its light smattering of hair against my cheek.

"And one more thing," he murmured. "You wanted this; you totally led me on. Everyone downstairs saw you come up here with me. So, if ever you say otherwise, I'll tell the whole bloody school you're a whore, and you were begging for it. Because that's how it was. You can't take a boy that far and then say no. Got it?"

I nodded again, flinching at a memory of the vicious belting I'd had, only for letting the boy next door kiss me at his tenth birthday party. My mother must never know about this. Ever.

Then his hands were gone; he was gone, thudding the door shut behind him. I was alone, and it was quiet, so quiet. As though the world had stopped to watch and listen in on my shame.

I had to get dressed and go home, but my mind wouldn't work. Eventually, I made it to the bathroom, bent over, bruised and hardly able to walk. As I glanced down the stairs, Scott was in the hall, holding the front door open and another, bigger, boy was halfway out. Cigarette smoke curled around Scott's head as he looked up at me, exhaling a wreath of it as he smiled. I rushed inside the bathroom, retching, and locked the door. And washed, and washed myself, sobbing at the blood, feeling I would never be clean again; shutting my eyes so I couldn't see my face in the mirror. *It wasn't my fault.* I repeated the words, like a mantra. But then, I'd gone upstairs with him, hadn't I? Let him kiss me and put his hand on my breast. Who was going to believe I'd said 'no' to the rest?

'So now go tell, and if thy tongue can speak.'

As I awoke into the present, the line was staring up at me from Jake's copy of *Titus*, lying open beside my laptop.

TWENTY-NINE

'…his guilty hand plucked up the latch,
And with his knee the door he opens wide.'

(The Rape of Lucrece)

Where on earth had I put my phone?

It was past four, and getting dark outside – and I really needed to talk to Mags. *Lost Voices* was finished and attached to an email addressed to Louise. I felt as though I'd climbed Everest; but I didn't want to send it without talking to my closest friend.

I was drained. My 'between the lines' exercise hadn't gone as planned, though it had added a whole new dimension to the play. I could barely believe that I'd managed to write so much for Elizabeth, but with my own memories still coursing through me, I'd produced a monologue for her that felt and sounded better than I'd ever dared hope. The problem was, it sounded far too modern, and try as I might, I couldn't force it into sixteenth-century-speak. So my solution was to switch the play between past and present by introducing a contemporary narrator, with her own story to tell. *Enter a modern Lavinia.* Key scenes could then play out alternately from different ages, one each side of the stage, each story fleshing out the other, bringing new depth to Elizabeth's lines.

I wasn't quite sure how I'd managed it, but as long as my narrator remained anonymous, my paralysing fear didn't raise its head. I could name her later.

The last section of the play still needed work, but I had to send it before I changed my mind – as soon as I'd spoken to Mags. I looked around for my phone again. I was certain I'd left it on the bar, but now it was gone. It wasn't in the kitchen, either. I spent the next fifteen minutes hunting: turning out my bag, my bedding, my bedside table. Nothing. Panic sprouted in my chest. Had I dropped it on the river path? *No.* I hadn't taken it out with me; I was sure of that. What on earth was I going to do if I couldn't find it? I ran downstairs and turned over my belongings again, but there was no phone.

My inbox pinged in the silence, and I hurried across to my laptop, hoping it was from Mr Norwich; then stilled in surprise at the sender's name. 'Aroma.tea@gmail.com.' I was about to delete it, and then I read the subject line.

Henry.

There was no message; just three images as attachments.

Don't open them, whispered a voice in my head. But I'd overreacted in the past; maybe it was someone in my cast. There had been images of Henry circulating on Facebook since the *Hamlet* workshop. Cautiously, I clicked on the first attachment.

Sure enough, a photo of a skull sprang up, a speech

bubble swelling from its mouth. I let my breath go. It was obviously a joke. The words inside the bubble were rather small, so I bent to read them, then shrank back.

Enter Lavinia.

Maybe it was Isla, messing about. The other attachments would doubtless solve the mystery. I clicked on the second, and the skull reappeared, but with a different caption. There was something macabre about it, as though the words were spewing from the skull's grinning mouth:

Let my spleenful sons this trull deflow'r.

It was one of Tamora's lines and Lavinia was the 'trull' or whore her two boys would rape and disfigure. No way could this be Isla. I should close this down, now. Delete it.

But I couldn't. My fingers guided the mouse pointer to the third image. Yet another skull, this time with a superimposed grey tongue curling out of its mouth as it 'spoke':

But when you have the honey you desire,
Let not this wasp outlive, us both to sting.

Tamora again, instructing her boys to kill Lavinia when they'd finished with her. Shit. This wasn't funny. Who the hell had sent it? Underneath was a message:

Still in the dark?

I sat down, trembling. I should call the police right now, while I still had some vision; but where was my bloody phone? I turned my eyes to the bar again, willing it to be there – and then spied the landline. Mr Norwich had talked about getting it reconnected in one of his last emails. Maybe he'd done it; if so, he might just save my life. I sprang up, knocking my chair sideways, and made my way to it, grabbing the receiver and pushing the 'call' key hard. But there was only a hollow click.

A sob pushed up into my throat as I stupidly clicked the button on and off. *What was going on?*

I rushed to the table where I'd left my coat when I came in from my run, and shrugged it on, shaking. Time to leave.

As I turned, another ping from my inbox fractured the silence. I stared at my laptop, knowing I should ignore it. Knowing I should get outside. But I didn't do that, either.

It was from the same sender. Again, I knew I should leave it… but the heading mesmerised me.

Time I came clean, Jenny Grogan Watson.

My tongue cleaved against the roof of my mouth. *Mark.* Mark or Ross. It had to be one of them; only they would use that name. *Please don't let this be Mark.* My fingers gripped the mouse, almost crushing it as I prayed for this to be just some stupid prank. I scrolled down, but there was no image this time, just a line or two of text.

Let's play 'tell me my name'. Are you good at riddles? All you have to do is take two times 'you' from my surname the wrong way around.

My mind was in freefall. *My surname?* This was insane. And as I watched, yet another email appeared. 'M. Radford'. It *was* from Mark. Dream-like, I clicked on it.

Hi, Jenny, Do you think we could talk? Sooner rather than later.

Oh, no, please. Surely he wasn't bitter enough to want to frighten me this much – just for revenge? And then I recalled his shrug when he'd deliberately hurt me; the constant flicking of that little knife when we'd talked about Scott.

Another ping from my inbox brought my eyes painfully back to the screen. It was from 'Amora.tea' again, with a heading that made my scalp crawl.

Nay, then; I'll shut your mouth.

And underneath was just one line: *Nice coat, by the way.*

I stared down at my black puffer jacket, and then wildly around the pub.

He could see me.

My vision began to pulse, and within seconds, grey and black patches were hovering at its edges, like microbes from some deadly virus, seen under a powerful lens. Everything in me was urging me to *run*: the word screamed through my nervous system like a fork scoring glass. But my legs wouldn't move.

I leaned forwards, hands on the table, panting, as a kaleidoscope of images streamed through my head. The man in the agency, in the olive-green hoodie. The strange texts. *You do realise by now that I made a mistake?* The coat; oh, God, Helen's coat. Nausea rose up. Her attacker had mistaken her for me. The note with the missing letter; the rosemary. Someone wanted to torture me... and the clue lay in those emails.

Nay, then; I'll shut your mouth.

"Stop still, or I'll bloody well make you." Those words hissed in my ear, just as they had when I was sixteen, paralysing my limbs while my mind fought to understand who was hunting me, and why. And then the pieces of the puzzle began to lift and shift in my head. The first was Demetrius's line, from *Titus*: Tamora's son, and one of Lavinia's rapists. The second, spoken by Scott Sutton, to me. But Scott was dead. I pushed my head into my hands. Think. I had to think. I needed to know this wasn't Mark.

Demetrius. I replayed George's answerphone message in my mind. *Dmitri! Dmitri Alexander.* A man using

Demetrius's name. Those last, taunting words on my screen seemed to glare at me. *Still in the dark?* Darkness, and light... *the electrician.* The smooth-shaven man in the Aran sweater at the auditions who had a 'bit of a beard' when George first met him – and who, according to Gordon, seemed well versed in a lesser-known Shakespeare play.

'Take two times you from my surname.' Understand this, and I would know who my tormentor was.

Whose surname? The electrician? *It didn't make sense.* And what did *Titus* have to do with him – and me? In some bizarre way, it felt as though the play itself was stalking me.

Two times 'you'. 'Double you'. But Alexander had no 'w', I thought, wildly. Who did I know with 'w' in their name?

My mind went back to that strange email address: 'Amora.tea@gmail', and realisation flooded me. *How could I be so stupid?* 'Tea' meant the letter 'T'. Move it to the front of the word, and it spelt *Tamora.*

The answer finally slid into place.

Norwich without a 'w', spelt backwards, was *Chiron.* Demetrius's brother. I remembered Mark's words, when I'd reassured him that Scott's death wasn't his fault: *'that's what Len said'.* Scott Sutton had a brother.

And as if on cue, the latch on the front door lifted.

My heart was pummelling my chest wall; I couldn't calm it and I couldn't run. But I wasn't going to give up, either. The only thing to do was get a message to someone; there had to be a way.

Wait. My email to Louise was still on screen, ready to send. My vision was failing now, but the laptop had a QWERTY keyboard. I'd never been so grateful in my life that I'd learned to touch-type. I felt my way into my seat, grasped the mouse and clicked on the message; then by pushing my nose almost into the screen, managed to position my cursor in the subject line. I ran both sets of fingers over the keys, anchoring them on the familiar middle row, feeling my way: left little finger slightly to the right of the broader caps lock key. Leave two keys clear. Then spread the right fingers.

Through the thrumming of blood in my head, I heard a distant knocking – from the back door this time. I was running out of time. Fingers slipping with sweat, I felt for the caps lock and turned it on, and pressed control/B for Bold; then concentrating so hard that my forehead ached, I typed in: HELP ME. SOMEONE TRYING TO GET IN. I THINK MY BOSS, ALIAS ELECTRICIAN – ASK GEORGE. REAL NAME LEN SUTTON.

I managed to position my cursor underneath, above the play's title, and typed the names I hadn't been able to bear seeing in print: Narrator: JW; S: Scott Sutton. This is my story. HELP ME.

The darkness was closing in around me. Groping for the mouse, I pushed my face close to the screen, found the 'send' button and clicked it. *Louise, please pick this up.*

I sat motionless in the silence, listening. George had said someone would need an axe to get through these doors, so maybe it was okay; the windows were bolted. I was safe. The knocking had stopped.

Then it started at the front door.

I felt my way shakily behind the bar towards the back room, an idea forming in my mind. The cellar had a bolt on the inside. Once I was in there, no one could get through. It was a better chance than rushing blindly out into the dusk.

As I reached the little lounge, a rush of memory made me gasp. My phone; I'd probably left it there when I had lunch – on the little table, under the window. I made my way to it as quickly as I could.

And then I saw him.

The pale shape of Henry. I could just make it out, through the clear holes in my vision, there on the table. I stretched out a hand to make sure, and shuddered as it came in contact with rough bone. He wasn't there this morning. Which meant... *whoever this was definitely had access to the pub.* I covered my pounding head with my arms. If that was the case, why was he outside, trying to get in?

A metallic clink brought my head up; the back-door latch this time. Then the knocking started again, and my body shook. My only hope was the cellar, but my legs wouldn't move.

"Jenny? Are you okay? Sorry to be a nuisance, but I can see the lights on," came a tentative female voice. And the world spun to a stop.

Tara? What was *she* doing here, in the dark? Tears of thankfulness and relief rushed and swelled towards my throat. She'd have a phone; maybe a car. I was saved.

Then a pair of arms came from nowhere: a hand clamped itself over my mouth; another snaked around my body, thrusting me hard against a warm, muscular chest and belly. I felt something sharp digging into my side through my coat, and my arms and legs stiffened, quivering like an arrow freshly buried in a target. I didn't have to see what was piercing my skin to know he had a knife.

"Quiet, now," purred a man's thick voice in my ear, tinged with Yorkshire and edged with grit. "There'll be time for screaming later."

THIRTY

'Remember me.'
(Hamlet)

"Stay still, or I'll slit your throat." Moist lips buzzed in my ear. "I can, you know. Me father were a butcher. I know just how to do it, for t'best effect."

My strength ebbed away. As I sagged against the body behind me, it shifted, and a hand stripped my coat over my arms and discarded it. The blade slid up over my sweater, and a rough thumb caressed the skin around my throat. I was desperate to scrape in some air, to swallow; but terrified in case the movement closed the hair's breadth between me and the knife's edge. I couldn't think beyond my next lungful of air.

"Are you going to stay quiet?" My attacker moved the knife away a few inches, so I could nod. I did so, very slightly.

"Good girl." He eased his hand away and I rasped in air. "Now, we can't have anyone raising the alarm before I've done what I came for, so you're going to open that door, and tell the girl who's out there that you're all good, but you're too busy to talk to her right now."

My knees weakened in momentary relief. He wasn't going to hurt Tara.

"If you don't do as you're told, she might get more than she bargained for," he said, in my ear. "Understand?"

I nodded again, carefully. The wild idea of making a break for it at the door died stillborn. Tara would never react fast enough, even if she stood a chance of outrunning him – and my vision was still blotchy. Then I remembered the cellar. If I could only distract him, I could make a dash inside, bolt the door and wait for help. Surely Louise would read my message?

But I couldn't risk any distraction involving Tara. I had to make sure she was safe.

"Good." He pushed me towards the back door. "Now, I'm going to be right here, behind this door, with this blade in your back. If you don't do as you're told, you'll end up in little pieces – and her, too." He leaned forward, and his lips brushed my ear. "*Remember*," he breathed. "You know who I am, don't you?"

I nodded, once. I only recalled Scott having the trace of an accent, but it was unmistakably the same.

"Jenny? Are you in? It's Tara." She banged on the door a bit louder. I had to answer.

I eased my bruised throat into a swallow, not sure if my voice would work.

"Okay, Tara, hold on a second." It was hard to keep the panic out of it, but I must have succeeded; I was still alive. My fingers felt for the bolt and drew it back, then I turned the key, feeling the blade slide away from my neck as the bulk of the man behind me moved sideways. He mustn't know about my sight.

Drawing the door open a crack, I peered out, my body rigid behind the frame, even though my mind was screaming to peel it open and run, as best I could. The security light juddered on, and segments of Tara's face swam into view. I had to act like hell now, to save her.

"Jenny, I'm so sorry. You weren't asleep, were you? Are you okay?"

"Oh, yes, yes; I'm fine. Only busy working." I rushed into speech, my mind racing. Had she walked over in the dark?

"Okay. I know I probably shouldn't have come." There was a nervous smile in her voice. "Only… I had something to ask you about the auditions, and didn't want to say it over the phone. I got a friend to drop me over after school."

My mind leapt. Her friend had a car? Could we both make a run for it?

"Are you… on your own?" I asked, forcing my lips into a smile. You could hear a smile, and I wanted to reassure the owner of that knife, for Tara's sake.

"No. Jason brought me on his bike. He's gone up the lane to find a postbox. Don't tell Mum, will you? She hates motorbikes."

My brief flicker of hope died. We couldn't all get away on a bike. Behind me there was a stirring of breath, and my heart rate spiked.

"Tara, I'm so sorry, but I've got some really important work that has to be done tonight," I said, keeping my voice light. I'd never been so glad of my mother's training. "Can I call you, in a bit?"

"Actually, it won't take a minute. Um... I only wanted to say, when you're casting, please can I not be considered for Lavinia? Because I know what'll happen. People will say you only picked me because of my... because she ends up..."

And I understood. She was talking about her scar.

"I was thinking... maybe the clown?" she added, hopefully.

The knife nudged my side, and I only just stopped myself from crying out. I had to get her to leave.

"Tell you what, let's talk tomorrow; I promise I won't decide till then." A wild idea slipped into my head. "But... you should think about Lavinia, Tara. The clown isn't much of a character. He's only on for a second, and really not important."

There was a surprised pause. "But..."

Shit. She was going to argue with me.

"Look, I've a call coming in, and a lot on. I must go. Sorry, Tara." I was rushing, but I couldn't keep this up much longer. "Have a read of Act 4, Scene 1 – it's a key scene for Lavinia. There's a word or two you'll have to look up, so ask Louise, if you need help. I'll call as soon as I'm free."

Her eyes and fingers went to her phone, and I tensed. *Don't look it up, now. Not till it's safe.*

"Listen; I've really got to get this call!" I said, brightly. "We'll speak later." Then with a quick smile I pushed the door shut and leaned my head against it. I had only a second's relief before Len's hand was back over my mouth.

"Not a sound," he murmured in my ear. We waited, his breath lifting the tiny hairs on my neck. *Please go, Tara.*

Her footsteps crunched away along the gravel at last, and I felt sick with relief. Now, I could only pray she'd understand my message… and that I could find a way of staying alive until someone came.

"Good. Let's get down to business."

I was dragged backwards to the cellar door and, with a jolt of terror, saw that it was already ajar. *This was the latch I'd heard lifting.* He'd been in the cellar all along.

"Well, then; you being so clever, you'll have worked out what those emails mean, by now?" he murmured. I stiffened, and he laughed. "Aw. Thought you were the only one who could understand a bit of Shakespeare, did you? You know, people have underestimated me all my life: the lad from Leeds, who'd never amount to much. But I'm quite proud of my little performances, as far as you're concerned. And I'm sure you'll appreciate the choice of setting. Very theatrical." He pressed his mouth to my ear. "The perfect place for your very own debut as leading lady. *Enter Lavinia.*"

The last two words were a whisper, but the pictures they conjured flushed the life from my legs, as the chink of my father's belt had done when I was a child. *Lavinia was raped and dismembered in a dark pit.*

As he freed my mouth to bolt the door, my body emptied itself of a scream that ricocheted off the walls and tore at my throat. In an instant, it was forced back inside my gullet, and I choked against his fingers.

"Please," I sobbed, as he relaxed them.

"Shut it." He kept my body tight against his shoulder. "I've waited a long time for this, and I don't want it to be over too soon." The hand around my waist moved down over my belly, and I flinched, all my muscles shrinking. "Fear," he murmured, in my ear. "This is what it feels like.

Utter loss of control. I want you to suffer like I have. Like my brother suffered. If he'd lived, the doctor said he would have lost all control over his body; did you know that? How does it feel to be that afraid, Jenny Watson? Shall we find out?"

The arm on my neck tightened, and I fought to breathe; blood pounding in my head. The world receded around me. I was going to die.

Then his arm loosened and air rattled through my swollen throat. I was barely aware of him hauling me backwards into the cellar; bumping me down the steps. My lungs were bursting, eyes staring wide. Through my mottled vision, I could make out jigsaw shapes of our shadows dancing like grotesque puppets on the wall.

My foot knocked against a candle as he pulled me off the bottom step. Random thoughts played in my head. *Candles.* Mags had unearthed a box of fat church ones last time she was down here. And everywhere around me, through a film of shifting vision, I could see candles flickering. They made the cellar feel like a cathedral tomb. Was I never going to come out of here? Or if I did, would I be…?

I kicked out against him. In a breath, I was slapped hard against the cellar wall, pain exploding through my head. The world turned liquid around me.

"Now you behave yourself, little lady, or there are things I can do with this sweet blade – oh, you can't even imagine – if you don't do as you're bid." His blurred face was only inches from mine. "And the wonderful thing is, you won't even die."

I slipped into unconsciousness.

The next thing I knew was a hard, lumpy surface beneath my back and a splitting pain in my head. As my eyes opened, fluctuating candlelight came into being around me. I could make out the shape of an old wooden ladder, propped against the wall nearby, and a pile of wooden packing cases. And with a start, I realised I could see. How long had I been unconscious? My fingers curled around lips of rough material beneath me. Hessian. It scratched against my bare legs: I was lying on sacks. A whole row of them, filled with something hard that was sticking painfully into my back and shoulders, and it hurt to move.

Bare legs.

Where were my jeans and panties? Then my memory flooded back, kick-starting my limbs into helpless shuddering against the sacks.

"There, there," said a soft voice, and Len Sutton's smooth-shaven face looked down into mine, candlelight playing on the caramel streaks in his hair. "You were out for a little while. I hit you a bit harder than I'd intended… but that's your own fault, isn't it? Perhaps you'll do as you're told now."

I screwed my eyes shut, dragging in breaths that never seemed to reach my lungs.

"Open your eyes. Come on; let's have a look at you."

Terrified of provoking him, I stared up into lion-brown eyes that were oddly bland and yet speculative, and my stomach jolted.

"Recognise me now, do you?" he said. "From the agency? And the auditions, of course. The accent's a bit different, but that's all down to training. They say you never really lose the voice you were born with."

'*I were born in Leeds.*' Scott's voice whispered through my head and I stilled, realising at last who I'd seen behind those eyes.

"You see the likeness, too, then?" Len said, as his eyes left my face and slid down over my neck and breasts, to my belly. "People always did say that Scott and I had the exact same eyes." I watched as the veil of blandness melted, and the predator seeped through. "You know, I'd been following you for a while, trying to work out how to punish you for what you did to Scott."

For the first time, I found my voice. "I didn't do anything," I panted.

"Shut it!" He pushed his face close to mine, grasping my chin with his hand, his teeth bared. I recoiled from the stale smoke on his breath, but he forced my head back. "This is all your bloody fault; *all of it*. You couldn't keep away from him, could you? I told him what you were, *and* he believed me. Then you went and fed him a pack of bloody lies about his father."

Mark. He was talking about Mark.

"I didn't tell him anything!" I choked.

"Like hell you didn't!" He spat, over my shoulder, and I screwed up my face against the droplets. "He wouldn't even speak to me afterwards. I kept phoning him, sending texts; but nothing. And then he told me. You had a meeting with him, didn't you?" I gasped, and a tremor ran over his face. "And I nearly killed that poor bitch by mistake, down by the river – all because you made me lose my sodding temper!"

Helen. I closed my eyes, in misery. Oh, God. She had been so close to death – and for what?

"Up until then, it were all just about fear and humiliation: I wanted to destroy every last thing you cared about – as you did for me." His top lip lifted, showing even teeth that seemed too white for his face. "But then I got Mark's text; and that changed everything." He leaned over me, his voice thick and soft. "As it happens, she'll live. But there's only one way our little story can end."

I stared up at him, my body beginning its involuntary shuddering once more.

"Please. I didn't tell Mark anything."

He grasped my hair and wrenched my head up, so my face quivered beneath his mouth.

"You didn't tell *Scott* anything, either, though, did you – about his kid?" he hissed, spittle dancing on his lips. "All these sodding years, and he had no idea he was a father!" His fingers closed over my skull. "If this were an egg, I'd crush it," he murmured. "How would that feel? The yolk of your brains all over my hand?"

For an eternal moment there was nothing except my thudding heart, his contorted face and that image in my head. Then my screams exploded, convulsing my body as it gave up its terror. He let me go and I yelped again as my neck and shoulders thudded back against the sacks.

When I opened my eyes, he was cradling his head in both hands, the flat of his blade pressed against one cheek.

"Scott raped me!" I sobbed, my voice raw. "I begged him and begged him, but he wouldn't stop. Do you think I would tell Mark that?"

He lowered his hands and slowly turned his eyes towards me. For a moment he stared, incredulously; then his face and body twisted in an eruption of rage.

"Liar!"

Pain sliced across my ear and down my cheek as his hand lashed it.

"Don't you bloody dare say his name!" he bellowed, and I curled up, wailing as his voice split the air around my head. "You left the poor little bugger in a home to fend for himself. You've no right to breathe the same air." His voice cracked. "You broke my brother's heart; the only person in the world I ever sodding-well cared about. I spent my whole life trying to protect him – and you go and destroy him in one day!"

"I didn't tell Mark anything!" I winced away from him as he leered over me, teeth bared.

"Don't you lie. Scott said you swore you were on the pill, you bloody whore!" He rubbed a fierce hand across his wet nose and eyes. "He wanted a boy, all his married life, but his wife couldn't have kids. How do you think she feels now, eh? It's destroyed her. So how many more people are you going to hurt, you useless bitch? Unless I put an end to you?"

No! I scraped myself up on my elbows. "He raped me!" I screamed. "And then he made me say I was on the pill. He threatened me!"

His hands landed on my mouth and neck, pressing down so that my voice died and I could barely breathe; then he watched me writhe until my strength ebbed and all I could do was pray that this wasn't it. That somehow I would be spared.

"So, my little brother raped you, did he?" he spat. I couldn't even turn my head from it. "When everybody watched you go upstairs with him, more than willing. Oh, aye. I saw the pair of you on that sofa, downstairs. He had his hand up your top, and you didn't seem to mind then, did you? That's your idea of rape, is it? Well, I tell you what; when I'm done with you, you won't be in any bloody doubt what's happened to you."

I heaved in air as he released me, my hands trying to scrub the wet from my face as he turned to place the knife behind him. Then he was at my feet, his hands around my ankles, hauling me towards him.

"No!" The scream was in my head; no sound came.

I bucked against him with all my strength and rose up; but he was all arms and legs and muscle, thrusting me down against the sacks. In an instant, the knife was back at my throat and I felt a thin sting along my collarbone, then a trickle of wet. When he raised the knife, the tip was laced with blood. My blood.

"Do that again, and I'll carve you up, like Lavinia," he hissed, through his teeth. "Tongue first. Understand?"

I nodded, my legs thrumming under his hands; my fingers gripping the open tops of the sacks beneath me as I fought to slow my breathing. It was the only way to keep my vision clear; and I had to try. Whatever I said, he was never going to believe me. And no one would get here in time to save me, either. I was alone. The realisation spread through me, and with it, a strange calm. Seeing my own blood on his knife had shocked me beyond panic, beyond numbness, to a new clarity. I had given in to bullies all my life; I'd hidden in corners and kept my secrets, for their benefit. I had begged and pleaded to save myself pain, and tried to make peace because I was desperate for love – all to maintain a status quo that, in retrospect, hadn't been worth protecting. But now I had something to live for. I was actually happy, and I'd fight for that until the last, precious second.

My fingers dipped into the mountains of sharp little crystals that filled the sacks. A memory stirred. Salt. I remembered George saying it was for de-icing the lane. The wisp of an idea uncurled in my mind. If I could just keep Len talking, delay him, I'd have a chance.

My mouth dried as he loosened his belt. "You won't get away with it," I whispered. "There's DNA testing these days."

He gave a crack of laughter. "Do you think I bloody care what happens to me, now? I haven't had a day's peace since Scott died. I'll make a run for it, for sure; but if they catch me, you won't know anything about it. The petrol will see to that."

My stomach dropped. *Petrol.* That was the faint smell I'd detected, earlier.

"There'll be a small, accidental fire, caused by one of the candles catching a thread from one of those bundles of material. With all the paper and wood down here and a couple of leaky cans of petrol – it'll be pretty explosive. You'll soon be overcome by the fumes." He ran a rough finger back and forth across my throat. "I'll be long gone out of the country before they ever link me with you." His mouth opened in a smile. "Because I don't suppose you told anyone about Scott or Mark, did you?"

I stopped breathing. He was right; or he would have been, up until this morning. But now, there was the email I'd sent to Louise, with the play that told my story... and revealed Len's name. Then there was my message to Tara, with the reference from the *Titus* rape scene. For the first time ever, I'd spoken out, and there would be a trail for others to follow, if… *no*. I gritted my teeth; I wasn't going to think about that. While there was hope, I'd hold on.

I closed my eyes, willing myself to lie still and passive as he laid the knife on the sacks beside me and started pulling my sweater and bra free of my arms. *This was my chance.* The second my head and arms were free, I thrust hard against him, and the blade went spinning to the floor as I fought to get up. I made it onto my feet before he overpowered me and pushed me back face-downwards on the lumpy sacks, the knife whispering over my ear.

"And that'll be enough of that," he panted. "So let's make bloody well sure you do as you're told in future."

There was a flurry of movement and the slip of leather through loop-holes, and my body sprang to life again, limbs thrashing. I screamed as the belt split across my thighs; piercing and burning my skin again and again until I prayed for unconsciousness.

"That was for my little brother," Len said, breathing hard over my neck. "The man whose kid you gave away, without a word to him. The man you *murdered*."

"No!" I choked into the sacks, struggling to turn my head to the side to snatch some air.

In the dimness, a streak of light ran along the cellar floor far away to the right, where the bar cellar was. I stilled, listening; praying for it to be someone coming to find me. But the seconds ticked past and no one materialised.

The belt dropped to the floor, and I heard Len's zip peel open. "Let's turn you over," he grunted, and flipped me onto my back. I cried out as the hessian with its traces of salt seared my bare skin. "I want to see your face when I do this."

I couldn't stop my sobbing, but now the pain had ignited something else: a roar of rage that flexed through my body with a primal force.

He thrust my legs wide, then reached behind him and stuck the knife into one of the sacks. It sighed as its contents flowed out.

I had one more chance. Digging my fingers hard into the salty crystals, I dredged up handfuls.

"Your brother raped me, you sick bastard!"

The words screamed up from my core, propelling me like a rocket as I rammed my fists into his eye sockets, flattening my palms and grinding in the salt. I kicked out as hard as I could at his groin, wishing I was still wearing my shoes. Bellowing like a bull in pain, trousers still down over his backside, he staggered back, tearing the knife from the sack as he went. I scrambled up, my legs like water, hardly believing what I'd done.

While he swayed, cursing, one hand over his eyes, I thrust my feet to the floor. I only had a few seconds before he recovered.

"You nearly blinded me, you bitch! Christ, I'll slice you into little pieces for this."

Run, I shrieked, in my head, *just run; anywhere, away from him.* Adrenalin was surging through me, but my legs tied themselves in knots as I turned and fell backwards, over a crate. On bleeding toes and fingers, I crawled across the filthy cellar floor and pushed myself to my feet... and there he was, crashing towards me, one eye still covered with his left hand, his right pointing the knife at my belly. There were obstacles hemming me in on both sides. I edged backwards and my heels hit the wall with a dull thud. There was nowhere else to run, and he was almost on me. In a last bid to avoid the blade, I threw myself sideways onto a pile of material, my head hitting the wall with a thud as my foot caught on a rough piece of wood. The room swam. I looked frantically around for something to help me fight, and saw the lump of wood I'd fallen over, lying at my feet. My fingers closed around it as he launched himself at me.

Then his arms shot forward; I screamed as his eyes dimmed into bloodshot blanks, and he came crashing down to the side of me, splintering a pile of empty crates.

I looked up to see Ben, panting, the bust of Julius Caesar cradled in his arms: his eyes enormous as he gazed down at Len's prostrate body. His mouth was moving, but I couldn't hear what he was saying.

The lump of wood dropped from my hand as he ran to me, peeling off his coat. And as he wrapped it around me, the smell of petrol filled my nose.

Unconsciousness claimed me as I sank into his arms.

THIRTY-ONE

'Give signs, sweet girl,
For here are none but friends.'
(Titus Andronicus)

I was vaguely aware of being lifted and carried... and of a gentle murmur in my ear that went on and on, comforting, monotonous.

"It's okay. You're safe, now, Jenny. Safe, now. I'm going to carry you upstairs. Hold on; let me find something better than this coat to wrap you in."

Safe... a vague unease swam through me as I drifted in and out of consciousness. Noises began to penetrate my mind. Footsteps. People talking.

"Hold on a sec, guys; I'll let you in." Ben. It was Ben's voice. Then a woman's, but I wasn't sure whose.

"It's great you're here. I need some help." Ben's voice, again. "No, I realise, but I daren't leave her down there with him, in case he wakes up."

Nothing connected; my mind was somewhere between dream and reality, carrying me along in a swirl of green water, my legs and arms dancing ahead of me in the current. I watched as they flailed in slow motion, trying to make their way back to me, while my mother's voice whispered through the reeds: *'You can never tell, Jenny. Do you understand? Not anyone. Ever.'*

A memory lit the darkness: my email to Louise. I'd done what I promised I never would, and sent my story out into the world. Mine and Henry's and Elizabeth's… and nothing could pull it back into its hiding place. It was free. I jumped as something dank and cold slithered over my skin, curling around me, pulling me down to where my mother was waiting. *'I'm not your secret, anymore,'* I said. And reached out to gather my drifting limbs.

More voices stirred in the liquid dark.

"Mark, any news on those paramedics?"

Mark. He was here? I stilled, listening for his response, but it was soft, and soon swallowed in other sounds.

Ben's voice cut through them.

"I did think I'd killed the bastard; that bust was heavier than I realised. No, there wasn't enough time, and I couldn't find anything else to hit him with. He's still breathing, anyway… yes, I'm afraid Jenny bumped her head on the wall as she went down. Knocked herself out."

Remember. I had to remember; but my mind was too heavy. I let the current take me upwards towards the light breaking through the water.

"Can he… get out?"

A girl's voice. Tara? She was safe…

"Not on your life. I've bolted it from this side, and the

delivery hatch is shut firm. George and I dragged the water butt over it. He's secure enough."

The rich, buttery crumble of George's voice stirred my consciousness. Memories flicked through my mind: the first time I'd grasped his hand; the feel of it. *Root ginger.* We were standing at the top of the cellar steps. *The cellar.*

"Henry."

There was a hush, then more voices. "She spoke. She must be coming round. Jenny?"

I strained to answer, but my voice couldn't penetrate the water above my head.

"Leave her be; she'll wake up in her own time." *George.* Then a hum of voices, and Ben's rising above them. "That was one of the reasons I came over. Mags was so insistent about this weird message she'd had from Jenny, about Henry disappearing... no; Louise called the police as soon as she got Jenny's email, but she was terrified they wouldn't get here in time. I wouldn't have made it myself, if it wasn't for Mags."

"Who was it? Do you know?" George, again.

"I'm not sure... thank God she managed to break away from that knife."

"He had a knife?"

"Yes. I didn't know how to tackle him without her getting injured, or... worse."

I tried to move, but everything ached. My legs were raw and my head felt as though someone had kicked it.

"You know, Jenny was so clever about all this. She gave Tara the scene reference from *Titus*, where Lavinia scratches the Latin word for rape in the sand." That was Nadine, surely? Tara's mother. I remembered her from the

Speak Out group. Something popped in my mind like a bubble; lighting me up inside.

"So that's how you knew!" exclaimed George. "What was the word, then?"

"*Stuprum*," said Tara and I together.

I hadn't realised I'd spoken aloud; but as I opened my eyes, a circle of faces shimmered into view and I blinked. They were all staring at me, wide-eyed.

"Jenny!" In a moment, Tara was on her knees, winding her arms around me, and I winced. Why did everything hurt?

"Woah; gently!" I heard Ben say, and I found I was lying in one of the big armchairs in the little lounge, wrapped in the quilt from my bed, with my legs up on a leather stool. As I lifted my arms, my fingers rubbed against the familiar softness of my nightdress, and a memory flickered of being in the cellar, and Ben coming towards me with his coat. There was something about that coat…

"That's the ticket. She's back," George said.

"Thank you so much," Tara wept into my lap. "You knew there was someone in here – and you sent me away. You were so brave."

I wanted to pat her head, but my arms wouldn't lift. Nothing seemed to want to respond, including my brain. I could see, though. Everything.

"Um, I think we need to take this very slowly, folks," said Ben, and there was relief in his voice. "Perhaps we should give Jenny a bit of quiet for a few minutes. If you could all go and make some tea, and keep a watch for the police and the ambulance?"

"Of course." Nadine rested a hand on Tara's shoulder. "I'll take Tara home. It's been an ordeal for her, too."

Tara clung to me briefly. "Thank you for saving me," she whispered. I shook my head, then closed my eyes as pain radiated through it.

"Has anyone got any headache tablets?"

My voice came out thick and strange, and I put my hand up to feel my mouth. It felt like a boxing glove. I looked up at Ben, mutely begging him for an explanation.

"Should she have some?" asked Louise.

"I don't think it would hurt."

"I'll see to it," said a voice that made my heart leap. Mark was standing in the doorway.

"You came," I whispered.

He looked at me, then quickly averted his gaze.

"Yes. I… I did message you, but you didn't reply," he said, awkwardly. "I'll go and get those pills."

"She'll be okay." Ben placed a hand on Mark's shoulder as he turned away. I couldn't believe Mark was here, but I also couldn't help remembering a certain remark he'd made – one repeated by Len, in the cellar. *"Nice coat, by the way."* Had he come with Len? No. Surely not.

"I'm so confused," I said, and my limbs began to shudder again. Ben and Louise were beside me in an instant.

"All right; you're all right, now." Ben eased his arms around me and lifted me, while Louise tucked my quilt around me. "I'm going to sit you by the fire, where it's warm," said Ben.

Everyone else melted away. When we got into the bar, he set me down on a leather armchair near the fire, and Louise wrapped her arms around me and held me while I gave myself up to the storm of shaking in my body; helpless against the memories that invaded my mind like scenes from a grotesque horror film. Len leering over me, lashing my legs and face, peeling down his zip. Wheeling towards me with eyes wide and senseless before he crashed to the floor at my side. Ben bearing down on me, holding out his coat.

I stared up at him, swallowing painfully.

"Your coat," I whispered. "The petrol."

He looked at me for a moment. "Yes, there was a spillage where I was hiding, waiting for the right moment to hit that bastard. I think the coat must have soaked some of it up."

The breath I'd unconsciously been holding broke free. *Oh, thank God. A spillage.* Then I shuddered anew as I remembered what the petrol was for, and buried my face in my hands, sobbing. Louise kept talking, stroking my hair and rocking me like a child until I began to calm.

"My head hurts," I said.

Ben knelt at my side. "Here. Mark brought you these paracetamols."

I hadn't even noticed him come and go. I took the tablets gratefully, while Louise held the glass for me and mopped up the water that spilt from my swollen lip.

"I'm afraid it'll be a little while before you can eat or drink properly," she said. "But it will heal, Jenny. It will all heal."

"Welcome back, brave girl," said Ben.

Fresh tears stung the back of my eyes at the tenderness in his voice. And as I looked up at his face, the skin around his eyes folded in that way I loved. I felt a surge of guilt for doubting him. He cared for me, it seemed, along with Louise, Tara, George, Mags and even Nadine. Why else were they here?

Wait. One of them wasn't here. "Mags!" I said, trying to sit up. "She doesn't know!"

"It's fine; I've told her you're okay. She'll be over as soon as she can."

Nadine appeared from the kitchen. "The ambulance is on its way, but there's a major hold-up in town." Her eyes wandered to my face and she winced.

"No worries," said Ben.

Louise stood up stiffly. "You get off, Nadine, and make sure Tara's okay. Jenny's in good hands."

"Thank you," I mumbled, hating the way my voice sounded. "And please, thank everyone for all they've done." Ben pulled a chair up next to me, as the door closed behind Nadine, and I looked tentatively up into his face. "You rescued me," I said. It was almost a question, and he smiled.

"Actually, a lot of people were involved. You have a good many friends, Jenny. And you made an impressive job of rescuing yourself, to be honest."

"How did you know?" It hurt to speak, but I had to piece together what had happened.

"Well, I'd just finished teaching for the day and was on my way over to the museum to do some research, when the college secretary rang me with Mags's number; she said it was urgent. Mags was pretty anxious. She kept going on about some answerphone message you'd left, asking if she'd moved Henry; insisting she hadn't. She'd tried getting you on the mobile or the landline, but there was no answer, and she was so certain something was wrong, I came straight over."

Oh, Mags. My eyes filled. She never missed a detail. I'd lost count of the times she'd rescued me over the last few years. My thoughts turned to Henry, no doubt still on the table in the little lounge. In one way or another, he'd helped to save my life.

I turned to Louise, remembering those last, desperate moments before Len closed in on me. "Did you get my email?" I asked.

She took my hand. "I did. I'd just got in from a workshop in Rushden, and rang straightaway – but like Mags, got no answer. So I called the police, then got straight in my car. Nadine rang me on the way to tell me how worried Tara was after she saw you. She didn't quite know what to do because, apparently, Tara can be a 'bit of a drama queen' – though don't tell her I said that!"

"And Nadine rang me," added Ben, "but I was already on the way by then."

Relief, warm and exhausting, began to soak through me.

"I got here at the same time as Mark," he said, "but as we suspected there was someone in the pub with you, we daren't knock, or call out. It was George who let us in. He'd seen the cars coming up the lane, plus a motorbike earlier, and decided to come and check on you. He managed to open up the old brewery hatch."

Mark. I realised that Ben had no idea who he was. "There's something I need to tell you," I began.

His eyes softened. "No need. Mark told me he's your son."

Despite my painful cheek, I smiled. It was good to hear those words. And yet I had to ask.

"Why did he come?"

"He said he'd received a text from his uncle that made

him really uneasy. He knew the man down in the cellar, though; looked pretty shaken up when I turned the guy over, to check he was breathing."

"I'll talk to him," I said, my throat tightening. *The conversation I'd never wanted to have.* Ben and Louise exchanged glances; God knows what they were thinking. And I remembered what I'd promised myself down in the cellar: if I got out of this alive, I would harbour no more secrets. My gaze went from Ben's gently smiling eyes to Louise's understanding ones. I thought of Mags and George, and all the people who had tried to come to my rescue, in one way or another since I'd come to Wethershall-End, and for the first time in years, knew I really wasn't alone. I thought of my mother, and my parting words to her, as I'd woken: *"I am no longer your secret keeper."* No; I was, and would be, far more than she had ever seen.

"Mark's father raped me." I forced the words out, eyes averted. "The man in the cellar is his brother. I was sixteen. My family persuaded me to have Mark adopted."

Louise came to kneel at my feet. "Brave girl," she whispered, clasping my hands.

But I wasn't looking at her. In the doorway, a fresh glass of water in his hand, was Mark. And I would have gone through every pain I'd endured again to wipe away the desolation in his eyes.

The paramedics were gentle and reassuring. One of them checked me over, while two others went down into the cellar with George, a couple of police officers and a detective to examine Len.

"We'll need to run a few tests in hospital, make sure that

bump on the head didn't do any damage. But your reflexes are all normal," said the paramedic who examined me.

I shot a quick glance back towards the cellar door, panic welling up. "I don't want to go in the ambulance with Len."

"Can I drive her up?" Ben asked. I looked hopefully at the paramedic, and he nodded.

"Yes, that would be fine. Don't leave it too long, though. And water, only, please, until the doctors say otherwise," he added, as Mark appeared with a mug of tea. Mark nodded, still very subdued, and I longed for some time to talk to him.

A string-thin young police officer and the stocky detective I'd seen earlier threaded their way into the bar, followed by George. The detective had a thick-set face and sandy, receding hairline. His grey wool overcoat just about fastened over an ample stomach.

"Aye, it's like I've told you," George was saying. "He came a few weeks ago – told me he were an electrician, here to look at the wiring. I'm the named key-holder, you see, till the property passes to the new owner – and Jake's solicitors said there would be a few tradesmen coming round to assess the condition of the place."

The detective frowned. "I'd like the name and number of these solicitors, please, when you've a moment. And this 'electrician' came back more recently, you say?" He glanced at the police constable, who was tapping away on his tablet.

"That's right," George nodded. "I'll have to ask the missus the date, but it were just before Jenny here arrived. He said he'd been asked to do a bit of work and would be here for a few hours. I left the keys with him, so he could lock up when he was finished, and drop them back. But he were still here at five, so I came up to check on him. That's when I asked to see his ID."

The detective frowned. "So he was here alone for some hours?"

George cast me an uncomfortable look. "I didn't mean to leave him all that time, but we had a call from the wife's sister, you see, to say she wasn't feeling well. So we ended up slipping over there, and… well, we were out longer than we expected."

"I see. It's safe to assume he probably had time to get the keys copied, then," said DS Barrett. George's ears turned red.

A second officer, square-shouldered, full-waisted and exuding efficiency, appeared at the detective's side. "Sir, we're just bringing the assailant upstairs," she said. I looked up, heart jumping.

"I've told them to take the stretcher out the back way." Ben gave me a reassuring smile. "You don't have to see him, Jenny."

I glanced at Mark, who kept his own eyes lowered. I wished I knew what he was thinking.

"I do apologise. Ms Watson, is it?" The detective turned to me, extending a stubby hand. "DS Barrett. This is PC Jenkins and PC Bhatt. We'll be needing to ask a few questions, I'm afraid – which we can either do here, or at the hospital, once you've been treated."

I looked at Ben. "Maybe now is better." *Get it over with.* But I didn't want Mark there.

"Good." DS Barrett got out a notebook, looking askance at PC Jenkins's tablet, which seemed to have frozen.

"Come on, mate." Ben stood up and put an arm around

Mark's shoulders. "Let's go into the kitchen and have that tea."

"So, the emails came from Germany, you think?" DS Barrett was still bent over his notebook half an hour later. "We'll need to take your laptop and the phone we found in the cellar, that Mr Whitaker said was yours? We need to gather what evidence we can from those, but we'll let you have them back as soon as possible."

I nodded. My head was feeling much better, now that the paracetamol had worked, but everything felt dream-like.

He got to his feet. "I'll get back to you when I have some further news, Ms Watson. And PC Bhatt will pop over to the agency and interview this girl, Denise."

As DS Barrett buttoned up his coat again, I looked up to find Mark and Ben hovering in the doorway, and Mark's expression told me that he'd overheard far more than I wanted him to know.

Ben glanced from my shocked face to Mark's. "Right. I'll show you out, Detective, and then I must get Jenny up to the hospital."

Mark and I were left alone in the silence.

"I… was really surprised you came," I said. It was still like speaking through a sponge.

He sat down on DS Barrett's vacated seat, trying not to look at my cut and bruised face. "Yeah. Well, when I called… you know, *him*… Len," he said, "to tell him I'd met you, he was really off with me. The things he said sort of didn't add up, now that I'd actually seen you. And then he sent me this weird text that said: *'She's lying to try and win*

your trust. Ignore it; she won't be bothering you for much longer.'
It made me pretty uneasy, so I called you. When you didn't answer, I figured I'd drive over and make sure you were okay. I'm glad I did."

Ben reappeared. "You need to pack an overnight bag, Jenny," he said. "Do you need some help? Louise stayed on, just in case."

I was relieved, not wanting to talk any more, and knowing that Louise would understand. One step at a time.

The hospital did keep me in overnight, but I was so exhausted that it was a relief to surrender myself to its caring staff. They gave me a thorough check and treated me for shock and cuts and bruising. While my external hurts were attended to, my mind wandered over my situation. I was effectively homeless; I'd have to move out of the pub. And then I found myself thinking about Henry. I wondered if the new owner would keep him, and if he'd ever get to feature in a tragedy – his lifetime dream.

My own dream was at an end, of course; the festival would have to be cancelled. I'd have to ask Mags if I could stay with her until I found a new job. I thought sadly of the friendships I'd made in Wethershall-End, and all the women at the Speak Out group. For the first time, I felt I could belong. But staying wasn't really an option; I'd have to get a job near Mags's house, in case it was a while before I could drive. A desolate little lump swelled in my throat. In the short time I'd been there, I'd become fond of Wethershall-End and The Old Bell. And moving away would mean leaving Ben, too.

Wait a minute. I sat up gingerly, as nurses bustled past in the corridor outside. My 'dream' hadn't dissipated, because of one man. If anything, it had become solid: I now had a set of goals that defined it. What was I doing, giving everything up, when I'd fought so hard to stay alive?

I nursed my bruised cheek. Okay, so I wasn't hired because of any extraordinary gift. But on the other hand, I'd proved I could get a play cast and the festival planned, *and* I'd run a couple of successful workshops: things I'd never have believed were within my grasp. And yes, I could bring off that production of *Titus*, especially with the cast we had.

Len was only posing as the owner of The Old Bell. So who *had* inherited it from Jake Reeve? And might they be interested in the festival going ahead? Even if they planned to sell the pub, it would be more attractive as a going concern. The festival could bring in lots of customers, with Diana at the PR helm. If they'd only agree, I could stay in the village a bit longer… and be near Ben. I didn't want to think too much about what that meant, or where Ben and I were going from here. All I knew was that I was lonely without him, and moving away was somehow unthinkable.

Maybe I could find a job, save up and pay to go to college again. Do a course in theatre studies; or better still, in directing! It would take a few years, but it was something to aim for. I quickened at the idea. The only drawback was earning enough money to find somewhere to live. I couldn't expect Mags to house me for years.

"We'll be along in an hour to give you that sedative, Jenny," said a nurse, popping her head around the door. "And the doctor who checked your sight has given you the all-clear. There's absolutely no damage, he says, and you just need rest. So rest," she added, severely, then smiled as I gave her a thumbs-up. But far from feeling sleepy, I was now wired – and desperate to keep my mind away from the last few hours. To sleep was perchance to dream.

A basket of yellow and red tulips appeared in the doorway, followed by a familiar figure, wearing her blue coat and gloves, her sharp nose pinched with cold. She stopped dead when she saw me, her face quivering.

"Oh, my God. Jenny," she whispered.

"Mags, it's okay." I quickly put out a hand. "Please, don't cry. I'm okay, honestly." My speech still sounded thick, and her pupils expanded. "Be even better when they give me my sedative," I joked. "Though a couple of brandies would do as well. You didn't bring any, did you?"

She dumped the flowers on the floor and rushed to put her arms around me.

"I should never have left you," she wept. "You're not safe on your own."

It took some time to reassure her that I really was all right beneath the bruises, and to even start explaining the events of the last few hours.

"I keep kicking myself for not calling you back," she said, mopping her cheeks with a massive blue hanky. "But my Dad was a bit poorly after his fall, and I've been preoccupied with him."

I gripped her hand. "Oh, Mags! Why on earth didn't you tell me? Is he going to be okay? I rang and rang, but couldn't get any answer. I even thought about taking a taxi over to see you. But then everything…" I shrugged and winced. "Listen: you get back to your Dad if you need to. You shouldn't have come."

"Don't be silly. Dad's fine, now," she said, gruffly.

"Veronica's with him. But I oughtn't to stay long; the nurses said only twenty minutes."

She started pulling her hand away, but I held on.

"No, don't go, Mags. Sit with me." We were in a small side-ward, which I suspected Ben had something to do with, and the other beds were empty as yet. Speaking was a painful exercise, but she was a trusted friend.

"There are some things I want to say; things I should have told you a long time ago. Pull up a chair for a little while."

Mags was with me until the nurses came in to give me my sedative, and I started to get sleepy. My face throbbed from talking, and she kept urging me to lie quiet, but now I'd opened up, I couldn't stop. I even told her about my father, and the day we'd planted the little willow tree; about the bonfire and the precious photograph my mother had burned.

"You know, I almost got George to drive me back to my old home, after my meeting with Mark," I said, "to see if that tree was still there. I even gave him the address, but then couldn't go through with it, so we turned around and came home. I've often regretted not taking a cutting after my mother died. But I was, well, too stunned, really, after what she'd said to me. You know." I voiced it at last. "That she never wanted me."

A nerve jumped near Mags's mouth.

"I never went back after that, and I guess the tree's probably gone by now. My mother was always on about getting someone in to do it. It seems she couldn't bear to have any reminders of my father – including me I suppose."

"Oh, Jenny." Mags turned away and blew her nose. "I can't believe you didn't tell anyone."

I shrugged. "I didn't want people feeling sorry for me. As a kid, I just wanted a normal life, so I invented one in my head. And as long as I didn't admit what it was really like, I got by. But do you know what *he* – Len – said, in that awful cellar? That if I didn't come out of there alive, he'd never be suspected, because I hadn't told anyone. About Scott, or Mark."

"Or your mother," put in Mags.

"Yes."

My face was aching too much to talk now, so we sat in companionable silence; I didn't have to tell Mags that I was terrified of being alone. And as my limbs grew heavy with the sedative, Ben's head came round the door.

"I wanted to be here when you fell asleep."

"I'm glad." I searched his eyes, silently asking him the question I daren't voice. And as though he'd read my mind, Mark appeared, a huge bouquet of mixed spring flowers in his arms.

"Hi," he said with a jerky smile. "I just wanted to see for myself how you're doing. And bring you these."

All I could do was nod my thanks.

"And... I, ah, wondered if you had any room for me to stay for a couple of nights? I don't have any lectures tomorrow, or anything planned over the weekend, and I'm happy to sleep in the bar."

All eyes were on me while I managed to croak out my response. "I'd like that."

"I'll make him up a bed on the floor in the costume room," Mags said.

Ben took my hand. "And when you're feeling better, there's someone who wants to talk to you. A lady called Dorothy Jessop. Apparently she owns the pub."

I stiffened, then winced. It seemed I couldn't move without something hurting. "Did she say what about?"

"Oh, for goodness' sake; don't tell her that, just as she's going off," exclaimed Mags. "You'll worry her."

She had a point. But as I looked around, a warmer feeling dispelled my anxieties. Mark had decided to stay; Mags was here. And Ben's gorgeous hazel eyes were looking at me so tenderly, as I fell over the edge of sleep. *Please don't let me dream.*

THIRTY-TWO

'No legacy is so rich as honesty.'
(All's Well That Ends Well)

"I'll wait here," said Mags, as I hovered outside the door of Dorothy Jessop's room the following afternoon. She was in a small private hospital in Hertfordshire, just under an hour away by road, so Mags had offered to drive me there as soon as I was discharged. I tried not to think about the fact that I was back in my home county. The only home I wanted now was a rambling old pub in Northamptonshire that needed some TLC. It was a few minutes before one; we could hear canteen trolleys clinking along the corridors as lunch plates were collected.

"I thought Ben was coming with us?" I said, simmering with nerves.

Mags frowned. "So did I. He even stayed at the pub last night. But then he went off in a hurry early this morning and wouldn't say where." She flicked her head towards the door. "Go on, then. She won't bite you. I'll meet you in the café when you're done."

I braced myself and tapped on the door.

"Come in," said a low, pleasant voice.

The door opened into a white room, brightened by vases of spring flowers. A pair of ice-blue eyes in a sunken face smiled up at me from a hospital bed, beside which was a green leather chair and a white plastic bedside table with a tray bearing a Perspex water jug and glass. Mrs Jessop was probably in her late seventies; it was difficult to tell. Her hair was pigeon grey with softening white streaks. Its sparseness had been given volume through careful brushing.

"Jenny Watson." She smiled, her eyes lingering on my cut and bruised cheek, and patted the chair next to her bed. "Thank you for agreeing to visit me. Come. Sit. Let me look at you."

She pulled a turquoise velvet bed-jacket more closely around her narrow frame. "I'm sorry to be receiving you here. But I won't be coming out of hospital for a while, and I needed to see you."

I perched on the chair, trying to ignore my aches; glancing around at the mass of 'Get Well' cards that adorned the white walls like many-coloured butterfly wings.

"So, you're the young woman trying to bring The Old Bell back into order."

She put out a mottled hand, as though to reassure me. "A Detective Sergeant Barrett came to see me last night. He had some questions for me, as you can imagine." She leaned back against her pillows. "You know, I still can't believe what he said. Or tell you how" – her eyes rested on my cheek again – "how utterly horrified I feel, at what's happened." I nodded my thanks. "I don't suppose you know: I was Len and Scott's foster mother for a time." I gazed at her, heart thudding. What did that mean? Was she going to defend him in some way? "Len was always difficult." She sighed. "I tried my best, but they'd both had a dreadful childhood: a sick, weak mother; violent father. In and out of care. The damage was done early on, I'm afraid. But I stayed in touch with them after they left. Scott settled down, but Len was still full of big ideas that never worked out."

His dreams, she meant. Stunted, like mine, by life. Perhaps that's why he'd known so well how to draw me in, to taunt me. Despite the warmth of the room, I shivered.

"I helped him to start up his own business as an electrician when the acting thing failed. So of course, when I learned that Jake had left me The Old Bell, I thought maybe I could put a bit of work his way, and he could have a look at the place while I was in hospital." Her stricken eyes met mine. "Of course, if I'd had any idea what he... what he was capable of, I'd never have asked him."

I stayed silent. Was I supposed to feel sorry for him? Mrs Jessop reached for her water glass and took a few shaky sips.

"I think you deserve an explanation," she went on. "I never expected to inherit the pub, you see. I was shocked to hear that Jake had died; we hadn't spoken for a long time. But, well, we were close, at one time." Her ribbed eyelids lowered for a moment. "Though not many people know that. We... married other people, you see, but that never stopped us both wondering what life would have been like together. We had some happy times, when we were younger, and The Old Bell is all I have left of his dear heart, bless him."

She drifted for a moment, her fingers playing over the sheet. "When I heard he'd left me that old place, I was surprised and rather moved, to be honest, that he still treasured those early memories of us. My husband only died two years ago, and I'd promised him I'd never contact Jake again." She picked at a loose thread on her white sheet. "That's why I didn't want any of the locals to know I'd inherited the pub, in case they remembered us. Jake and I," she added, a sad little smile hovering on her lips. "I caused my husband enough pain, and I wouldn't want his name caught up in any gossip after his death. Though I wish I'd had the chance to say goodbye to Jake; he was a good man."

I understood. The Old Bell had been their occasional sanctuary, even while she was still married. Everyone had their secrets.

"I wasn't well enough to go over and see the condition of the place, let alone make a decision about whether to sell it," she went on. "But I thought I'd go ahead and get some quotes done, so that after the operation I could move forward. Jake's solicitor, Mr Arnold, offered to liaise with the key-holder, to save me the worry, and well…" her eyes met mine. "That's how Len came to be involved. Unfortunately, just after that my health took a turn for the worse."

She glanced at me, under her lashes. "DS Barrett said that Len was posing as the pub owner, in order to lure you there?" I nodded, feeling myself flush. My fragile dream had made me an easy target. "But what I can't get over is the nerve of him," she said. "Even the job agency just accepted his word; but then of course, he knew the name of Jake's solicitors, because I'd mentioned them to him. Though surely he must have realised he could get found out at any time."

I thought of all Mags's concerns. And I'd ignored them. But then, if I hadn't, I wouldn't be here, with a play written, and a flicker of hope that I could convince Dorothy Jessop to keep me on.

"Len always was reckless," she mused. "DS Barrett said he probably thought it was a risk worth taking. If he never came out into the open, the only person who would get into trouble was you, for living in the pub under false pretences. He could easily disappear if the alarm was raised."

I moved uncomfortably in my chair; I didn't want to hear any more.

She surveyed me thoughtfully. "But this is not why I asked you here. You've been so patient, and now I'd like to know your side of the story – if you can bear to tell it, my dear. And then perhaps we can find a way through this mess."

My mouth dried to a crisp. Now was the time, if there ever was one, to trot out my painfully rehearsed speech.

"Yes. Of course. But... I've been wondering," I said, clasping my hands tightly together. "If there was any chance I could stay on at the pub till the summer? I know you may still decide to sell it, but I'd love to do the festival, just this once. The play's all cast, you see, and if we can sort out the licences, I could run the pub with a couple of friends who say they'd love to help, so you wouldn't lose money. George used to be the barman, and he's offered to help with the licences and insurance *and* run the bar while he trains me up. That's if... if you're agreeable, Mrs Jessop." I knew George was bursting to get involved; he and Mags had talked about it last night.

"Dorothy, please, my dear." Her thin eyebrows rose as she surveyed me. "Is that really what you want?"

"More than anything."

"I see." She eyed me for a moment, and I waited, heart pumping. "You know, I wasn't sure about selling anyway. How about… we set up a proper contract of employment, and you become my manager, for the time being? Of the pub and the festival? We'll have a meeting with this friend of yours, George, as soon as you're feeling up to it, and sort out a way forward."

I gulped. "You mean, I can stay?"

"Well, yes! We'll have to see how it goes, of course," she said. "If you manage to turn a profit. And I need to consider those repair quotes; the pub needs a fair bit spending on it. It may not be worth keeping. But we'll do our best."

It was more than I'd dared hope for.

"And there's another thing that might help. My friend and I have started a costume hire business, and we've already made a profit." Mentioning that was Mags's idea. The Mile-End Players hadn't paid us yet, but Mags said we could easily set up an account and advertise the costumes online.

Dorothy burst out laughing, and her face was transformed by her bright, youthful smile. "You're nothing if not enterprising! How much were you expecting to get paid?"

I told her, and she nodded. "I think we can stretch to that. I'll see you're paid for all the work you've done so far, too. Now, tell me exactly what's happened over the past two weeks."

Blood was singing through my head. I could hardly thank her enough, and though it was hard to go through the whole story again, it was just a tiny bit easier than with

DS Barrett. She listened, her face a mask; and when I'd finished, she sat back, her eyes glinting.

"You're clearly stronger than you look. I can see, now, why DS Barrett seemed so impressed with you."

I stared. DS Barrett? He'd shown no emotion whatsoever in my presence.

"But there is something I need to tell you," I blurted. If we were going for honesty, she had to know. And I poured out all about my sight problems, and the Speak Out group. "Louise, the leader, honestly thinks that drama workshops, especially the Shakespeare ones, could help women with low confidence and self-esteem. We could put on performances on a regular basis, to give them a goal to work towards. So, I was wondering... would you mind if we held the workshops at the pub? Because for the first time in my life – I know what I really want to do, and this is it."

Dorothy's eyes gleamed. "Well, now you have me really interested. Why don't you come and see me again next week, when you're fully recovered? And in the meantime, I'll get my solicitor to draw up a proper contract. Here, write your details on this pad."

I did so, then got to my feet, ignoring my protesting aches. Nothing mattered now, other than having a job I loved, a home, and friends – and a son – to go back to, even if it was only for a few weeks.

When Mags and I got back late that afternoon, I found the little back lounge of The Old Bell arrayed with flowers. There was a huge basket of red and white roses from the Speak Out members; sunflowers from Gordon and Diana and the Mile-End Players; and a posy of carnations from

Nadine and Tara. I'd been longing to go home, but fearing it, too, in case my memories of Len would outweigh happier ones. But as I looked around, I felt only hope.

Ben emerged from the cellar, followed by Mark. They were both wearing navy overalls splashed with fresh white paint. Ben kissed me on the cheek, and my insides hummed with pleasure and nerves. Mark hovered awkwardly nearby. He didn't hug me, but he was still here. It was an almost perfect homecoming.

"Hello, sweet," said Ben. "We're transforming the cellar. You won't recognise it when we're finished." I attempted a smile. The last thing I wanted to do was think about the cellar, but I forced myself to fix my eyes on its door. It was not going to become another memory I couldn't face.

"Ah, here she is." George appeared round it, wheezing a little from his climb, and clasping a square wooden box that looked as though it belonged in the props department for *Treasure Island*.

"Here, let me help with that." Mark was there in an instant, and the two of them carried the box to the table under the window.

"Jenny, why don't you sit down?" said Ben, as he helped me off with my coat. "We've a real surprise for you." He exchanged a look with George and Mark that bristled with anticipation. "You'll never guess what we found this morning." Mark pulled out a chair for me opposite the box and I eased myself down, my eyes still on Ben's face. It had to be something good; they looked as though they'd won the lottery. Ben nodded towards the box.

It was bound by a tarnished metal panel, in which two keyholes were still visible at the front. Three bottle-shaped metal bands ran up from the back and down over the lid, the larger middle one overlapping a lock that was half consumed by rust. The rim of the lid was nibbled away like a sea-worn groin, showing splinters of umbered wood that had once been golden brown.

"We've cleaned the dust off, though we had to be incredibly careful," said Ben, the trace of a tremor his voice. "Mark spotted it tucked away in an embrasure in the cellar wall. It must be reasonably dry down there, to be so well preserved. But look, Jenny."

His hand moved to the right of the lock. Three letters, curled and blackened, had been scored into the wood. *JHC.*

"John Henry Coates," breathed George. "It were here, all along, and none of us even suspected."

I reached out a finger to touch each letter, imagining the flesh-and-blood hand that had made them, lifetimes ago.

"That's oak, that is," George said, in satisfaction. "Probably worth a bit now. And built to last, which is just as well, with what was in it."

Ben nodded at Mark, who slowly lifted the lid, and a familiar, sour odour rose up. In the bottom of the box was a small roll of grey, suede-like material stained with light-brown patches. I glanced at Ben and his eyes lit in response.

"It's some sort of animal skin. Maybe calf." He held out a pair of white cotton gloves. "Here, I borrowed these from the museum. Handle it carefully."

Fingers trembling slightly, I donned the gloves and stretched in a hand to pull up the roll. As I did so, several fragments of what looked like bone clattered across the bottom of the box.

"From Henry," nodded Ben, as my gaze flew to his. "I've already sent a piece off to Aaron for comparison. It seems that Henry was once stored in this box."

Mark carefully closed the lid of the box and lifted it away. My imagination racing, I laid the material on the table and teased back its edge. Beneath was a small roll of yellowing parchment.

"It was bound up in a number of other papers that disintegrated when George unrolled them," said Ben. George cast him a guilty glance. "But they seemed to be blank; we think they were only there to preserve this one. Go ahead; it's sound."

With a gentleness that was at odds with the adrenalin pulsing through me, I unfolded the parchment. The ink was faded, but unmistakably written in the same spiky hand as the Bennington papers.

"I imagine Edward Bennington copied this out," Ben said. "Maybe it was him who managed to recover Henry; who knows? Anyway, whoever it was sealed this in with his remains, doubtless intent on preserving his story."

The title of the poem had letters missing, but I recognised it. *The Fool's Prophecie*. And at the bottom right of the page was a date: 1596.

"Three years after he died?" I whispered.

"Just about right for recovering the skull and linking it and the poem to John Henry Coates and Edward Bennington," said Ben. "Sadly, we'll never know who the poet was."

"It belongs in the museum, really," George said, "but we wanted you to have your own moment with it, seeing as you're the one who uncovered his story."

I looked from George to Ben, then Mark, my throat

bursting with a joy I hadn't felt since I was seven years old and knew I could write stories. And now that knowledge coursed in me with a new certainty.

"Come on; let's make tea. I've brought some scones and jam," said Mags, breaking the moment and making us all grin. "There's another surprise on the patio. The cast of *Titus* had a whip-round and bought an outdoor heater for the pub. It's waiting for you to try it."

While Mags was in the kitchen, Mark wandered outside and sat opposite me. After we'd exchanged a few bland remarks, he looked resolutely into my eyes.

"You weren't going to tell me, were you?" he said. "What my father did."

My insides flushed with anxiety. "No."

He shook his head. "You know, when I saw Len Sutton, he was pretty brutal about you. That's why I found it easy to believe you never wanted me. I'm... sorry I was so judgemental."

"Oh, Mark." I instinctively reached out, sorrow for him radiating through me. "I never wanted you to find out."

He jumped at my touch but recovered quickly and laid his hand over mine, giving it a brief squeeze.

"No. You didn't want me to know because you thought I'd feel bad about having a father who did something I'm sure he wasn't proud of afterwards," he said. "So you removed the blame from him, for my sake."

I turned my head to where the river shimmered along in the late sunshine. "I didn't want you to be unhappier than I'd already made you. Listen, Mark; I know I have no rights, but—"

"Do you know something?" His eyes searched mine. "You are a nice person. You're also a rare one, and I'm proud of that. Because what you did was an act of unselfishness that means only one thing to me. There aren't many folks I know who would have kept silent for that reason."

My face scorched under his words. I should be glowing with happiness, but I couldn't tell him about the guilt that still coursed through me, stinging me whenever memories of the past haunted me. If only I hadn't given in to my own weakness and gone to that party; if I hadn't tried to make Ross jealous; if I'd stood up against my aunt and uncle and my mother. My own fear had carved out my son's life indelibly.

"I think it's time you stopped blaming yourself," he said, softly, as though he had read my mind. "Sometimes we can't help what life throws at us. And you know, I think I had a much better time growing up than you did, so perhaps you didn't do as badly as you think." Then I knew Mags had been talking, but I was grateful. There were things I'd never be able to bring myself to say to him.

Mags, Ben and George appeared with trays of tea, cakes and scones, and a straw for me to sip through, and in the burst of inconsequential chatter I surreptitiously wiped my face and steadied my spirits. Mags took charge of my phone, which had been returned to the pub earlier that morning by PC Jenkins, and continually buzzed and rang with messages. Ben patiently fielded them for me, until one call took him by surprise.

"Just a second. I'll see if Jenny can have a quick word. It's a woman called Denise, from your agency?" he added.

I took the phone. She was probably calling to tell me I no longer had a job.

"Jenny?"

I was surprised at the anxiety in her voice.

"My God, are you okay? The police have just left. I can't believe what's happened; we were all completely taken in by the guy. Though I guess we should have been suspicious when he insisted on no contact except for email. I feel terrible!"

"It's okay," I said, hoping that my words were intelligible over the phone. My face still felt stiff and painful. "He fooled everyone. Did any of you actually speak to him?"

"Yes. The policeman asked us that. I did. He sounded very well spoken, a typical businessman; and well, lovely, to be honest. I can't believe…" her voice caught. "I'm really sorry, Jenny. It was such a perfect job. And now—"

"It's okay," I said again, and told her briefly about my interview with Dorothy. She sounded as though she was going to burst into tears.

"Oh, that's wonderful! Well, listen, the policeman who came reckoned they've got a lead on the guy who sent the emails: an old school friend from Yorkshire, they said, who now lives in Germany. So don't you worry about a thing. And Jenny, please let me know when the play is on. I'd love to get a ticket. We'll all come."

Touched, I ended the call as Mags appeared with a bouquet of mixed roses and a frown.

"Jenny; these have just come from Helen."

I gasped as she laid the flowers in front of me. "But she shouldn't be sending me flowers! I didn't…" tears blocked my throat. "I've wanted to see her, ever since I realised…"

Mags put a gentle hand on my shoulder. "The coat. I know. I was stupid not to have picked that up. But listen:

she brought them herself. I told her I didn't really think you were up to seeing any more people at the moment."

I was up and gone before Ben or Mags could protest. George was just shutting the front door when I got there, and I slipped out as Helen reached her car.

"Helen?"

She turned, and a tremor ran through her when she saw my swollen face.

"I'm so sorry," I said, my voice catching. "Sorry you got hurt by mistake; and that the police suspected your husband. It should never have happened."

She walked towards me, all her usual gracefulness gone. "Jenny, don't be silly. None of this was your fault. The flowers are just to say... well, I can only imagine what you went through, too." She put her arms awkwardly around me as though hugging an ice sculpture. "*I'm* sorry I didn't pass your audition stuff on," she said. "Your video is... really good. Impressive. If you need any help organising *Titus*, you know where I am."

I watched her walk slowly back over the gravel to her car, seeing her from a new perspective.

"What was all that about?" asked Ben, appearing at the open door.

I waved as Helen drove away. "Building bridges, I think."

"Ah. Speaking of which." He came towards me, and took both my hands in his. "If we're to build any ourselves, there's something I need to say. I wasn't completely honest with you, the night I said I was going up to Leicester." I stiffened, wondering what was coming. "I, um, was in a relationship, a year or so ago," he added. "For about six months. She was much younger; in her late twenties.

When I realised that the age gap was a problem, I thought it best to end it, and did it as kindly as I could. But she'd previously been through a divorce and took it badly; she keeps contacting me. So last Saturday night, she texted me to say she was depressed and thinking about… well, taking an overdose. I completely panicked and went shooting over there. I called her parents on the way, and they were already in the house when I arrived. To cut a long story short, she was okay, but they told me it was best I didn't see her. I still feel terrible about it."

I put a hand up to his face. "It wasn't your fault, either. Thank you for telling me."

He looked down at me with such tenderness that my insides contracted. "I don't want any secrets between us, if we do start seeing each other on a regular basis. And we should take it really slowly this time."

"I'd like that," I murmured, and he kissed the side of my mouth that wasn't bruised.

In the early evening, we all gathered for dinner in the lounge bar. George went home to fetch Vera, and Mags and I were eager to see the woman who had been mentioned so often but never seen. We were surprised when George ushered in a figure half his size, with a tiny pointed face and straight grey hair. In her rust-coloured wool jacket and brown slacks she reminded me of a robin, whose bright, watchful eyes flicked constantly from one face to another. She said very little, though her voice was light and musical when she spoke, and she was economical with her smiles. George said she was "shy of strangers", a remark that earned him a sharp glare of reproof.

"Just because I don't rattle on all the time," she murmured to Mark, who she clearly liked. I could see from Mark's ready smile that he'd taken to both of them. I was content to watch and listen to Mark talk, soaking in the tone of his voice, the tilt of his head; the way he rubbed his nose when he was thinking, or threw back his head when George made him laugh. After dinner, we ventured bravely outside onto the pub patio under the heater, wrapped in our coats and drinking coffee and brandy; listening to the gentle lapping of the river. Then George bore Vera off home, 'before she took a chill'.

"I'll come with you to the car," said Mark. "I need to stretch my legs." Ben got up too.

"I've something for you, Jenny; I was saving it for the right moment. Bear with me."

He disappeared around the corner of the pub, and I raised my eyebrows at Mags. She shrugged. "I haven't a clue."

"Okay," I said, dubiously. "But while he's gone, there's something I need to tell you. Mrs Jessop – Dorothy – seemed really pleased about the costume hire business idea. How do you feel about running it, and helping me with the pub, once we're open? At least until we know what's happening to the place?"

Her face split into a smile that wavered between joy and tears. "Oh, Jenny, that's wonderful! As it happens, I was going to tell you: my Dad's decided to move in with Veronica. He always got on better with her, so I'm not really that surprised. I was a bit down about it, but perhaps now it'll work out better. Are you sure?"

"Mags," I said, awkwardly, "you've done far more for me than any sister ever could. It's fine."

She threw her arms around me, and then let me go as though I was a kettle of hot water.

"Oh, God, Jenny; I'm so sorry. Did I hurt you? No, don't laugh. You'll make it worse."

Ben returned at that point, carrying a twig in a plant pot.

"What on earth's that?" exclaimed Mags. "It looks dead!"

"Jenny knows." He smiled as I ran my fingers over its bumpy grey buds.

"It's a cutting, from a willow tree," I said. "From this one?" I looked towards the river, and he shook his head.

"No. Mags and I had a chat late last night over a bottle of wine, about quite a lot of things; the tree you planted with your father, for one. And how you didn't have anything to remember him by. So, I went to visit your old childhood home. The tree's still there; it's pretty big, now, and the new owners are a nice couple. They let me take this."

A hot, pricking sensation spread from my crown, down over my face and arms.

"And while I was there, the old guy next door came out to see what we were up to."

"Mr Roberts? He's still there?" My voice brittled. He'd always been kind to me.

"He is. He's seventy-nine, now," said Ben. "And on his own; his wife died five years ago. He was lonely, and welcomed a chat; in fact, I'm sure he'd love to see you. Of course, I ended up telling him that you don't have even a photo of your father, and the next minute, he was off into the house, and found this. There's just the one, of him and your Dad in the garden, having a pint together one summer's evening. His wife took it, he says. He's very happy for you to have it, for old time's sake."

My fingers closed on the small, rectangular image he held out. I was afraid to look down. Afraid it could never be what I hoped. But when I did, there was my father's dear face, smiling back at me. Memories of the picture I'd lost to the fire filled my mind, and with them, bitter-sweet snatches of the conversations we could never have again.

I reached out a finger and traced my father's face carefully with its tip. Mark peered over my shoulder. "Your Grandfather," I said.

He raised an eyebrow. "The photographer? Yeah. I can see the likeness, to be honest. To you, I mean."

"Actually, I'd have said there was more of a likeness between him and you," Mags said, scanning Mark's face. "Something in the expression." She was right. I realised that the elusive memory I'd caught that day in the café was my father's smile.

Sitting there with the heater warming us and the mellow light from the old pub swelling at our backs as the evening dimmed into dusk, it was so perfect that I wanted to box it; to hide it away under my mattress, so I could always go back to it if life changed.

Ben looked up from my phone as Mark appeared with another tray of Prosecco.

"Another member of your cast, asking about when he'll get his script."

Mags frowned. "We'll think about that tomorrow."

"You're right. Let's enjoy the moment," Ben said. "You don't get many like this."

We raised our glasses to the stars, and then each other.

"To all our tomorrows," he said. "Welcome home, Madam Director."

EPILOGUE

'And tongues to be your being shall rehearse,
When all the breathers of this world are dead.'

(Sonnet 81)

Five months on, under a late August sun, Mags, Ben and I gathered with our friends by the river. Now Gordon was handing out glasses of bubbly.

"Old Jake would have loved this," said George, coming towards us in his best Sunday suit. He leaned over to kiss my cheek. "Well done, my dear. You're a star."

I blushed. "Not me," I said, holding up my glass. "To all the people who contributed to our success: the cast and crew of *Lost Voices*. I can't tell you how proud I am. And to Louise, who entered it in the Summer Festival. Thank you for having faith in us."

Cheers rang out as glasses clinked, and everyone echoed the toast.

"Where's the trophy, Jenny?" called Louise. "It should be in a place of honour."

Mags held it up, to a burst of clapping.

"But this morning is also about remembering some other people, without whom our journey would never have been possible," I said, when it was quiet. "So we've had a couple of plaques made to commemorate them. The first one is for Janet and Ann Bray: Elizabeth's sisters. It's just across the river where, according to the folk legend, they were hanged. And the other plaque on this willow tree is for John Henry and Elizabeth Coates. On both plaques we've added a line from one of Shakespeare's sonnets."

"*And tongues to be thy being shall rehearse*'," read Sam. "We certainly did that. You gave them a voice, Jenny."

"To be honest, it was more the other way around." I glanced towards the patio, where Ben had placed Henry on his pedestal in the sunshine. Without Henry and all his words had taught me, my own story could have turned out very differently. And now here I was setting out on a new chapter, in which Ben already played a part. It wasn't always easy, but we were making progress. *I* was making progress.

"What's the other plaque on the cherry tree, Jenny?" asked Gordon.

"That's in memory of Jake Reeve and Dorothy Jessop. Dorothy chose the quote, herself: *Journeys end in lovers' meeting*'."

"I'd say that's perfect." George gave his eyes a surreptitious wipe. "It's a shame poor Dorothy never got to see your play – but at least she was there for *Titus*, and she loved that."

A pang of sadness stung momentarily. Dorothy had had so little time to 'tie up the loose ends of her life', as she'd put it, before illness claimed her again.

"No need to worry yourself," murmured George, his hand on my shoulder. "She were over the moon about the festival, and everything you've achieved."

I looked along the river, remembering the line of boats ferrying passengers up from the village between the strings of twinkling lights that George and Mark had spread through the trees; hearing the strains of baroque music from the speakers installed in the branches; seeing the pub come alive again with chattering people, and the costumed figures of actors nervously warming up in the barn. Diana's sterling publicity had even brought a local TV crew to film an excerpt for the news. And there, as now, Henry had sat, atop a rough, wooden pedestal that resembled a miniature gallows. At its foot had coiled a thick, hessian rope. George had done a superb job with effects. Instead of light reflecting off the skull, it eased up underneath him in green swathes and seeped into the hollows of his eyes and nose, spiking out through the uneven teeth; casting long, sharp shadows. I heard the voice-over again, read by Adam in a silence broken only by the river. *'My name is John Henry Coates. I was born here, lived and died here. And this is the story of my death.'*

"It were a rare success," sighed George, bringing me back to the present.

"We could never have done it without you, George." I kissed his stubbly cheek.

"Is Mark coming this evening?" Denise appeared at my side. I smiled at her; here was another unexpected friendship I'd come to value.

"Tomorrow. He's working today." I ran my fingers over a letter in my pocket: his first one to me. Apparently he shared my love of the written word. I cherished its opening: *Dear Jenny-Mum.* He'd started to call me that during the festival, and it had eventually got shortened to 'JM.'

"Have you got your car back yet, Jenny?" Gordon came up to refill my glass, jerking me out of my reverie. I shook my head, wishing he wouldn't always draw attention to what I hadn't managed.

"You can't rush these things," Denise said, squeezing my arm. "It'll happen. And I'm delighted the pub's doing well."

Yes. That was the most important thing. And I hadn't had a vision disturbance for weeks.

Tara came up, her eyes full of news. "Oh, Jenny, I wanted you to be the first to know! I applied for a late place at Durham Uni to do English Lit in September – and they've accepted me. They asked me all about *Lost Voices* at the interview, so I'm sure it helped. I'm going to join their drama society."

I enfolded her in a hug. "That's wonderful, Tara."

Nadine stood behind her, with eyes full of love. Her hand came out to stroke her daughter's hair, as though storing the feel of it in her body for the times they would be apart.

"She'll be fine," I said, and her mouth twisted.

"I know. The only thing is, she's so worried about having to fit in again." The words rushed out, and Tara's face retreated instantly behind her sheet of hair, but not before I'd seen her mother's words reflected there: the fear of facing a fresh cohort of people who would judge her face before they listened to her voice. I put my hands on her shoulders and gently turned her to me.

"It will be different, this time," I said. "Because you have something for yourself. Something you love and are gifted at."

The corner of her mouth quivered. "I know. I want to teach drama eventually. I've known since the night we came to the *Hamlet* workshop."

She threaded her arms around me and we hugged for a long time in silence. Then she was gone, running to tell her friends the news.

Nadine wiped her eyes. "She'd never have had the courage to do this before. Thank you so much, Jenny."

I smiled awkwardly, her gratitude like a present I had no idea what to do with.

As Nadine disappeared after her daughter, Isla collected the trophy and Ben snapped photos.

"Speech, Jenny!" called Isla, and I shook my head.

"After Henry's service," I said. It seemed a bizarre thing to have a celebration followed by a burial, but somehow I hadn't wanted Henry to miss our gathering in the sunshine. He was part of our success.

George brought out the small willow casket we'd all contributed to, for his last journey, and I held it while he laid Henry gently inside. Then I added a new facsimile of *The Fool's Prophecy* and a brief summary of Henry and Elizabeth's story, sealed in an oilskin tube. Mags took my arm and we walked together, Ben and George carrying the casket between them, along the river path in the sunshine, to where the Vicar of St Mary's was waiting to receive us. It was an honour, George said; no one had been buried in the churchyard itself for over a century.

While the Vicar told Henry's story and asked God for

His blessing, a single church bell tolled and, as George and I laid Henry down in the darkness, I whispered my thanks to the man over four centuries old, who had brought so much light to my life. Part of me couldn't bear to watch him sealed away from the life he'd fought so hard to illuminate, yet I knew somehow it was the right thing, this last, silent rest.

He'd achieved his dream: Helen's production of *Hamlet* last month had made sure of that; and I couldn't face the thought of him on a museum shelf. We had his words, as we had Shakespeare's; the essence of their living thoughts, if not the timbre of their voices.

"Any more news on the trial?" asked Gordon, as he and Diana fell into step with Mags and me. I shook my head.

"Len Sutton's defence counsel are building a case of diminished responsibility, based on his mental health," I said. "I've been told it could take another year to get a date for the crown court. And would you believe, he's contesting…" I stopped. Now was not the time for that disclosure. "Anyway, as long as he's kept away from me, it can take as long as it takes."

Diana nudged Gordon, and he fell silent. I was glad; today was about triumphs and conclusions, not loose ends and bitterness.

When we reached the pub again, I wandered down to the river, wanting to be alone to reread one last time the letter that Dorothy's solicitor had given me only a week ago. I would tell everyone else the news in a moment; but this was for me, before it became official. I crinkled open the pale lavender paper, covered with Dorothy's last words to me, in her fragile hand.

My dearest Jenny,

I trust by now your play has been an enormous success, as I knew it would be. You have a great talent, my dear, and it should never go to waste. I've also seen the way you've helped others, and indeed, what you're achieving is very close to my heart. I've therefore decided to gift you The Old Bell *in my Will, because I can't think of anyone more deserving to be its owner. I know you will love and care for it as Jake did, and return it to what it was. That makes me very happy. It was a privilege to know you, my dear. Had I been able to choose a daughter… well, I don't have to say any more, do I?*

Take care, Jenny; live life to the full, and be brave. Yours in memory Dorothy L. Jessop

I stared into the green water as it churned around the knots of grasses growing out from the bank, untangled itself and slipped away on its onward journey. Not even Dorothy's considerable gift of property matched her final words. I had never felt worthy as a daughter; and the realisation that I'd made Dorothy happy, as I had never made my mother, was a piercing joy.

Ben's hand on my shoulder made me jump; he jerked his head towards the group gathering on the lawn, clutching their drinks.

"I think now's a good time," he said, and I folded Dorothy's letter up and nursed it tightly in my hand as I told my friends the best news of my life. *I had a home. And the job I loved so much was mine, for as long as I – we – could make it pay.*

"And before Dorothy died, she and George and I decided that we'd like to change the pub's name," I said, my voice quivering at their delighted faces. "So, it will be called *The Cap and Bells*, after our own actor-clown who was born here." Then I turned to Mags, unable to wait another second to say what I'd longed to, so many times. "Mags, I want you to have the costume business for your own – with all the outfits. Everything. But you can run it from here, of course." She'd never have room in her little house.

"You… *what?*"

For a moment, she looked like she'd woken up on a Christmas morning to eclipse all others.

"You don't mean it? Oh, Jen!"

"*Winter's Tale*, here we come!" said Gordon with satisfaction. "I thought perhaps one of those fur-lined cloaks for Leontes, Jenny. What do you reckon?"

"Oh, for goodness' sake, Gordon," hissed Diana.

Mags let me go and Ben took her place, stroking my face with his hand and cupping my mouth with his so tenderly that he took my breath with him when his lips pulled away.

"Congratulations, sweet," he said, and his eyes held a glow and a promise for the hours to come. Then he went off to rescue a couple of glasses of bubbly from Isla, who'd brought out a fresh tray.

"Louise, I'd like to make the pub a permanent home for Speak Out," I said, as she came up. "And maybe run some new workshops."

Her eyes softened. "Well, by the looks of things, you'll be turning this legacy into one of your own, Jenny."

"I'd like that," I said.

But it wouldn't be easy; I knew that. The pub needed money spending on it – a lot of money. We couldn't do indoor performances until it had been made regulation-safe. But if my time here had taught me anything, it was a willingness to fight for what I loved, and who I wanted to be. Part of me would always be the damaged shell my mother's words had forged; but that would never be the whole story. The rest was in my hands.

I turned back to survey the old building, glowing russet red in the summer sunshine, loving it as I never had my childhood home. Dorothy's gift offered me a new chance at my dream, and I'd pay that on in the future in as many ways as I could. But the greatest legacy of all, I thought, watching my chattering friends, came from their love and support; and from the voices that had given me hope. The random comment of a stranger at the end of a school play; an extraordinary playwright, whose iridescent words had brought a roar to my heart that would never be silenced; and an actor and his love, whose story had helped me find my way out of my own darkness.

Your monument shall be my gentle verse,
Which eyes not yet created shall o'er read;
And tongues to be, your being shall rehearse,
When all the breathers of this world are dead;
You still shall live, such virtue hath my pen,
Where breath most breathes, even in the mouths of men.

From Sonnet 81,
by William Shakespeare

ACKNOWLEDGEMENTS

Dear all

Writing this book has brought me so much pleasure, so I hope you have enjoyed it, too! I'd like to thank the great team at Matador for their care and patience in making it happen; my lovely husband, David, and son, Johnny, for their even greater patience, love and support; my friends Jennifer, Maureen, Lucy and Gaye for all their helpful notes; and my sister, Tina, who has never wavered in her faith in me.

If you'd like news on my plans for the next book in this series, please visit my website, contact me on Twitter or Facebook, or sign up for my email newsletter!

Thank you for reading *So Now Go Tell* !

ABOUT THE AUTHOR

Susan lives in Bedfordshire with her husband, where she enjoys writing, reading, spending time with her family, and directing plays for local drama groups! She also runs Shakespeare acting workshops, has a PhD in Shakespeare Studies, and is a Honorary Research Associate at Royal Holloway, University of London. *So Now Go Tell* is her debut novel.

Website address: www.susansachon.co.uk

Facebook: www.facebook.com/susansachonauthor

Twitter: twitter.com@DrSusanSachon

Milton Keynes UK
Ingram Content Group UK Ltd.
UKHW021618030823
426158UK00011B/37

9 781803 137606